Wild, Wild Women of the West II

Wild, Wild Women of the West II

Delilah Devlin
Layla Chase
Myla Jackson

𝒜

APHRODISIA

KENSINGTON BOOKS

http://www.kensingtonbooks.com

APHRODISIA BOOKS are published by

Kensington Publishing Corp.
850 Third Avenue
New York, NY 10022

All Kensington Titles, Imprints, and Distributed Lines are available at special quantity discounts for bulk purchases for sales promotions, premiums, fund-raising, and educational or institutional use.

Special book excerpts or customized printings can also be created to fit specific needs. For details, write or phone the office of the Kensington special sales manager: Kensington Publishing Corp., 850 Third Avenue, New York, NY 10022, attn: Special Sales Department, Phone: 1-800-221-2647.

Aphrodisia and the A logo Reg. U.S. Pat & TM Off

ISBN-13: 978-0-7582-2386-9
ISBN-10: 0-7582-2386-2

First Trade Paperback Printing: May 2008

10 9 8 7 6 5 4 3 2 1

Printed in the United States of America

CONTENTS

ONCE UPON A LEGEND

DELILAH DEVLIN

1

Serendipity, Montana, 1883

Prudence Vogel didn't want to miss a thing.

She wet the tip of a sharpened pencil on her tongue and steadied a writing tablet on her lap, ready to capture the last moments of her journey. But as was her nature, her mind wandered, and instead, she began to write the adventure playing out in her imagination.

Katarina's nose wrinkled at the smell of stale beer and dust as she slipped behind the saloon and peered into the darkened room—

The stagecoach jolted as a wheel slipped into another deep rut on the rough trail, sending her pencil scraping off the edge of the pad.

She sighed, resigned she'd have to commit the final moments of her journey to memory and pick up her heroine's adventure after she arrived at her destination.

She slid her tablet into the pocket of her valise behind her dog-eared copy of *The Adventures of Katarina*, her latest, well only, publishing credit. She'd kept the novel in clear view in hopes of drawing a comment to give herself an opportunity to sell one of the many copies she'd brought with her.

Not the dog-eared copy, that one contained penciled notes of the details she'd gotten wrong. For that was the purpose of this journey. Prudence Vogel had never traveled outside the city of Chicago, yet her first novelistic experience was an adventure tale set in the wild frontier, featuring a tall, handsome hero she'd only fantasized about. She needed to know whether she'd been wrong.

For all she knew, the real Jake White Eagle was a short, squat man who could suck his whiskey through the space where his front teeth ought to be. She'd braced herself the whole journey for disappointment because she'd built such high hopes he'd be the hero she'd envisioned—the kind of man a real "Katarina" would admire.

Tales of his wild youth, his talent with a gun, his time spent scouting with Buffalo Bill Cody for the Fifth Cavalry had fired her imagination since she'd come across the first mention of his name in the *Chicago Tribune*.

After that she'd scoured every newspaper she could get her hands on, searching for a description of the man and his exploits.

Physical descriptions had been hard to come by; "burnished skin" and "the deadly stare of the black-eyed Indian" hadn't told her whether his jaw was square or rounded, or his nose was a sculpted blade or broad and bumpy. And it would have been helpful to know whether Katarina would have to lift her patrician chin to kiss his lips. Since she'd lacked definitive answers to her questions, in her mind she'd created an image of the man she wanted him to be.

However, news of his dangerous exploits had been much

easier to find. The man had earned quite a reputation as a gunslinger as he'd roamed the western territories. Then last year, for some reason, he'd settled in Serendipity, Montana. Not Deadwood or any number of more recognizable wild, western towns, but an unknown place with a whimsical name.

In her research, she'd missed the reason for his inexplicable move. Now she wanted the truth for the sequel to her book and detailed descriptions to bring her wild, western adventures to life.

Prudence pulled back the curtain to take a look outside, blinking against a cloud of dirt stirred up by the stage's team of horses.

Bright sunlight dispelled the gloom in the interior of the stagecoach. Everywhere around them endless blue sky filled the view. The golden tips of the prairie grass rimming the trail waved in a slight breeze. Cottonwood trees swayed in the distance.

"Close that curtain! You're lettin' in the dust."

As if we aren't already wearing a coat of gritty trail dirt? Prudence bit her tongue against the retort. Ever since Mrs. Waters had boarded the stage in Helena, she'd offered a contrary comment to every one of Prudence's actions.

Prudence firmed her lips into a polite smile and turned to the stout woman sitting on the opposite seat. "Aren't you the least bit curious about what's happening outside this coach?"

Mrs. Waters snorted. "Curiosity killed the cat."

Prudence lifted her brows, which sent her spectacles sliding down her nose. The woman had repeated the same tired old cliché as Mrs. Lake in the opening scene of her dime novel.

Just like the character of Mrs. Lake, the woman had a cliché for every occasion and nary an original thought.

Another coincidence! An odd prickling raised the fine hairs at Prudence's nape.

While some of the less important details—the flora, the

fauna, and the ruggedness of the trail—had mostly been wrong, the events in her story had been strikingly similar. The string of similarities between Katarina's adventure and her own true-life adventure had at first amused Prudence, who'd been convinced she'd simply done her research and was an apt pupil of human nature.

But this time, the words were repeated as though they'd been scripted in advance.

As well, the more Prudence thought about it, Mrs. Waters was an exact physical replica of the irascible woman who'd complained throughout that first scene of her adventure novel.

Even Mr. Stanton who slept beside her resembled the handsome, debauched gambler who'd managed to snore throughout the last leg of the fictional journey despite the bone-rattling thuds of the lumbering stagecoach.

The one jarring detail that didn't match her story was the character of the heroine. Prudence was a far cry from the beautiful and spirited Katarina. Sadly, she wasn't brunette, or possessed of a pure, porcelain complexion and soft, curvaceous figure. Her own hair was a muddy blond, her nose sprinkled with an unfortunate quantity of mud-colored freckles, and her figure was as straight as a boy's. And she wasn't the least bit adventurous.

Still, if the story was somehow unfolding . . .

A loud banging sounded from the top of the coach. "Folks, we're comin' up on Serendipity," came the call from the driver.

Mrs. Waters patted her hair while Mr. Stanton snuffled and opened bloodshot eyes as he refastened his string tie.

Surreptitiously, Prudence reached for the edge of the window casing and held on tight . . . just in case.

Shots rang out, the coach jerked forward and back, and then shrill whinnies filled the air as the team lurched again and shot forward, sending a screaming Mrs. Waters headfirst into Mr. Stanton's lap.

Prudence suppressed a squeal of fright and held on. Then just as quickly, she relaxed, suddenly unafraid, because she knew how this would end.

A hero rode to their rescue.

Sure enough, shouts sounded outside—from the driver and another man whose horse ate up the distance between them in a staccato flurry of sharp hooves.

Gradually, the team slowed, snorts and frightened whinnies settling like the dust sifting underneath the flapping leather curtains, until at last the stagecoach came to a stop.

Just like in her story.

Only Prudence didn't wait for their rescuer to fling open the door. She stood and grasped the door handle, nervous but determined to see whether the object of her obsession was indeed on the other side.

The door gave way unexpectedly, bringing her along with it, and she toppled out of the coach and straight into the arms of a very tall man. Thick, strong muscle surrounded her as he swept her off her feet and held her close to his solid chest.

Startled, Prudence glanced up, but his rasping breath fogged the lenses of her spectacles, and she groaned.

Why, oh why hadn't she put them away? Better to be blinking at the man than looking like a startled, befuddled mouse. Around the rims of her glasses, she noted the breadth of his wide shoulders and the dark shadow from the hat shading his face.

"Ma'am, are you all right?" His voice was a deep, raspy bass that seemed to wrap around her like a raw caress.

"Jake?" she whispered, more sure of his identity than she'd ever been of anything in her life. She knew his voice—had heard it speaking in her imagination.

Naturally, he smelled of sage and soap. She'd written that as well.

"Do I know you?" he asked, amusement in his voice.

A wide, tremulous smile stretched her lips, and she slowly wound her arms around his shoulders. "No, but I know you, sir," she said, too excited to give more than a passing thought to her forward behavior.

His head tilted as though he were scrutinizing her. "She bump her head?" He directed the question to the people stepping from the coach.

"I don't think so," Mrs. Waters said, her voice trembling and affronted at the same time. "But she's a very strange young woman."

"Ma'am, think you can stand on your own now?"

Prudence sighed dreamily. "Must I?"

A soft snort and his arms tightened for a second; then he set her on her feet, his hands settling at her waist to steady her.

Prudence sucked in a deep breath at the intimate touch. The heat of his hands caused an immediate warming in her nether regions. Her breasts peaked against her thin chemise. If just a simple, helpful touch could do this to her, what havoc would a more intimate caress wreak?

"Well, damn," he said softly, quickly removing his hands and standing back.

"Wait—" Prudence reached up for her glasses and took them off, blushing as she searched for a pocket to hide them away. When she squinted upward again, he was gone.

His boot steps thudded, growing softer in the distance and mingling with the sounds of other people moving along the boardwalk.

She realized that for that short space of time, no one else had existed for her. All thought had stilled in her busy mind. He'd been exactly as she'd imagined. Well, as tall and strong as she'd imagined. And she was pretty sure he still had his front teeth because he hadn't lisped.

He'd acted the hero, putting his own safety at risk to slow the stagecoach. He'd behaved exactly as she'd expected.

Again, Prudence was reminded she was no Katarina. Her heroine hadn't swooned into the hero's arms. She'd given him a brilliant smile and said something equally brilliant, which Prudence couldn't have remembered at that all-important moment to save her life.

She'd been so filled with a vibrant, glowing heat that she'd forgotten her purpose—and the fact that maybe she had the means to avert certain disaster.

She patted her pocket for her spectacles and choked on the dust she raised. No wonder the man had fled in such a hurry! She was filthy and smelled as sour as old milk.

Glancing back at the coach, she decided to check into the hotel and give herself a quick scrub before setting out to find Mr. Jake White Eagle. She had a good idea where he'd be.

The man needed her insight into his future. But would he listen to her?

Another question burned a hole in her belly—Was he as handsome as her heart and body said he was? As she'd imagined back in Chicago when she'd penned her novel in the wee hours of the night inside the tiny room she'd kept above her uncle's apothecary?

Of course, he was. His hands had felt her over and found her wanting. He must have his choice of beautiful ladies.

If only she were as lovely as Katarina. In *her* first meeting with the hero, she'd rendered Jake speechless as he'd searched her fair countenance and committed it to memory before shaking himself out of his daze. He'd remembered at the last moment to extend his hand to help her glide gracefully from the stage.

Katarina had shivered delicately as she settled her soft palm in his broad, calloused palm and given him a blinding smile.

The smiling part Prudence had managed to get right. Although likely he'd stared at her puffy lips and wondered if she'd kissed a bee.

She sighed, hoping to earn at least his gratitude, if not his admiration, when she gave him the news that tonight he'd be drawing on a killer.

Jake White Eagle tied the reins to the hitching post in front of the sheriff's office and stomped up the wooden steps, feeling as ornery as a horse with a burr beneath its saddle. First order of business was to find out who fired the shots that spooked the runaway stagecoach.

Maybe then he could forget the softness of the woman he'd held in his arms as she'd melted all over him like sweet, warm molasses.

The first sight of her tumbling from the door of the coach hadn't inspired so much as a spark of interest. She was mousy. Her blondish brown hair straggled from its neat bun. Her scrawny figure was hardly worth noting.

However, close up, the sight of her slender nose dotted with golden freckles and the misting lenses of her wire-rimmed spectacles had forced a grin.

The smile she'd returned had been brilliant, scorching as summer sunlight. Suddenly, she'd felt light and fit just right in his arms. The way she'd wrapped her arms around his shoulders had sent an arc of electric heat straight to his loins. For a moment, he'd thought she returned his interest.

Until he'd set her on her feet and held her tiny waist between his large hands. Her sharp gasp had felt like a splash of cold water.

She'd been shocked a breed held her tight.

Reminded he was tolerated for his skill with a gun, he withdrew quickly, leaving her blushing and glancing away at the impropriety of his touch. Townfolk might turn a jaded glance when he diddled with a saloon whore, but decent folk would look askance if he set his sights on a young, marriageable white woman.

Her smile had been one of relief, not of interest returned. He'd do well to remember that and give the woman a wide berth. Besides, he had enough problems on his hands—drunks to turn out of the jailhouse, a wild young town to tame.

As he walked into the dim interior of his new office, he flipped the sign to let folks know he was in and reached for the keys hanging on a peg.

He had what he wanted right here. A chance at respectability after a checkered past. One reed-slim woman with lush pink lips wasn't going to put a spoke in his wagon's wheel.

2

A quick, darting glance around the edge of the window and Prudence spied her target. The gunslinger had his back to her and was talking to a large man who tucked his wrinkled shirt inside his pants and hitched up his yellow suspenders.

When they moved toward the door, she quickly drew back and straightened the hem of her neat, gray-striped jacket. She'd settled on a staid, professional outfit. No use in trying too hard to win an appreciative glance.

She'd only look desperate.

In her hand, she held a copy of her novel. Not the precious dog-eared copy that had been the first to roll off Beadle's printing press. This was a fresh copy. She intended to give it to him along with the warning that, however unlikely it sounded, the events within its pages were coming true.

She wouldn't mention she was the novelist. That would be far too embarrassing. After reading it, he might guess correctly at her infatuation.

Oh, why had she extolled his beauty and gone on and on about the strength in his taut, leanly muscled body? He'd wonder how an innocent maiden would know about any fires that heated the loins of the heroine at just the sight of his manly physique.

Never mind he'd figure that out quickly if she couldn't remember how to breathe. She was about to get her first clear view of that impressive body and handsome face, and her insides trembled like jelly.

The door opened and the burly man with the yellow suspenders stepped onto the planked walkway, wincing at the sunlight. "Dammit, Jake. A man could go blind this time a day."

"Quit grousing, Caleb. Next time watch who you pick a fight with when you're drunk."

"Who'd a guessed that little pipsqueak had fists like a hammer." He rubbed his swollen jaw. "Must a caught me by surprise."

"I saw the whole thing," Jake said flatly. "You swayed right into his fist."

Caleb winked. "Must have felt sorry for him."

"Whatever makes you feel better. Now get along."

"Sure have lost your sense of humor since you pinned on that star."

Prudence's eyes widened, and her gaze fell to the shining silver badge on Jake's chest. In her story, he'd been newly elected to the position.

Caleb's glance passed over her, then paused. He grimaced as he reached to tip his nonexistent hat. "Howdy, ma'am."

Prudence nodded absently but kept her gaze on the hard-eyed man standing at the doorway with his arms folded over his chest. Her heart fluttered like a butterfly's wings, and her palms grew moist. Gazing at last into his face, her breath caught.

She hadn't begun to do the man justice. Feeling a little light-headed, and more than a little intimidated by his male perfection, she looked her fill, just so that she could recount this moment later.

But how would she ever capture his masculine, sensual essence?

Standing hatless, his eyes squinting slightly against the bright sunlight, he took her breath away. His thick hair was as dark and shiny as a crow's feathers. Tied back, it only accented the sharp edges of his face, scraped clean of any softness by years of living in the outdoors. His cheekbones were equally sharp-edged and set high; his eyes black and brooding; his lips a firm, straight line.

While his features marked him as Indian, his skin color was tanned and olive, a testament to his mixed heritage along with his unusual height.

Gradually, she realized she'd stared too long. The remoteness of his expression chilled her. She didn't dare drop her glance below his square jaw, although she was tempted beyond common decency to do just that. Instead, she lifted her chin and returned his hard glare.

His mouth slid into a small, mirthless smile, and his glance fell first, skimming over her frame, resting a moment on the slight curve of her breasts, before quickly dropping down her length and rising again to meet her widening gaze. She hadn't missed the insult in that slow perusal, and her back stiffened.

Determined not to be the only one discomfited, she gave him a slow, assessing look that trailed down his broad chest. However, the insult she intended to return fell away as she quickly forgot why she'd engaged in the challenge.

The black vest he wore over a pale pin-striped shirt lovingly followed his shape, emphasizing the broad chest and narrow waist and hips. Her breath grew ragged as she paused over the juncture of his thighs, noting the large bulge that started beneath the placket of his dark pants and trailed down the right leg of his trousers.

Her gaze snapped back up to his.

One dark brow arched. "Is there something I can do for you, ma'am?" he drawled.

Prudence gulped. Something he could do? Kiss her breathless? Strip her naked? His glance had already accomplished both.

Thank goodness she had some experience in the carnal delights, or she'd be entirely overwhelmed by his . . . maleness.

Barely suppressing the urge to fan herself, she stepped inside his office and thrust out the hand holding her novel.

His brows knit in confused irritation. "Thank you, but I'm not one to read that sort of story." His thumbs slid into the front pockets of his dark trousers, his long fingers bracketing his impressive sex.

He was unnerving her, drawing her attention to the part of him she most wished she could explore—and the bastard knew it! Feeling flustered and angry because he'd managed to turn her curiosity against her, she huffed a breath. "You're in it," she blurted, holding the novel higher.

He hesitated, his frown deepening. "All right, I'll have a look. Later." He lifted one hand, sliding it slowly over the outside of hers before tugging the novel from her numb fingertips and dropping it on the desk behind him.

As she let her hand drop to her side, her skin still tingled from the contact. So much so, she cupped her hand against her trembling stomach. "Everything in that book is coming true." She paused, then cleared her throat as his expression sharpened. "I know I sound a little . . . touched, but I felt I had to warn you."

"I'm pleased you sought me out, whatever the reason," he said, with that low, growling rumble that passed for a voice. He stepped closer, reaching beyond her to close the door, his knees nudging hers through her skirts.

Her heart skipped a beat. Had he intended to do that?

"Is there anything else I can help you with, ma'am?" he asked silkily, not moving away, but giving her a look that melted her insides like butter on a griddle.

Although propriety demanded it, Prudence didn't want to step back. The contact of his hard thigh sliding along the inside of hers was too . . . decadent. Her knees shook, and she clamped them shut, trapping his thigh between hers. A little whimper tore from her throat as her cheeks flooded with heat.

His snort, soft and masculine, accompanied a tightening of his features. Suddenly, he seemed truly dangerous. Wholly male.

Close enough now his breath brushed her lips, a ragged sigh slipped from her. She closed her eyes. This was Jake, after all.

"Damn," he whispered. Then his lips smoothed over hers. The kiss was sweet, but not nearly enough to quench the riot of feelings swelling inside her.

She murmured and leaned closer, letting her aching breasts brush his chest.

His hands settled at her waist, then began to roam, gliding up along the sides of her breasts, then downward to curve around her bottom. At her startled gasp, his tongue stroked into her mouth.

Her thin, aching moan was muffled by his deepening kiss. Then his thigh rose between hers, surging deeper between her legs, pressing higher, until it grazed the moistening juncture.

Without thinking, she loosened her grip on his leg and settled onto it, riding the hard, muscled thigh as it pressed upward to rub against her feminine folds until they heated with the friction and liquid arousal seeped through her pantalets.

He murmured against her mouth and gripped her bottom harder, rocking her back and forth on his thigh.

Slowly, Prudence lifted her hands to grasp his shoulders, sinking her fingernails into the sharp corners. Her mind reeled as she tasted coffee on his tongue and breathed in the soft scent of sage mixed with the tang of fading tobacco that clung to his skin. Her body tightened while blood rushed to swell her heated sex, and her inner walls clenched.

His mouth lifted from hers, and she moaned a protest. Her eyelids fluttered open to meet his heavy-lidded gaze.

His nostrils flared. A muscle flexed along the side of his jaw; then he blinked—and drew sharply away, his leg withdrawing. Once again, his hands gripped her waist to steady her as she swayed. "You've done your civic duty, ma'am. I'm much obliged."

"Duty?" she whispered, trying to gather her scattered wits.

"Your warning."

His words, rough as sandpaper, caused a delicious shiver. "Oh, yes, my warning." She shook herself, and added a bit of starch to her own raspy tone. "You'll read it?"

"Every word," he said, staring at her mouth.

"Quickly, though," she said, her breaths panting like an overheated kitten as she struggled for aplomb. "Tonight, there'll be trouble at the saloon."

His eyes narrowed; his head canted slightly. "Who are you?"

Her stomach lurched. She'd rutted against him like a cat in heat and they'd never really been introduced! "Prudence Vogel," she croaked.

"Prudence?" His gaze skimmed her face. "Seems a fitting name."

She wrinkled her nose. *Meaning it's plain, like me?* Or was he mocking her after she'd all but begged him to take her—here in broad daylight in full view of anyone walking past his office. She wished again she were more like Katarina—more beautiful, more poised. Katarina wouldn't be at a loss for words after the passion they'd shared.

His hands gripped her shoulders and turned her; then he gave her bottom a slap.

She yelped and glared over her shoulder, the sensual haze

that had held her tongue-tied lifting at her flare of anger. "What was that for?"

"So you'd know better than to stir up any trouble tonight. And stay away from the saloon."

"I'm not going anywhere near the saloon! There's going to be a shooting."

One dark brow rose and his gaze hardened. "If there is, I'll know exactly who's responsible, won't I?"

Prudence's mouth gaped, heat flooded her cheeks, and she rounded on him. "You think I'm playing some sort of game?"

"I think you're trouble. And I don't abide anyone stirring up my town."

Watching angry color flood her cheeks, Jake grimaced, wishing he could adjust his cock.

The woman stirred up more than trouble.

Why the hell had he tried to intimidate her? He'd thought sidling up close would turn her on her heels to flee, but she'd gasped, her head tilting back, her eyes fluttering closed. He hadn't been able to resist tasting those full lips. Damn, but they'd been every bit as soft and pliant as he'd imagined.

The fact she'd let him do much more than kiss her had shocked him. Didn't the woman know the danger she courted?

However, this ridiculous claim of a dime novel telling the future made him wonder what her real purpose was. Was she just trying to get to know him better and seizing on a slim excuse? The thought was flattering, but he didn't want to dismiss the possibility of some more sinister reason.

Although the last thing she seemed was menacing or dangerous. She was reasonably attractive with an innocence that had glowed in her wide-eyed stare even as she'd invited his kiss and let him touch her intimately.

That air of innocence was belied as well by how quickly she was recovering her poise. Sure, her cheeks remained reddened, but her glance didn't slide away, and she didn't seem ready to turn her sweet tail and run.

Her looks were growing on him by the minute. He took in the golden brown hair that curled in soft waves she'd tried to wind into a tight, staid knot. His fingers itched to tug it loose and slip his fingers through the glossy thickness.

Sure, she was scrawny as a wet hen, but her waist and sweetly curved rump had felt firm, and he wondered if the rest of her would feel the same. His glance slid again to her breasts. Little more than two fried eggs. But his mouth watered wondering whether her little nipples would spike like short penny nails when he sucked on them.

Her dress rustled as she stomped her foot, both hands resting on her slender hips. "Sir, I'm trying to avert trouble."

He shoved his hands deeper in his pockets, attempting to subtly relieve the pressure building in his balls and cock. "I said I'd read it. But right now, I need to find out who fired the shots that caused that runaway stagecoach."

"You promise you'll read it before tonight?"

"I'll try," he said, not wanting to outright lie. He had more important things to do.

She blew out a deep breath and narrowed her eyes. "I hadn't dreamed you'd be this stubborn," she muttered.

He reached past her for the hat hanging from the wooden coat rack next to the door, and smiled as her breath caught when his shoulder brushed so close she had to reach up to cling to him rather than topple backward.

"Sorry about that, ma'am," he said, tucking his hand around the curve of her trim waist to steady her once again. "I'm kinda in a hurry."

Then he swept past her, turned the sign, and opened the door.

"Is it true Buffalo Bill Cody asked you to appear in his traveling show?"

The question was sharp-edged and so disconnected from their previous discussion, he shot her an irritated glance. "Yeah."

"Why'd you turn him down? He was your friend, wasn't he?"

"Friends don't ask friends to prostitute their heritage," he bit out, and slammed the door behind him, leaving her inside his office. He may have been raised in the white world, but that didn't mean he didn't give a thought to where he came from.

The door opened and shut behind him, but he was already heading fast down the planked sidewalk. Her question soured his stomach while not easing his growing arousal one bit.

Sharp taps sounded on the walkway as she scurried behind him. "I'm sorry, I didn't mean to offend you," she said breathlessly. "Maybe he didn't realize you felt that way."

"You think he's some kind of hero?" he growled, shooting her a glare over his shoulder.

"He scouted for the Fifth Cavalry . . . so did you," she said, trotting to stay with him.

Despite the fact she'd touched on a sore subject, her persistence began to amuse him, so he widened his strides to see whether she had the salt to keep up. "We hunted buffalo, killed everything that moved, and left rotting carcasses across the plain. What's so damn heroic about that?"

"I . . . guess I never looked at it . . . that way," she said, her breaths growing more ragged. "Did it . . . sour you?"

"Might say that. Don't like talking about those days. And, lady, if you ask about the shootout with Blackjack Mulligan, I won't be responsible for my language."

Her chin lifted. "I'm not so . . . lily-livered."

Sunlight hit the golden strands in her mud-brown hair and glinted in the gold flecks in her brown eyes as she kept apace.

He couldn't help himself from responding. The woman

wasn't much to look at, but her curiosity and dogged determination, added with her interest in him, stirred up a mighty heat, which licked along his thickening cock.

The woman didn't realize just how close he was to grabbing her and dragging her into an alleyway, just to see if she'd let him kiss her again.

Which made him mad as hell. The woman didn't have an ounce of commonsense. He slowed his pace, his thoughts quickening.

Was she this open, this intensely focused on every male she met? Did she knowingly leave herself vulnerable to a man's advances?

Then again, she was from the East. Perhaps men there weren't quite as raw or as accustomed to taking what they wanted.

In the back of his mind was the seductive thought that perhaps she knew exactly what she was asking for. "Did you already find yourself a room?" he ground out.

"Why yes," she said, "At the Pendergast Hotel . . . the second floor—"

"Fine." He was sure she would have given her room number by the nervous way she blurted the information.

"I hope you're comfortable during your stay," he said formally, wondering if she'd take the hint she ought to mosey along before he gave into the urge to hurry her into a dark place.

"Actually, Mr. Pendergast still has my trunk behind the counter. He was waiting for a boy to come and take it up for me."

He stopped in his tracks and stared. Was she asking him up to her room? He sighed, exaggerating his inconvenience, and turned toward the hotel, letting her follow once again in his footsteps.

As he entered the hotel, Mr. Pendergast's eyebrows rose. "Mornin', Sheriff."

"Mornin', Simon. Miz Vogel has a trunk you need some help with?"

"Yes, I was waiting for my bellhop to get here. No tellin' where he's got himself off to this time. Back's out again, or I'd have done it myself."

"I'll take care of it for you." Jake walked stiffly behind the counter, grabbed the large trunk by its leather straps, and hefted it onto his shoulder, giving Prudence a nod. "Show me where you want it."

Her eyes widened. "I didn't mean for you to go to all this bother."

"You didn't? I thought all that hemmin' and hawin' about your room was the whole point," he growled.

"Sir, I was just making conversation," she said, blushing.

Mr. Pendergast gave them both a sideways glance.

Prudence blushed and turned with a flounce to precede him up the stairs, her head held high. At the top of the landing, she turned to stalk down to the end of the long hallway.

Jake eyed the exit door at the very end of the hall. "He gave you this room? You know, anyone could walk in from the outside staircase."

"Well, I have a key, and Mr. Pendergast assured me this is a safe little town now you're in charge." Her hands shook as she unlocked the door. Once she managed to fling it open, she stood aside while he entered, clasping her hands nervously in front of her.

"Where do you want it?"

Her cheeks flushed strawberry red, but she indicated with a wave of her hand that he should lay the trunk on the bed.

"What do you have in this thing?" he asked, dropping it on the mattress. "Rocks?"

"Some books," she said, her blush deepening.

"More of those dime novels?"

Her lips pressed into a straight line.

He took her response as a yes, not questioning her taste in literature. "What is your business here, Miss Vogel?"

"Um . . . research. For a publisher."

That explained the books. And the questions. So maybe she hadn't been so much interested in him as a man, but as the western legend. Which made him madder. He tipped his hat and strode toward the door.

As his hand reached for the knob, she said quickly, "You will read the novel today, won't you?"

Glancing over his shoulder, he replied, "Like I said, I'll do my best."

She stood looking as though she wanted to say something else. "Maybe if you just read the passage about what happens tonight . . . ?"

He gave another long sigh and turned, leaning his back against the door. "Why don't you just tell me the short version about what's supposed to happen tonight."

Her eyes widened. "Well, I guess I could." Her eyes shut for a moment and her brows furrowed as she thought. "Two men will be sitting at a table playing poker. One of them will toss his cards in the center of the table, and say, 'If I didn't know any better, I'd say you had that ace up your sleeve. No one's that damn lucky.'" Her eyes popped open. "That's when the other man will start to rise, and his hand will go to a gun he has in a holster inside his jacket. It's hidden because no one's allowed to wear a sidearm in the saloon."

"That's right," Jake said, his eyes narrowing on Prudence. "So, why don't you save me the bother of waiting until that happens and just give me their names?"

"Because their names won't be the same as in the story."

She said it so matter-of-factly, with such confidence, he had no doubt that was exactly what would happen that night.

Question was, why did she need it to happen? To draw him to the saloon? For what purpose? What kind of con game was the lady working?

The whole time she'd told the story, her face had been illuminated, as though relishing the argument and the man drawing on the other gambler. She was a bloodthirsty little thing.

He hadn't had any plans on being in the saloon that night, but seeing as how she wanted him there so badly, he was curious enough to make a point to be there. However, first he'd give her a chance to come clean about her scheme. "Miss Vogel—"

"Prudence," she said, beaming at him. "I mean, I've already called you Jake."

Despite his suspicions, her name tugged at the corner of his lips—because the longer he knew her, the more *un*suited her name appeared to be. He shook his head. Damn, maybe he should just let her scheme play itself out. He changed his tack. "You do know Mr. Pendergast is counting the seconds I remain in this room."

"I suppose you should go then." She bit her lip.

"Is there anything else you need?" he asked softly. "Before I go?"

Another strawberry blush brightened on her cheeks. "I was just wondering why you did that . . . before."

He knew damn well what she was asking, but the devil in him made him want to force her to say it. "When I did what?"

Her lips pouted with irritation. "When you kissed me."

Jake lifted one brow. "It seemed an easy way to shut you up."

Her mouth gaped and fire leaped for a moment into her gaze. Just as quickly, she gave him an assessing look. "You're teasing me, aren't you?"

He let a slow, easy smile stretch his lips. "You think I didn't want to kiss you?"

"Well, I know I'm no beauty."

"That's true. But you've got gumption. Makes a man wonder how far it'll lead you."

Her golden brown gaze glittered with a dawning excitement, and she drew a deep breath and blurted, "Mr. White Eagle, what if I told you I wasn't a virgin?"

3

Jake froze, sucking in a deep breath. The thought she'd given herself to another man clawed at his gut. He didn't know why the fact angered him so much—it wasn't as if he had a right to be jealous. Wasn't as if he knew anything about the woman, but he'd felt a connection the first time he'd held her in his arms.

Ridiculous as it seemed, the thought that another man had caressed her intimately, molded her slender curves with his rough hands, and enjoyed her passionate responses made him feel sick to his stomach and ready to kill.

As the anger roiled inside him, he reminded himself, she wasn't what she appeared to be—sweetness and innocent curiosity. Her lack of innocence meant he didn't have to be so careful. "You're very direct."

Her chin lifted. "I don't see any reason to pussyfoot around this. I'm attracted to you . . . and if you're attracted to me, well . . ."

His body tightened as he got her meaning. He crossed his arms over his chest and feigned a nonchalance he was far from feeling. "You'd risk your reputation to be with me?"

"I won't be staying here," she said softly.

"I see," he said, nodding slowly. "Is it just because you want to see what it's like having an Indian?" he asked, not hiding the bitterness that rose to burn the back of his throat.

She blinked owlishly. "I thought you were half."

"I am, but a drop's too much for most."

"Well, it's not because of that." Her expression filled with mild reproach, her full lips pursing. "What a silly reason that would be."

"Then why?"

A shrug accompanied a sudden glistening in her eyes that made him uneasy. "You're a very attractive man."

"Do you make it a habit to proposition every attractive man you meet," he bit out.

Her breath huffed and the glistening became a welling of angry tears. "Of course not."

His jaws ground together. "Just how experienced are you?"

"Well, I've done it once."

Once. Damn near a virgin. He stared at her, sure she was telling the truth. "Just to be clear . . . Are you asking me to take you to bed?"

Her gaze held his, despite the shimmer that turned his insides to mush. "I'm just letting you know," she said softly, "that if you're interested . . . I am too."

"I appreciate the honesty," he said slowly, carefully. "But you see, I have . . . peculiar tastes." He waited to see how she reacted, the muscles of his belly bunching tight, his balls hardening in anticipation.

"Peculiar?" Her gaze shifted away then back to him again, her brows knitting in a frown. But rather than sensing any trepidation, the woman's curiosity gleamed from behind her wire-rimmed glasses.

Dark amusement filled him as he watched her. "I would need to discover whether you share a similar peculiarity."

"How would you do that?" she whispered.

"I think we only have a couple minutes more before Mr. Pendergast decides to investigate what's taking so long. So this will have to be quick."

Her breath caught. "You mean now?"

He nodded, letting his jaw firm.

"But it's daylight." Her hands fluttered, then clasped together again over her stomach.

He shrugged. "You wanted to know."

Her glance shot to the sashes at the curtained window. Bright sunlight streamed through the glass. Her eyes closed briefly; then her gaze returned to him. "What do I have to do?"

His chest rose with his deeply drawn breath. His heart galloped like a runaway horse. "I want you to open your jacket."

Her hands trembled as she quickly opened the row of polished horn buttons.

"Now, I'd like you to open your blouse to your waist."

A riot of pink spread from her cheeks down her neck, and he was about to see whether the blush extended to the tops of her small breasts because she quickly flicked open the next row of tiny buttons.

"Spread open the edges, let me look," he said, already cursing himself for his own curiosity because his cock was pushing hard against the placket of his pants with little hope for relief anytime soon.

When her gaze rose to his, he said, "I want you to push down the top of your chemise until I can see your nipples."

Her nose wrinkled. "And this is a peculiarity? Mr. Hanson wanted to see them too."

He ground his teeth at the mention of her previous lover.

But she did as he asked and pushed down the thin muslin to the top of her hard-boned corset, exposing her breasts.

He'd been right. Her breasts were very small, dainty actually, but rounded—just enough to fit in the centers of his palms.

Her nipples spiked sharp and long, and the color was a deep, reddening peach.

His mouth watered to know their taste.

"This is all you wanted?"

He lifted one dark brow. "No, it's not all. Pull up that stool from beside the bed," he said, lifting his chin in the direction of the stool.

She did as he asked, then glanced back up.

"Now, I want you to reach under your skirt and take off your underthings. Step out of them, and then pull up your dress and let me look at you."

Her breath rasped shallow, but once again, she did as he asked, bending to reach beneath her skirts. For long moments, his belly tightened at the rustling sounds that accompanied the actions she tried to hide beneath her long skirts, her breasts quivering above her corset with each tug, until at last, she drew out her pantalets and tossed them to the bed.

Then without looking at him for further instruction, she bunched her skirts in front of her as she pulled them up slowly, exposing her long, slim legs. When her skirts reached the tops of the garters holding up her stockings high on her thighs, she hesitated.

Despite the fact his body was wound tighter than a spring, he kept his stance casual, shook his head, and tsked. "Don't stop now," he said softly. "I want to see your pretty pussy."

Her mouth dropped open. "Looking at my, um . . . that will please you?"

Damn, it'd do a helluva lot more than just please him. The sight might kill him. His cock stirred against his thigh. "Maybe I'm just takin' a look at what you're offering."

Her chin came up and her lips firmed. Angry blotches of color stained her cheeks, and he held his breath, sure she'd back down any second now.

But she drew a deep breath and raised the fabric the last few inches, letting him gaze on the pale brown thatch of hair between her legs.

His mouth went dry, and he swallowed. "Put your foot up on that stool."

"But that will—"

"Yeah, it'll open you up," he purred.

She shook her head. "I must be crazy. You're doing this to make fun of me."

"Believe me, lady, the last thing I feel like doing is laugh. Do it."

Again, her stubborn little chin came up. She held his gaze steadily, even as her lips trembled. Then she lifted one slender, booted foot and set it on the stool, angling her leg to open herself further.

The curls clothing her outer folds were damp and glistening.

Jake dropped his arms, and he straightened away from the door. He strode toward her, wiping his face clean of any expression. His heart thudded loud and dull in his ears as he stared, raking her with his gaze from her trembling lips to her whitened knuckles as she clasped her skirts to her waist, and lower to where fluid gleamed in her brown curls and along her slim, pale thighs.

When he drew close, he saw the near-panic widening her eyes. Raising a hand to his hat, he slowly took it off and dropped it to the floor. Then he slipped a hand around her neck and pulled her forward to kiss her hard.

Her mouth opened under his and their tongues met, touching, lapping together. He canted his head and nudged her glasses with his nose. He leaned back and reached up to remove them.

She drew away and shook her head. "Please, I won't be able to see."

That pleased him. Maybe they were better suited than he'd thought. Better than he'd hoped.

Prudence held her breath as Jake knelt beside the stool, his face drawing level with her . . . *pussy.* Not something Mr. Hanson had been interested in seeing—he'd been in such a hurry to bury his "scabbard," as he'd called his cock. Everything had been accomplished with clumsy haste in the darkness after he'd looked at her breasts.

Jake seemed content to stare and . . . breathe in her scent! Thank God, she'd bathed before seeking him out.

Then he lifted his hand and slid his thumb between her nether lips, gliding into the moisture gathering in ever-increasing volume. An embarrassing amount, really. She'd drenched the fabric of her underpinnings earlier with just the nudge of his knee. Now, he slid upward, gathering her dew, pulling up the skin to expose the tender little knot at the top of her sex.

Prudence sucked in a deep breath, anticipation curling tight in her core. Lord, he wouldn't . . .

He did! He leaned close, dragging in more of her scent, and ignoring her gasp, sucked the hard little knot into his mouth.

His deep groan vibrated against her turgid flesh.

"My word!" Prudence had never felt anything this delightful in her entire life. And the thought that this rugged, dangerous man had his head buried between her legs, his lips tenderly encircling her most intimate flesh, was a heady thrill.

"When you said you had peculiar tastes, I had no idea!" she gasped.

A sound that resembled a strangled laugh gurgled in his throat, and he released her little nubbin. A grin tugged at his lips as he raised his glance to meet hers. "Woman, you say the damnedest things."

The heat that burnished his cheeks and the slow, sensual dip of his lids as he returned his attention to her feminine mound left her breathless.

Really. She swayed on her feet and opened one hand still holding her skirts to grab for his shoulder.

"That's right. Hold on, baby girl." His tongue slipped out and licked at her folds, dragging along her outer lips and into the creases where her thighs framed her sex. Over and over, lapping and swirling, until her hips followed his motions and her fingertips dug hard into his shoulder.

Just when she thought he couldn't do anything more wicked, more shocking, he drew the leg perched on the stool over his shoulder, opening her further.

Prudence couldn't move, couldn't breathe as he brought the fingers of one hand into play to part her folds and thrust two fingers from his free hand inside her, stroking deep.

She drew in a jagged breath, trying to calm her racing heart as he thrust in and out, twisting his knuckles inside her channel. A low, keening moan broke from her as another finger filled her, stretching her.

"You're so tight, so hot. Damn, you're sweet," he said, and leaned close to draw her little button into his mouth again.

A flurry of sensations bombarded her, too many to keep track of, not that she would recount any of this in her next novel! But she wanted to remember each stroke of his fingers entering her sex, each swirl of his tongue on the rigid little knot, each rasp of his breath as he suckled and licked and thrust— until her body tightened impossibly more, and her back arched, her head falling back . . . and she was falling . . .

Over the edge of a dark chasm where thought and sight weren't important, only the darkening heat that exploded like a burst of black fire to cloud her vision and set her body trembling.

When she came back to herself, she found his hands clutching her bottom, holding her upright as she leaned away, his mouth still suckling, now gliding along her folds, gently laving her in soft, soothing laps as her wits and her breath returned.

Good Lord, is that what the fuss is all about?

The muffled laughter from between her legs told her she

must have said that last aloud. She groaned and sank her fingers in his hair to drag his mouth away from her sex. If he worked on her any longer, she had no doubts he'd send her crashing again.

Which would be truly wonderful, but he had seemed concerned Mr. Pendergast would find them together. He must be worried about his reputation as a new sheriff.

Jake pulled away, giving each of her inner thighs a quick kiss before lifting her leg from his shoulder and setting her foot on the floor; then he tugged her bunched skirts from her nerveless fingers to drop them, effectively cutting off his view.

When he stood, his lips curved in a small, wry smile. His gaze swept her face before settling on her lips.

She knew he would kiss her again, and her head tilted, a soft sigh escaping as his lips rubbed hers, molding them to his kiss. When he drew back, she found his hands had settled at her waist, and his cock was poking at her thigh.

The length and width of him rising inside his pant's leg startled her, and she reached to trace the shape of him. Lord, was that really all him?

His groan was half laughter half pain. "I'm going to have to take the backstairs. I can't walk through the lobby like this."

"Is it painful?" she asked, cupping her hand to follow his thickening shaft where it rose beside his thigh, tightening his trousers. She smiled thinking he would indeed make a spectacle of himself walking around with this poking at his pants.

"Yes," he winced, halting her hand with his. Then he seemed to change his mind about pushing it away. Instead, he moved her palm up and down his cock, squeezing her hand to tell her he needed a harder grip.

"Wouldn't it be better if you . . . adjusted it to ride upward?" she asked, rubbing him, feeling her cheeks heat as his gaze sharpened on her expression.

Did he think her beyond sinful? She hoped so. She didn't

want him hesitating due to her lack of experience. She knew now her breaching in the dark had not been lovemaking. It hadn't been mutually pleasurable, hadn't given her an ounce of the sensual heat Jake's narrowed gaze gave her now.

"Let me?" she asked, suddenly breathless.

His hand tightened on hers, and his head turned toward the door as though listening. Then he whipped back around and nodded sharply, dropping his hand away from hers.

Prudence went first for the leather belt slung low on his hips. She'd never touched a gun before, wasn't sure how to remove the holster, but she bent and untied the leather strings that held his holster close to his thigh, reaching between his legs to draw them away. The leather strap was easier, as she tugged to free the two prongs from their holes and gently pulled his gun and holster away, dropping them to the ground beside them.

Breathing a sigh of relief she'd managed that without his tensing, she undid the buttons of the suspenders that held up his waistband, letting the straps slide up beneath his vest. Then she reached for the buttons at the front of his trousers and, one by one, flicked them open with her thumb and forefinger.

His stomach jerked with each flick of her fingers, and Prudence smiled to think she had that much of an effect on him. When she had his pants opened, she gave him a quick glance from beneath her lashes, then reached inside, smoothing a hand downward to grasp his filling cock and gently bring it upward from where it strained against the fabric pulling tight around his leg.

When she brought it into the opening of his trousers, she stared. His sex had felt impossibly hot and heavy in her hand. The sight of it was even more imposing—more delicious. The skin surrounding the thick shaft was stretched tight and shone like a soft, worn satin. Bluish veins formed shallow ridges along his length. The bulbous, mushroom-shaped crown was redder than the darker tan rod, and felt soft and cushiony beneath her thumb. The eyelet hole at the top glistened with a pearly drop of fluid.

Proof of his excitement. Not copious amounts like she'd released, just a drop.

The thought brought a niggling challenge that straightened her shoulders.

Jake drew a deep, inward breath when she didn't let go. His glance was piercing, his cheeks darkening with a flush of heat. "You just gonna look at it?" he growled.

She knew what she wanted to do—she had to demonstrate a similar "peculiar" taste.

She let go of his sex for a moment and smoothed her hands around his waist and pushed down his pants, just far enough to free his straining cock.

He should have looked foolish. Buttoned-up vest and shirt, his pants caught around his hips. But the expanse of pale olive skin and the largeness of his straining sex only made him look more dangerous, more sensually devastating.

Again, Prudence was taken aback. All that perfection bared for her gaze, her touch. Her pussy clenched, fresh arousal seeping freely to wet her naked thighs beneath her skirts.

However, as much as her body wept for him to fill her, she had to prove something to the man . . . and to herself. She might be inexperienced, but she wasn't missish, wasn't squeamish about her needs and wants.

She'd traveled halfway across America to meet the man, she wouldn't pause on the brink just because she was embarrassed . . . and unsure what she should do next.

Prudence took a deep breath and lifted a finger. "Just wait one moment. Don't move." She turned and walked toward the stool, grabbing it up between her hands, then returned to him. She set it between his braced legs.

His chest rose and fell quicker, his breaths noisier, deeper. His hands rested on his hips. "Just what do you have in mind?"

Evidence of his rising excitement, his anticipation, gave her a little more confidence. "I think you know, but I may need a little advice," she said, biting her lip.

His glance fell to her mouth.

Enough of a hint to tell her she was heading in the right direction.

4

Jake had never seen anything as lovely or sexually exciting as Prudence Vogel with the bit between her teeth.

Her gaze focused on his cock. Her white teeth nibbled at her lower lip. Her cheeks glowed with faint embarrassment.

So focused was she, he wondered whether she remembered her blouse was still open, her little breasts trembling with her shallow breaths. God, he still hadn't felt their drag across his tongue. Still hadn't tasted them.

He waited, his hands on his hips, his cock rising between his legs, painfully full. He hoped she meant to take at least a nibble to let him see her lush mouth stretch around his manhood.

Not that having a woman making a meal of his cock would be a new experience for him, but somehow knowing he'd be Prudence's first "meal" only made him harder.

And she'd asked for advice. He snorted. She could do anything her heart desired so long as her wet, warm mouth swallowed him *now*.

She knelt gingerly on the stool, taking the time to tuck her skirts under her, and then motioned for him to step closer.

His lips curved, and he moved his feet, one at a time, bringing his cock directly in front of her mouth.

She blinked behind her glasses and shoved them to the top of her head, then lifted her hands to run her fingers along his shaft as she continued to stare.

"I like my balls rubbed," he said, firming his lips against a smile.

Her little gasp and the deepening flush that reached her little breasts made him feel pretty powerful. Made him want to growl like a bear.

With another nibble of her lip, she cupped him in one hand, rolling his balls tentatively on her palm before wrapping her fingers around him and tugging.

"Gently," he gritted out, groaning when she softened her grip and squeezed. "Take 'em in your mouth."

Her eyes widened, but she didn't hesitate, moving closer and wetting her lips with her tongue before opening her mouth and sucking on one of his balls like an ice cube, working him with her mouth, her tongue stroking tentatively against his ball.

"That's it. Just right," he gritted out, feeling his body harden, wanting to rut against her, but afraid he'd frighten her if he just reached down and guided his cock straight into her mouth the way he wanted.

He'd take her one step at a time, teach her just how he liked it. Even if it killed him.

Her jaw widened and she took his ball into the cavern of her mouth, moaning around him, the sound vibrating as she glided her tongue around him. One small hand reached up and grasped his cock; he closed his hand around it, fisting her tight against his cock, and moved her up and down his shaft, sliding the skin over his steely rod while she laved his ball.

Damn. Damn.

When she moved to his second ball and sucked it quickly, greedily, into her mouth, he cursed out loud and rutted, jabbing his cock inside their clenched hands, helping her stroke him faster.

She pulled away, gasping, and rose higher on her knees. Guiding her hand, he pointed his cock at her mouth and she opened wide, her tongue coming out to take a swipe around his head, taking another drop of his gism into her mouth and closing her eyes as she tasted.

Then her mouth opened again; he let go of her hand, gripped the back of her head, and forced her closer, groaning as her full lips stretched around him.

He flexed his buttocks, driving himself along her tongue, then pulling away, only to stroke deeper the next time.

She gurgled around him, but gamely widened her jaws, careful to fold her lips around her teeth. She could have scraped the skin off his cock and it wouldn't have mattered.

Her hot, steamy mouth was everything he'd dreamed. "Suck on it, sweetheart," he ground out.

She murmured, tried to nod, then started to draw on him.

Jake's legs shook. His balls drew tight against his groin, pressure built, and he knew he wouldn't last much longer. He needed to move. Needed to stroke deep, needed to fuck her mouth hard. "Have to move . . . Don't fight . . . Relax," he rasped.

Her hands gripped the notches of his hips, and her gaze rose to meet his.

Jesus, the look of her, her gold-flecked eyes wide, her reddened lips dragging on his cock, had him deepening his strokes. He reached down to grasp the base of his cock, moving upward to gauge the depth he'd go so he didn't choke her. Then with one hand holding himself and the other cupping the back of her head, he let loose.

She milked him with her mouth, all the while moaning around him as he stroked faster. He twisted his hand around his shaft, adding friction to the steamy heat of her mouth until he felt the tightening of his balls and lunged, jerking now, finally feeling the scrape of her teeth as he let loose, thrusting faster, deeper, butting the back of her throat and pushing further.

When at last the scalding liquid release pulsed from his cock, it was too late to pull out, too late to remember he shouldn't let himself go like this. Not her first time.

As the blackening fury receded, he realized she still suctioned his cock—and her throat worked at the back of her mouth, caressing his head with her gulping motions, drinking him down, clasping around him hot and wet, like her pussy would when he finally got inside her.

His fingers released their fierce grip on her hair, and he slowed to a stop, shivering and jerking still in the aftermath, his chest heaving like a billow.

Prudence suckled him now, working her head forward and back, slowly backing off him. She learned damn fast.

When she finally drew off him completely, she leaned back and kept her head down. Her shoulders rose and fell; the tops of her little breasts quivered.

Jake hooked his hands into her armpits and lifted her high until her face was level with his so he could read her expression.

No repulsion, no fear. Only a softening wonder that glowed in her eyes and on her cheeks.

"Did I do it right?" she whispered.

Jake's jaw tightened, unable to speak he was still so taut, so raw. The woman had gotten to him fast. Instead, he angled his head and kissed her hard.

Her mouth opened readily, and he struck his tongue into her mouth, tasting himself on her tongue. Something primal rose inside him, fierce and strong, and he crushed her body to his.

The sound of footsteps stomping in the hallway brought him back to reality. He jerked his mouth away, cursed, and set her on her feet.

A knock sounded on the door.

Prudence's eyes widened, and she glanced down at her naked chest.

She rushed quietly across the room, before calling out, "Yes?" breathlessly while her hands worked feverishly to close her blouse and jacket.

"Is everything all right in there, Miss Vogel?" Simon Pendergast asked, his mouth very near the door.

Jake knew he probably had his ear pressed against the oak and held his breath.

"I'm fine. I'm just . . . taking a nap."

Jake's eyes sliced a glare her way.

"Uh . . . just wondered," Simon said. "I didn't see the sheriff leave. Thought there might be a problem with the room."

"Oh, no problem," Prudence said, her cheeks flaming. "He let himself out the side door."

"Oh! Well, I'll let you get on with your nap."

"Thank you, sir."

At the sound of receding footsteps, Jake let out the breath he'd held.

Her hands stilled on her clothing, and she looked up with a slow grin wreathing her face. The buttons had been closed in the wrong holes. She lowered her glasses and slid them up her nose. "You know," she said softly, "he thinks I'm taking a nap."

Jake narrowed his gaze. The little witch had mischief gleaming her eyes. He knew where this was leading, and hell, his cock was already tingling, hardening again so quick he wondered if she'd cast a spell. "I have rounds to make."

Her lips pouted, and her shoulders slumped. Then she lifted her hands to unbutton her clothing. "Well, I don't want to keep you," she whispered. When she'd finished unbuttoning the jacket, she drew it slowly off her arms and dropped it on the floor beside her. Without looking up to see whether he was even watching, she did the same with her blouse.

Jake couldn't help himself. He should be looking for the ya-
hoos who'd shot up the town. He should be doing any number
of things, but he stayed rooted to the spot as she reached behind her, undid her skirt, and let it drift to the floor around her
ankles. Her petticoats went next.

Then she unwound the laces of her corset and breathed a
deep sigh of relief as it too fell away.

When she pulled the chemise over her head and stood nude
except for the dark stockings that clung to her long legs, he finally moved.

His hands tore at the buttons of his vest and shirt. He drew
both off and flung them aside, shaking his arm to free one sleeve
when it snagged on his wrist. Then he toed off his boots, shucked
his pants, and walked in his socks to stand in front of her.

Her eyes were eating him up, raking his body up and down,
seeming to find a hundred places to linger before moving along
to the next.

His gaze fixed on her tiny breasts. He wasn't going to wait
another minute to get a taste.

When he was close enough to reach for her, he picked her
up, sliding an arm beneath her knees and another under her
shoulders, and crossed to the bed, laying her down gently on
the patchwork quilt. He crawled right over her, laying on her
like a blanket, warming her head to toe, drinking in her heat,
her shallow breaths, and floral-scented musk.

"Is this done?" she whispered.

"What?" he asked, settling his cock between her legs.

"Doing this in the middle of the day."

"Only if a body's lucky."

Her nose wrinkled. "We still have our socks on."

"Want to lose them?"

She nodded. "I don't want to miss a thing."

Jake smiled and lifted off her, coming to his knees between

her legs. He took his time, smoothing his hand down one long, slender leg, then back up. The lacy garter slid off first; then he rolled her stocking down her leg, taking his time to smooth his palm down her length. By the time he started stripping the stocking from her other leg, her sex was soaked again, her curls drenched, her sweet fragrance deepening.

He drew off the stocking and lifted her leg to run his lips along the inside of her calf, then her knee. When he set it on the bed, he bent to kiss her inner thigh and steal a taste of the moist arousal gathering on her folds.

The first intimate caress had her widening her legs, lifting her knees so she could plant her feet on the bed and lift her bottom—an invitation he couldn't resist.

He licked and prodded her pussy with his tongue, swirling his thumb over her nubbin as her thighs quivered. She was ready again.

But he still hadn't kissed her sweet breasts. He moved up her body and cupped one small mound.

"They're not much," she said, her voice small.

He thumbed one lengthening stem. "They're perfect."

Her snort said she didn't believe him. "You still have your socks on."

"Are you trying to distract me?" he asked, looking up to catch her gaze.

She'd slipped an arm beneath her head to raise it so she could watch him. "I'm just saying. I'm naked—so should you be."

"Lady, everything that matters is naked." He plumped up one little breast. "You don't want me staring at these, do you?"

"No," she said softly.

"If I told you I eat my green beans first, my apple pie last, will you believe I like them?" he asked, rubbing his calloused thumb on her nipple.

Her eyebrows drew together in a slight frown. "I guess."

"You just want me to hurry past 'em now."

A pout puckered her lips. "I'm thinking there's more interesting ways to spend our time."

"I promise I'll get to the best part soon." Only he liked that the urgency was building slowly this time. Time to savor. He'd never cared much for bedroom talk, but she amused him.

"Think highly of yourself?" she asked, her tone pert.

"I think we're well suited for this sort of sport," he said, teasing her.

"Why would you think that?"

"Well, we both have all the right parts."

"Any man and woman would," she said, her tone flat.

"I love the way you taste and smell. You all but swallowed me whole."

"Oh! I can't believe you mentioned that!"

"Wasn't that your throat gulping me down?"

Strawberry spots reddened her cheeks. Her teeth worried her bottom lip. "Did you enjoy it?"

"Oh yeah," he whispered.

"They're not too small?" she said, in a tiny voice.

"Is that what that other man said?"

"He never said, and he only took a quick look."

"His loss." He dropped his gaze to her chest again. "You want to keep talking?"

"No."

"What do you want me to do?"

"Um . . . will you kiss them?"

"I will. Will you let me suck on them too?"

She groaned and gave a little laugh. "I think I'd like that."

"Then hush." He bent over her and stuck out his tongue, aware she stared as he dragged his tongue over the distended tip.

Her breath caught, and her thighs tightened around his waist.

From the corner of his eye, he saw a hand clench around the quilt and pull. She liked it all right.

So did he. He licked again and this time drew the whole nipple into his mouth to suckle, savoring the velvet-soft texture. She was tiny, delicate, but completely female. A mewling cry broke from her throat when he tugged it gently with his teeth.

He cupped the opposite breast as he continued to work her breast, liking the way her hips rolled beneath him. He thought he might be able to make her come with just his mouth sucking on her tit, and again, he felt a surge of powerful lust fill his loins.

He released her nipple, gratified at her moan of protest, and licked a path across her chest to latch on to the other nipple while his fingers twirled and squeezed the tight stem he'd nurtured into full arousal.

Her back arched, forcing her breast deeper into his mouth, and both her hands sank in his hair, tugging away the leather tie. He liked the way she raked his hair with her fingers, and he groaned around her breast.

Soon the pressure in his cock became too insistent for him to ignore, and he released her breast and scooted farther up her body.

Her eyes opened, meeting his gaze. He liked the sleepy, dazed look of her, the way her lips had reddened beneath her nibbling bites as she'd held back her moans.

He wanted to see her face when he sank inside her, claiming her. Whoever she was, whatever her purpose, she'd challenged him, drawn him irresistibly with the purity of her open-eyed curiosity.

He sensed she didn't see the red man, didn't give a damn about the darkness of his past. She thought he was a hero, despite the stains that niggled at his own conscience.

She wanted *him*. The wetness of her sex caressing the head of his cock was pure sexual attraction. "That other man . . . was he made like me?" he asked.

"Hmmm?" she asked, her eyes focusing finally behind her misting lenses.

"Was he as big as me?"

Her forehead wrinkled as she thought. "I don't know. It was dark."

"You didn't touch him? Hold him in your hand?"

"No."

Jake stifled a groan. He guessed that other bastard had pushed up her skirts and taken her without a bit of care or preparation.

He'd have to take it slow. He came up on his elbows. "Bring your knees up, sweetheart."

Prudence gave him a look of total trust and raised her knees on either side of his hips.

With his cock poised at her entrance, Jake ground his teeth and slowly pushed inside, circling his hips to stretch her as he entered.

Her mouth opened around a tiny whining moan. She drew in a deep breath. "Oh my." She was tight, and her inner muscles clamped around his cock, resisting his invasion.

"Relax, breathe," he said, although he'd forgotten how to do that himself. He fought the urge to thrust into her, and although he was only a couple of inches inside, he pulled back. He rested his forehead against hers. "Do you trust me?"

"Of course."

"There's no of course," he muttered. Didn't she have an ounce of self-preservation? Anger rushed through him, hot and fierce. She was going to let him fuck her, but she didn't know a thing about him other than whatever she'd read or heard.

He knew his anger wasn't with her but with "Mr. Hanson," who'd taken her but hadn't really shown her what it was all about.

Everything Jake had done with her so far had been fresh and

new to her. Since the moment they'd met, she'd opened herself to him. Why him? If he hadn't stopped her headlong fall from the stagecoach, would she be in bed with some other man?

Right now, he couldn't think too much on it. His balls ached, and his cock felt as tight and full as it had ever been. Damn, he was going to hurt her if he didn't take it slow.

"Is something wrong?" she whispered.

He snorted and lifted his head. "Best not to talk."

She blinked and sighed, pressing her lips together. Her thighs snuggled tighter around his hips.

"Best not to move."

"I thought that was the point," she murmured.

A laugh caught him by surprise. "Anyone ever tell you not to tease a bear?"

"Why would they tell me such a silly thing?" Her head canted. "Are you feeling growly?"

"Lady, I'm trying to gird myself. Let me concentrate."

"Is this such a trial?" she asked, her voice tightening.

He blew out a breath and aimed a glare at her. "Not for the reasons you're thinking."

Her brows furrowed in a frown. "No one's forcing you to make love to me, you know." Her legs loosened around him, and her hands pressed against his shoulders.

"Dammit, don't move," he bit out. "Don't you know I'm trying not to hurt you?"

"Well, I'd say it's a little too late," she said, shoving at him now. "All that comparing me to apple pie—"

"Shit!" He ground his teeth hard and groaned, releasing his iron hold on his desire to move. He flexed his hips and pushed into her again, cramming himself into her tight sheath.

She winced, and her breath hitched. "That didn't feel so good. Maybe we should stop."

"Jesus Christ! It's a little late now."

"You're mad at me?"

"No, I'm not mad," he said slowly. "I'm hard as a post, and I have to move."

"You really want to do this . . . with me?"

Jake sighed and cupped her face between his hands. "I really do. With you."

Her lips trembled. "Is it going to get better?"

"God, I hope so. Now, will you be quiet?"

5

Prudence wondered what she'd done that had gotten him so ornery so fast. Although she did seem to have that effect on a lot of people.

Jake was braced up on his arms, his sex pressed just inside her entrance, and he trembled—but was it rage or passion?

And the questions he had asked her! Her cheeks burned with the thought she'd actually told him so much about her one experience.

So she hadn't actually seen Jerry Hanson's cock. No, she hadn't held it in her hand—*or her mouth!* But she knew from the way Jake's cock stretched her tender inner tissues that Jerry couldn't have been even half as large.

With Jake, she felt like she was embarking on a sensual journey for which she'd prepared herself very poorly indeed. She'd thought she needed to know what sex was all about. She'd agreed to let Jerry breach her maidenhead, because, deep down, she'd wanted to be the sort of adventurous woman someone like Jake would want.

She hadn't wanted to be a scared little virgin who didn't

know her way around a man's body. But it seemed she hadn't chosen the right man to initiate her.

So she lay beneath Jake's body, her own frame trembling with trepidation, as well as a burning, unfurling desire. "It really doesn't hurt all that much," she said quietly, offering him a smile.

He snorted again, his eyes closing tightly for a moment before glaring down at her. "Liar."

"Some parts have been wonderful . . ."

"I'm going to start moving," he said, grinding his teeth audibly. "If it's too much . . ."

"I'll be sure to yell."

"Damn." He gave her a tentative thrust, moving just an inch or two deeper.

Her back arched and she gasped. "That's not so bad."

"Sure. And you always grit your teeth when something pleases you?"

"All right," she huffed. "It hurts . . . a little. Will you just get on with it?"

His lips curved in a feral smile. He looked more like a wolf than a bear now. "Put your legs around me. The ride's gonna get a little rough."

That growling, rumbling bass did things to her. Wicked things. A fresh wash of arousal glazed her channel and the head of his enormous cock.

Somehow that seemed to ease his entry, and he grunted as he glided deeper and pulled away. Then he came back, pressing inward, circling his hips to screw himself into her, stretching her channel, pumping softly while sweat broke on his forehead and upper lip.

Prudence noted every change in his demeanor as he went from taut, angry hunger and eased into a smoldering, sliding rapture. She could tell how he felt by the way his muscles trembled then tightened and by the way his face went from reddening strain to a slackening glory that said he'd forgotten who was beneath him as he stroked harder, deeper.

Her own body softened and moistened, perspiration beading on her own face and glazing her breasts and belly, easing his gliding movements as his whole body ground and chafed and plunged against her, into her.

Her arms came up to circle beneath his arms, around his back so she could flatten her palms on the muscles that flexed and tightened, reminding her of the power he still leashed inside him. Slowly, as her body eased and stretched and accepted, she became hungrier, needier for all that power to let loose inside and over her.

How could she convince him she was ready? Her tight channel clasped him tight, rippling along his shaft. Dear God, she could feel that too!

"More, please," she groaned.

"Damn, girl. Let me do this right."

"Please," she keened, curving her hips upward and digging her nails into his backside, urging him deeper.

He thrust faster, his strokes more gloriously punishing, prodding deeper, cramming tighter, grinding slightly at the end of each sharpening thrust.

Prudence felt that curling lick of heat tighten around her womb and arched her back, crying out, "Now! Oh God, please now!"

"Damn!" Jake ground out. Then he reared up, hooked her thighs beneath his arms, and lifted her buttocks from the mattress.

With his hot, feral gaze holding hers captive, he slammed his hips into hers, over and over, shaking her whole frame with the strength of his thrusts.

Her belly and breasts quivered and shook; her breaths grew short, labored, rasping. The friction of his thick sex thrusting endlessly inside her burned and melted her inner channel.

Creamy fluid eased his powerful thrusts. His belly and groin slapped in the wetness pouring from inside her, seeping down between her buttocks to puddle beneath her.

She didn't care, couldn't think. Only felt—the burning heat, the sharpening thrusts—until the curling, tightening blackness swept over her again, and she cried out, arching, strung taut as a bow string while she exploded—too overcome with sensations, one atop the other, to capture.

His guttural groan soon followed, and he abruptly pulled out, leaving her empty.

She opened her eyes to see him pulse his hips, his cock thrusting into air, stripes of pearly fluid spurting from him to land on her soft belly in silvery ribbons.

His head was flung back, his arms quivering beneath her thighs as his movements slowed, and he drew a deep, ragged breath.

When his eyes opened, his gaze seared her with heat. Here was her fierce warrior. The one she'd dreamed of—his face taut and sharp, his eyes as black as midnight.

He blinked and slowly drew his arms from beneath her legs and lay over her, supported on his elbows so that she could breathe freely. Their chests billowed against each other.

"Are you all right?" he asked.

She drew a deep breath and offered a smile. "Better than all right."

"Not too rough?"

"Just rough enough."

His lips curved into a smile of pure masculine satisfaction. He framed her face with his rough palms and leaned over, brushing her lips once, then he drew away, climbing off the bed to stretch his back. His arms reached high, then dropped to his sides. "I'll be busy today."

Was he giving her an excuse not to linger in her bed? The

thought stung. Obviously, what had happened between them hadn't been as cataclysmic for him. "Me too."

His gaze narrowed, raking over her naked body. "Stay away from the saloon tonight."

She resisted the urge to pull the coverlet over her. Now that her body was cooling off, embarrassment rose to sting her cheeks again. "I don't have any intention of being there. You'll be careful?"

"I'll be prepared." He reached for his clothing and started to dress.

She was thinking what a shame it was she didn't have more time just to look her fill. His body was so interesting—so well formed. When he pulled his pants over his waning cock, he winced, and she smothered a grin.

What would Katarina do at a time like this? Prudence rolled to her side and rose on an elbow, striking a feminine pose that emphasized her meager curves. "Will I see you later?"

His expression darkened, his gaze sweeping from her breasts to her hips before meeting her eyes. "Depends on you, I guess."

"If I tell you, I'll answer your knock?"

He drew a deep breath. "Look, Prudence . . ."

She steeled herself for rejection. He'd already given her so much. She shouldn't be greedy. But Lord, she wanted more. "It's all right. You don't have to if you don't want to."

A dark brow rose as he shrugged into his suspenders. "Oh, I want to. I'm just wondering if you have anything else you want to tell me." His steady gaze honed sharp as a steel blade.

Her breath caught. "There's more. But you really should read that story."

He paused, looking as though he wanted to say more, then shook his head. "I have to go." He turned and strode toward the door.

"Be careful."

He shot a glance over his shoulder. "I always am."

Then he left.

Prudence eased up from the mattress and grimaced. Her body ached. She was a sticky mess. She'd love nothing better than to take a long nap and maybe let her mind wander back over what had just happened. However, she had a mission. And a cliffhanger ending she had to wrap up.

Tonight, if everything happened the way she'd written it, then tomorrow would have worsening consequences. A chill raised goose bumps on her naked skin.

She stared at her trunk, wondering whether she had the power to influence the ending.

Jake strode into his office, spied his deputy engrossed with a slim volume, and closed the door behind him with a slam.

His deputy, Billy Wells, jumped, his gaze lifting from Prudence's dime novel. "Hey, boss. Where ya been?"

"Did you find out anything about those gunshots?"

"Sure did," he said, laying the open novel facedown. "Geezer Fenton and his boys came into town, hootin' and hollerin'. I took their weapons away from 'em."

Jake nodded to the book. "I pay you to spend your day reading?"

His young face flushed red. "I was just passin' the time waitin' for ya. Um . . . boss?"

"Yeah, Billy?"

"This book's about you."

Jake blew out a deep breath in exasperation. "It's a book. A story written by someone who's never even met me."

"But . . . it sounds like you. The way you do things . . . even talks about a runaway stagecoach you stopped. Just like you did today."

"And your point is?"

"Don't ya think it's a little strange? Um . . . did you happen to meet a woman on that stage?"

Jake's gaze narrowed. "Maybe, why?"

"Well, she sounded mighty pretty. Just wondered if her name might a been Katarina."

"Now, you see? There wasn't any Katarina. Just Mr. Water's wife returning from a visit with her sick sister and Miz Vogel."

"Was Miz Vogel pretty?"

Jake rubbed the back of his neck. "Pretty? I guess." Prettier naked than she was in clothes, that was for damn sure, he thought, remembering her little peach-colored nipples.

"Name 'Waters' is awful close to 'Lake.' And Miz Waters is a might grumpy."

"What the hell are you talking about now?"

"Just that I got a really weird feeling reading this story. It says you're the new sheriff, but you only got elected a few weeks ago—how'd they know that was gonna happen?"

"Mayor's been at me for months to run for office. Maybe the writer caught wind of it."

"There's a shooting in the saloon—the same night the stage arrives with Katarina."

"I've heard all about it."

"You gonna check it out tonight?"

"I suppose." Jake glanced again at the book. "Why don't you make the rounds. Make sure everything's quiet."

Billy grabbed his hat, eager as ever to do whatever Jake asked of him. As soon as he'd cleared the end of the walkway, Jake slid into his seat behind the desk and turned over the novel.

With Prudence's floral scent, as well as the fading aroma of the sex they'd shared still on his skin, he settled down to read.

Prudence had no intention of entering the saloon.

She'd thought she might casually stroll by and peek into the window; but when she got there, she felt a little foolish loitering near the entrance.

The men who passed to push through the swinging doors gave her strange looks; one even asked her if she might be lost.

Maybe she did look a little conspicuous. The sun had set, and daylight was dwindling. Not the time a lady ought to be on the street.

But she was dying to find out whether any gamblers were playing cards—and whether Jake had heeded her warning.

She'd dressed in a dark gray skirt and jacket. If she kept to the shadows inside the saloon, maybe no one would notice her. She glanced around her once, then stiffened her spine and pushed through the doors.

All heads turned her way.

So much for no one noticing. She took a deep breath, forced a tight smile on her lips, and looked around for an empty table. As luck would have it, one sat empty in a darkened corner that provided a perfect view of the entire room. She walked hastily to the table and slid into a seat.

"You sure you want to be here, ma'am?" a soft, musical voice said next to her.

Prudence grasped her valise in her lap and stared up at the painted woman. Her dress was tawdry, a bold green satin with cream lace along the low neckline. Her generous breasts nearly overspilled the top.

Aware she stared, Prudence's face heated. "Is there a problem?" she asked a little sharply.

The woman shrugged. "Guess not. Can I bring you something to drink?"

Prudence blinked. Although she'd had the occasional glass of wine, she wasn't familiar with most of the spirits a saloon might carry. She brightened. Here was a chance to fill in a few more pesky details. "My name's Prudence. What would you recommend?"

"Mary, pleased to meet you," she said, a shy smile tugging at her lips. "Do you drink much?"

Prudence pursed her lips. Should she err on the side of caution? *What would Katarina do?* "I'll try a whiskey."

Mary's eyes widened. "Would you like it watered down a tad?"

Prudence took Mary's surprise into account and nodded. "Please. However you would drink it."

"Danny waters all the girl's drinks down so's we don't get too drunk to work. I'll ask for one of those."

Prudence gave her a grateful smile and turned her attention back to the room that had fallen strangely quiet. And no wonder—every set of eyes was trained on her! When Mary slid her glass on her table, Prudence's hand shook, but she raised her glass to the men. "Bottom's up!"

Now, why had she said such a thing? They all continued to stare until she realized they waited for her to drink down her glass. Steeling herself, Prudence lifted the glass to her lips and poured it down her throat, not letting her nose take too long a whiff of the revolting drink. It burned all the way down, but she didn't stop until she'd emptied it and slammed it on the table.

Her eyes teared as she fought the urge to throw it back up. The men exploded with laughter, lifting their own glasses and bottles. But thankfully, their attention returned to their own activities.

"You feeling all right?" Mary whispered next to her. "Do you feel like you wanna turn your insides out?"

Prudence blinked up at Mary and smiled. "Actually, I feel fine. It burned a little going down, but it does warm a body up." She pulled at the tight collar of her blouse to ease it from her skin.

"Do you mind me askin' what you're doin' here?"

Prudence swung her gaze back to Mary, and the room whirled. "I'm here to see a shooting."

Mary's eyebrows furrowed. "Um...that sort of thing never happens here. Danny has a strict rule about firearms in the saloon. Takes 'em all up if the sheriff doesn't get 'em first."

"Someone's going to pull a small Derringer from inside their coat."

"How do you know that?"

Prudence opened her valise and pulled out a copy of her dime novel. "Page twenty-two," she said, handing it to the other woman.

Mary's wrinkled brow mirrored her doubt. "You think something's gonna happen because it's in this book?" She eyed Prudence as though she were a card shy of a full deck.

"Mary, everything that book has said so far has happened. I guess I'm just seeing tonight if it's coincidence or real."

"Do you mind if I look at it?"

"You can have this copy."

"Thanks." Mary's gaze rose beyond Prudence and her eyes widened. "Don't look now, but trouble's headin' your way."

"What do you mean?"

"The sheriff just walked in, and he looks mad as a bear with a hangnail. Gotta go!"

Feeling defiant, and just a little queasy, Prudence lifted her glass, then remembered she'd already polished it off. From the corner of her eye, she saw dark-clad thighs bracing apart beside her.

What would he do if she ran her hand along the inside of one of those thick, muscled thighs? Prudence plucked at her collar again. Lord, it was getting warmer.

A hand gripped her elbow and hauled her out of her seat.

She didn't have any choice but to rise or make a scene, so she stood and faced him, swaying slightly on her feet.

"What did I tell you?" he bit out.

This close, she couldn't miss the tic that pulsed at the side of his eye or the angry heat in his narrowed glance. Odd, but even though her stomach jumped with trepidation, her sex clenched and moisture began to flow.

Jake's hard gaze looked her up and down. "Prudence," he said, his voice softening, "how much have you had to drink?"

She shook herself, realizing that once again he'd caught her staring. "Not much. Just a watered-down whiskey."

"You ever drink whiskey before?"

She shook her head and blinked, his face suddenly unfocused. Maybe she had finished it off a little too fast.

He lifted a finger and pushed her glasses slowly up her nose. "I'm going to take you to the hotel. Right now."

Prudence's head tilted back as she swayed nearer his broad chest. "Are you going to stay with me?"

He grimaced. "Do you say everything that comes to your mind?"

"Of course not. If I did I'd have asked if you would stay and get naked with me again."

A muffled laugh sounded beside her and she turned to see Mary holding another whiskey.

"Why thanks, Mary," Prudence said, reaching for the glass.

Mary held it away from Prudence. "Actually, it's for the sheriff, sweetie. How's about I bring you some sarsaparilla?"

"You heard what I said, didn't you, Mary?" Prudence whispered loudly.

"I swear I didn't hear a thing," she said, giving the sheriff a wink and walking away.

Prudence groaned and hid her face against his chest.

"Ahh . . . Prudence."

It took a moment for her to realize what she'd done, snuggling up to him in public like this. She threw a glance over her shoulder, and sure enough, the whole room watched them with interest.

"I'm so sorry," she said, pulling away. "I didn't mean to embarrass you."

His brows furrowed. "You're worried about my reputation?"

"You are the new sheriff."

"Lady," he said softly, leaning down to whisper, "I'm afraid yours is the one in tatters at the moment. Not only did you tell the room you wanted to get naked with me again, you snuggled up to me like you had some practice at it."

Prudence stared at his stern mouth. "Is that bad?"

"It is if you don't want to be branded my woman."

"Would that be so bad for you?"

"I can take care of myself." His hand started to cup the back of her head; then he straightened, letting his hands drop to his sides. "I wouldn't want anyone to hurt you. Which doesn't mean I'm not still mad as hell you're here. Pick up your bag; we're leaving."

"But what about the shootout?" she hissed. "The gamblers."

Jake leaned down, his glare searing. "There won't be any shooting here tonight."

Just then the sound of something crashing to the floor drew their attention to a table on the far side of the room.

"No one's that damn lucky!" a man said, standing beside the chair he'd overturned.

"What are you saying?" Mr. Stanton from the stagecoach said, slowly rising from his seat.

"I'm saying, I think you had that ace up your sleeve."

Prudence's eyes widened as Mr. Stanton's hand slid inside his coat.

Jake shoved Prudence behind him. "Get on the floor!"

6

Jake tipped Prudence's table to the floor and pushed her behind it as tables flipped around the room and men dove for cover.

The sting of excitement flooded his muscles with steely strength as the moments seemed to slow. In that instant, he could account for every man and woman in the room, could take it all in from the corners of his eyes as he strode slowly toward the two men frozen, half out of their chairs.

"Mister, if your hand comes out of your coat with a gun in it, I'm gonna have to shoot you," Jake said, raising his voice just loud enough to be heard over the sound of falling furniture and the rustle of clothing as those around them clung to the planked floor.

He hoped like hell Prudence was cowering behind the table, her hands covering her eyes. If he had to draw, he didn't want her watching.

The gambler rising opposite of Geezer Fenton paused, his hand still buried inside his tailored coat. His cheeks were flushed, and anger narrowed his eyes as he glanced from Geezer to Jake. "Don't want any trouble with you, Sheriff. This is between me and the gentleman who just called me a cheat."

"We have laws in this little town. The sign in the window here says 'no guns on the premises.' I'll have to ask you to remove your hand from your coat—nice and slow."

The gambler's gaze dropped to the gun still sitting deep in Jake's holster.

"I'll clear leather and have a hole through your heart before you even squeeze your trigger," Jake said softly, steel in his tone. He didn't blink, didn't move; his whole body was poised for the moment.

The gambler sighed. "I'm gonna take my hand out."

"Nice and slow."

The gambler's hand came out, a gun in his open palm.

"Just set it on the table." Without taking his gaze from the two men still frozen in place, Jake said, "Billy, take the gun from the table, then escort the gentleman to jail."

The gambler's lips twisted in a tight smile. "That won't be necessary. I'll just clean up my winnings and head back to my room."

"You were gonna draw on a man. The least you'll do is spend the night in our jail. As soon as I can arrange passage on a stage, you're out of here. As to those winnings, I think drinks tonight will be on you."

Billy picked up the gun and put it in his pocket, then indicated with an overly polite gesture for the gambler to precede him out the door.

When he'd left, Jake slapped his hand on Geezer's bony shoulder and pushed him into a chair. "What'd I tell you about gambling when you've been drinking?"

"Now, Sheriff, the man was cheatin'!" Geezer whined.

"I've half a mind to put you in a jail cell next to him for the night. After shootin' up the town this morning, and now this . . ."

"I done turned my guns in to Billy. I was just lookin' for a little fun. It's been a month since I been in town."

"Tell you what. You finish your drink, get yourself a room upstairs—but I want you out of here in the morning."

Geezer's thin shoulders slumped. "All right. I'll leave the boys to get supplies, but I'll be out of here soon's I wake up." His gaze slipped beyond Jake. "That little filly you was sparkin' on is about to get away, Sheriff."

Jake glanced over his shoulder just in time to see Prudence slip between the swinging doors. "Thanks, Geezer. Remember what I said," he muttered, already moving toward the door.

"Woman like that needs a firm hand, boy!" Geezer called after him.

"More like a firm hand and a red bottom!" someone else hollered behind him.

Jake stomped down the planking, keeping the woman in his sights as she rushed down the darkened road, her skirts twitching faster.

A slow burn heated his anger and his lust. She'd gone too far. Not that she had anything to do with instigating the little scene back there in the saloon. Geezer would have accused his own mother of cheating at gin rummy after he'd had too much to drink.

The woman had meddled, put herself at risk for all kinds of ugly things by walking into a saloon. She'd risked her reputation, invited slurs from any man who knew she'd not only entered, but drank a glass of whiskey in their presence. Then she'd topped it off by letting every man in the place know she'd been naked with him.

As she opened the door of the hotel, she glanced over her shoulder. Her eyes widened when she spotted him. She slipped inside, no doubt making a beeline for the stairs.

Jake bypassed the entrance and instead headed to the side stairs, taking them two at a time, before flinging open the door. Prudence had just rounded the top of the staircase. When she saw him, she dropped her valise and turned on her heels to scurry back down the steps.

Jake smiled with grim satisfaction and caught her around the waist before she cleared the third step. "Not so fast," he whispered as he reeled her in, locking her against his chest.

"Let me go!" she hissed, wriggling like a fish on a hook and shoving at the arm gripping her waist. "I can't breathe."

"Liar." He hefted her over his hip, grabbed up her valise, and stalked down the hall.

At her door, he held up the bag. "Give me your key."

As she hung at his side, she swiped at her bag and reached inside, coming up with the key. "If you'll put me down, I'll unlock the door."

Jake snorted and held out his hand.

Her hand trembled as she laid the key on his broad palm.

At least she had enough sense to know she was in deep trouble now.

Jake unlocked the door and dragged her inside the darkened room, kicking the door closed behind them. He stomped toward the bed and slung her like a sack of potatoes onto the mattress, then stood back with his hands on his hips, glaring.

Prudence pushed her hair out of her face and eyed him warily as he stood over her, his face darker than the shadows enclosing them. "That ended well at the saloon, don't you think?"

His gaze glittered dangerously in the darkness, and a rumble that sounded more like a growl slipped from between his gritted teeth.

Growing more nervous by the second, Prudence swung her legs over the side of the mattress, determined not to be at a disadvantage for the coming argument, but Jake stepped closer.

She scurried back on the mattress and came to her knees. "I

don't know why you're so mad. We averted real trouble back there. No one was hurt."

Jake shook his head and reached for his gun belt, quickly ripping away the ties around his thigh and flinging open the closing at his waist. He hung the belt over her brass headboard, his gaze never leaving hers.

As he shucked his boots, one at a time, Prudence's nervousness slid into a dewy anticipation. Her breasts swelled against her chemise; cream slid from her body to slick her feminine folds. Lord, he looked angry—savage. Maybe she did like that part of him—even thrilled at the thought of the Indian falling upon her, ravaging her.

What a wicked thing to think? How depraved was she? But she couldn't help hoping he'd be rough—take her rather than seduce her.

While she wanted to rip away at her own clothes, ready herself for what came next, she didn't want to show her growing excitement. She wanted him to do all the taking—let him lose some of the red-hot anger that burnished his features as he ripped her clothes from her body.

Maybe by the time he had her naked and under him, he'd get over being mad.

What would he do with her? Punish her with a little rough loving? Pummel her body with his powerful thrusts? Her breaths hitched, growing more ragged as he stripped away his shirt and trousers and stood gloriously naked in front of her.

In the shadows, he seemed larger, more menacing, his cock rising like a great, thick trunk from his body.

About now, she was wishing he'd think about lighting a candle or two because his silence was unnerving her, and she needed to see his features clearly to gauge his thoughts. "Um . . . Jake? I take it you're angry with me." As soon as the words left her mouth, she cringed.

Soft laughter rumbled from him as he circled the bed, heading toward her wardrobe. He opened the doors and reached inside, dragging out clothes and rumpling them between his hands when he didn't find what he was looking for.

Prudence had had enough of kneeling on the mattress like a scared mouse. She reached for the little table beside the bed, fumbled until she found a match and lit a candle, sighing with relief when it flickered brightly, filling in the oppressive darkness.

When she glanced back at Jake, he held a nightgown in his hands and ripped it apart from the neckline all the way to the edge of its pretty embroidered flounce.

She didn't dare voice a protest. The look on his face was grim and determined. She swallowed to wet her dry mouth when he stalked toward her, climbing onto the mattress. Instead of leaping to the floor, she backed up against the rails of the headboard.

A smile curved his thinned lips. Not a friendly one. It did nothing to calm her nerves. He lunged suddenly, snagging one of her wrists, and wrapped a strip of fabric around it, then tied it to one of the rails behind her.

Prudence's jaw dropped. "What in Hades do you think you're doing?"

His response was to grab her other hand and tie it to a rail. There was plenty of give in her restraints, and she wondered about that, but she didn't have time to form a question because his hands began to rip away her clothing. First her jacket, then her blouse. The buttons pinged against the wooden floor as the fabric rent.

"You know," she said breathlessly, "it would have been smarter to strip me before you tied me up. Now, how are you going to get them off my arms?"

His smile broadened and he held up a small, closed knife. With a deft twist of his wrist a blade gleamed, long and slender. He inserted it at the edge of her wrist, the dull side sliding up her arm, the fabric parting like butter beneath a hot knife.

Lordy, she was in for it now.

Quickly, one piece at a time, he cut her clothes from her upper body, popping the laces at the front of her corset until he could pry the sides apart, slitting her chemise to her waist to expose her chest.

Her breasts quivered in the open air as she sucked in a deep, frightened breath.

He reached beyond her and thrust the knife into the wall between the spokes of the headboard, then straddled her body, his hands cupping her small breasts.

Naked, his thighs spread over her hips, his cock rising close to his flat belly, Prudence's lustful gaze raked over him. Tanned skin above pale hips, a darkening cock that thickened as she stared—she'd never been so consumed with desire.

She tugged hard at her restraints, and whimpered when she couldn't reach for him and draw his body closer. "Please," she begged.

Instead, Jake scooted down her legs and rucked up her skirts, reaching underneath for her thin pantalets and ripping them away. Her legs drummed the mattress as she fought to free herself and spread her legs wide for him, but he wasn't done being in charge.

He ripped away her petticoats, letting them drift like torn, white clouds to the floor, then reached for the waist of her skirt and pulled it until the button gave and swept it down her legs.

With only her shoes and stockings left, she was sure, now, he'd take her.

But Jake knelt outside her legs and rolled her, her hands twisting in their ties; then he lifted her over his bent knees.

Suddenly, she knew what he intended, and she bucked. "I am not a child to be punished, Jake White Eagle!" she gasped as his palm circled one globe of her bottom.

His hand landed in a sharp slap. *Thwack!* "This sweet little bottom's mine, Prudence."

She gasped, the sting taking away her breath. She wriggled like an eel, her arms stretched above her head, bucking against his lap, working her legs like scissors—to no avail.

He anchored her against his thighs with one arm and continued to deliver his sharp retribution. The slaps fell harder, faster, warming both globes of her bottom. As she realized she wasn't going to escape his punishment, she quieted, her breaths sobbing now, hoping he'd work off his anger on her abused bottom.

Gradually, she began to notice the changes in him as he spanked her. His cock hardened against her hip. His own breaths grew labored, harsh.

Finally, when tears slipped down her cheeks and she hiccoughed, his hand settled on her hot skin.

"Dammit, Prudence," he said, his voice roughened and thick. "This isn't a game. This isn't some story in a dime novel. What you did was dangerous."

"I just wanted to help."

"You wanted to see if you were right."

"And I was," she said petulantly, a sniffle ruining the sharpness of her retort. With her hot face pressed into the bedding, she collapsed, giving in to the urge to cry, her shoulders shaking with her sobs.

Jake dragged in a deep breath beside her, his hand smoothing over her bottom, a soothing caress that did nothing to cool her buttocks.

She squirmed, parting her legs to ease the ache that had grown between them, unrecognized until now.

His hand stilled.

So did her breath.

Then his fingers glided down between her buttocks, glancing against her back entrance, which elicited a small, shocked gasp from her.

He glided lower, his fingers parting her folds and sinking into the wetness that spilled from inside her.

Prudence smothered a groan against the bedding. How demented was she? He'd abused her, spanked her like a child, yet she was melting from the inside out, yearning for more of his touches.

While his breaths deepened, her body began to writhe across his thighs. She parted her legs, dug her knees into the mattress and lifted her bottom into his hand, begging silently for a deeper penetration.

"Yes, baby, I'll give you more." He stroked inward, slipping another finger into her, stretching her as he twisted his hand.

When a wet thumb slid over her little, forbidden hole, she bucked.

"Shhhh . . . let me. You'll like this. I swear it."

He hadn't been wrong yet. Not about anything dealing with her body, anyway. She turned her head away, unwilling to give him a glimpse of her tear-stained face or the rapture that was painting her cheeks with a new, carnal heat.

Her hands clutched at the ties and she wrapped her fingers around them, then lifted her bottom just a fraction higher, giving him permission to proceed. She wished she'd never lit a candle, because he could see her, see where his fingers played. She'd never be able to look him in the face without the memory of this act burning her cheeks.

As his long fingers swirled inside her, his thumb tunneled into her little hole. She couldn't help tightening around him. She couldn't believe it pleased him that she let him do this, and she couldn't relax. The foreignness of the concept brought an embarrassing clarity that she had little will to deny him anything. Would he think her easily led by any man?

How could she tell him that only he had ever tempted her to surrender completely? Even Jerry Hanson hadn't convinced her to let him look at more than her nipples in the light. She'd felt ashamed during the whole act, somehow less.

With Jake, she felt free to explore his body and her own reactions. Even this sordid little act didn't carry the deep sting of shame.

The realization returned a little confidence. He wouldn't be so keen to take her this way if he didn't derive some pleasure from the act. Perhaps it even fired his own lust. The evidence pressed strong and hard against her hip.

He shifted beneath her, his fingers delving deeper into her pussy, sliding in and out. His thumb swirled into her, coaxing the tight ring to relax beneath the pressure until the burning discomfort changed and she had to move, had to press forward and back on her knees to ease him deeper.

"I'm going to come up behind you. Open your legs so I can climb between." His fingers withdrew and Prudence moaned, rolling her face against the coverlet as she protested.

His body shifted, his thighs nudging her off; then his hands caressed the backs of her legs and pressed them apart. He gripped her hips and lifted her until her bottom stuck in the air.

"This is better?" she asked, sure she'd die of embarrassment any moment now.

"It is for me," he murmured. His hands rubbed over her warmed buttocks and parted them; his thumbs pressed open her folds.

He was staring at her. Into her. She could feel it.

She tugged hard against her ties. "Is this part of the punishment too?" she muttered. "You trying to embarrass me? Because it's working."

His laughter soughed over her like a caress. Then his hot breath licked at her bottom before he pressed open-mouthed kisses to her buttocks.

If Prudence could have pulled free at that moment, she would have reached between her legs to rub the ache building there. He was killing her. The ache intensifying. She knew where he was heading. She shouldn't allow it.

His tongue licked between her buttocks, following the crease, at last stroking over her little hole.

She groaned, partly from a hideously, deepening shame, mostly from an arousal that spurred a fresh release of cream from inside her. It seeped out to coat her nether lips, which clasped and opened noisily, wetly, the succulent sounds blending with his moist sounds as he swirled around her asshole.

"God, please don't," she said, achingly near to cresting. How wanton was she to enjoy this? She needed more, needed him to pierce her *there* again. She rubbed her breasts on the coverlet, letting the fabric abrade her aroused nipples. She rubbed and writhed beneath his hands, heat building between her legs, moisture streaming now from within her.

One of his wicked hands ground into her pussy, his palm rubbing her lips and the hard little nubbin—all at once. She squirmed to rub against his palm, coating him with her fluids, easing her motions as she pumped down and up, down and up, her thighs trembling as she tried to find just the angle to set off the explosion hovering just beyond her reach.

And then his mouth slid lower, his lips drawing on her folds, his tongue stroking into her, and Prudence became desperate for him to come inside her. Her thighs widened, trembling so hard she hoped she didn't collapse before she reached the summit.

Then he drew away again and she sobbed, unable to voice her protest, to beg for him to take her.

His thighs pressed hard against the backs of hers, his thick cock falling between her buttocks, sliding down as he dragged it along her crease. The thick, blunt head stroked over her asshole, and Prudence gasped noisily, caught between a sigh and a moan.

"Let me have you here, Prudence," he said, pushing softly at her entrance.

"You can't. It won't work."

"Don't you trust me yet?" he said, softly rubbing himself on her. She felt moisture drop between her buttocks, and his crown swirled in a tightening circle.

She hung on to her tethers, limp and shuddering. "You're asking too much."

"I promise I'll stop if I hurt you."

"This pleases you?"

"It will please you too." A hand slipped around her hips, fingers slid into her folds and speared into her pussy.

Prudence lunged backward, pressing on his cock, seeking a deepening penetration from his fingers. Heat curled deep in her belly, tightening like a watch spring. "Do it," she whispered.

His hips flexed forward, the thick tip of him pushing against her constricting muscles.

A slap landed on one side of her bottom, and she groaned, but her pussy opened and clasped around his fingers, and her asshole eased.

He slipped inside.

"Wicked!" she shouted. "Wicked man! I shouldn't want this!"

"But you do. Don't you, sweetheart?" he asked, his voice roughening, tightening just like his thighs were against hers. He ground into her, pressing inexorably deeper, stretching her beyond pain . . . straight into a dark pleasure that rippled throughout her body.

His hips pulled back. She followed him. When he flexed forward again his cock crammed deeper inside her, impossibly thick and hard.

"Jesus!" she cried out, her voice thin and high.

His fingers stroked into her pussy, tunneling deeply in the wetness. He added another. Was his whole hand inside her now?

God, she couldn't take any more. She was too full, stretched too tight, her pussy and her ass burning and rippling.

"Let go, baby. I can tell you're there, you're clamping like a bear's jaws around my hand and my cock. *Damn!*"

"Faster!" she said, her words strangling in her tight throat, she was so near to screaming.

Jake shuddered behind her; then his fingers pulled out, his palm cupping her pussy and pressing hard as his hips bucked against her bottom, pounding into her, faster, deeper. So hard her whole body shook and the bed squeaked noisily beneath them.

But she didn't care, couldn't think beyond the pressure building in her womb.

When Jake shouted, Prudence let go, her face dropping to the mattress, her mind opening to the darkness that blanketed her as her body convulsed beneath the thrusts of his powerful body.

When at last he slowed, Prudence wept.

"Damn, damn, damn." He pulled slowly out of her, then left her.

Her sobs deepened. When something wet slipped between her legs, she quieted. A cool, moist cloth soothed her swollen tissues, stroked away the moisture from her pussy and her inner thighs.

When it glided between her buttocks, she moaned.

"I'm sorry, baby," he said, his breath gusting against her neck. "I lost control. I didn't mean to hurt you."

Prudence shook her head, her face crumpling. "Well, you did."

7

Jake tossed the cloth to the floor and closed his eyes, sickened by his own actions. He never should have touched her. Not with anger ruling his body.

What had begun as punishment for her reckless behavior had quickly turned to dark, ruthless lust.

He'd wanted to claim her. Mark her as his. Make sure no man would ever touch her as deeply.

He'd succeeded beyond his dreams.

He lifted a hand to caress her, to soothe her, but stared at the darkness of his skin as it hovered above her delicate, pale shoulder.

Her breaths were jagged, tears had choked her voice. He'd done that. While everything inside him urged him to lie down beside her and take her in his arms, he held himself away. He'd done enough damage this night.

"I'll go."

"Oh, Jake. I'm sorry."

"I'm the one who needs to apologize."

She looked over her shoulder, her glassy gaze boring into his. "Untie me," she said quietly.

He reached over her and untied the knots at her wrists.

No sooner was she loosed, than she rolled toward him, coming up on her knees. She flung her arms around his shoulders and buried her face against his chest.

Jake closed his arms around her and hugged her close at last, rubbing his hands over her back.

Her lips opened on his collarbone, and she kissed him. "It didn't hurt that bad," she whispered.

"Of course not. You cry every time a man makes you happy."

"It wasn't the pain that made me cry."

He breathed deeply, hope flaring inside his tight chest. "Why then?"

"Because I've never been so . . . overcome. I felt too much," she kissed him again. "I'm going to hate for this to end."

"Does it have to? Do you have to go back?"

She grew still inside his arms. "Are you asking me to stay?"

Jake was tired of looking at the top of her head. He gripped her hair and tugged, tilting back her head. "Yeah, I'm asking."

Her gaze searched his face. "I know we hardly know each other, but is this all you want from me? I have to know."

"Being with me won't be easy," he said. "The folks in this town are good for the most part. But they might give you a hard time, because of me."

"Because you're part Indian?"

"And part outlaw."

"But they respect you."

"They respect a gun. They needed mine when the last sheriff decided to ranch. I was all they had."

"Are you trying to talk me out of staying?"

"Hell no. I'm just warning you."

"Jake, I'm stronger than I look. And not nearly as naïve as you think."

"You wrote that book, didn't you?"

Prudence wrinkled her nose. "How'd you guess?"

He snorted again, a satisfied smile stretching his lips. "That Katarina couldn't keep her eyes off my manly chest."

A grin stretched her lush mouth. "Neither can I."

"This is the good part, you know. The sex. The getting to know each other . . . that might not be as easy."

"I'm willing to stay. To try."

He swallowed. "All right, then. But you have to promise me a couple of things."

A smile started at the corner of her lush lips. "Anything."

"Don't say that before I even tell you what you have to do."

"I trust you."

"Even after what I did?"

"After what you did?" Her brows furrowed. "Do you think I didn't like that?"

"I hurt you."

"Sure, you did. But that doesn't mean I didn't like it."

"I made you cry."

"That's because it hurt so damn good. Can we do it again some time?"

Jake snorted, still not believing her. "Just don't get me mad like that again. I can't seem to keep my hands off your backside when you do."

"Honey, I'm afraid that's one promise I won't want to make."

Her lips slid into a wider grin, and Jake couldn't resist their invitation a second longer. He dipped his head and kissed her, mashing lips and teeth together.

"Did you like me warming your backside?" he growled when he came up for air.

"Well, it's not something I'd like every day of the week. I'd never want to sit down."

"But you liked it."

"Yeah, it made me feel everything more deeply. Guess that's why I cried."

He brushed her lips with another swift kiss, then leaned away. "Are you going to be in a hurry for me to say some things to you?"

A shadow crossed her face, but she didn't look away. "It's okay if you don't love me yet."

Relief, sharp and swift, filled him. When it came to saying it, even thinking it, he thought he might be downright yellow-bellied.

Suddenly, her eyes widened, and she stiffened in his arms. "Jake, I forgot to tell you something. About tomorrow morning—"

"This another scene from your dime novel?"

"Yes, at the end of the story there's this big—"

Jake pressed his finger to her lips. "Sorry, sweetheart, but you aren't interfering again. Besides, I have better ways to keep that mouth of yours occupied 'til dawn."

"But—"

"Tell you what. You can tell me later. Before I leave."

Prudence blew out a deep breath, her worry apparent in the depth of the frown wrinkling her forehead and the thinning of her full lips. "Promise you'll let me tell you before you go?"

"Of course, sweetheart." Then he rolled over her, stretching his body over hers, noticing once again how well they seemed to fit: chests rubbing together as if breathing the same breath, his cock settling naturally between her spreading thighs, her liquid arousal easing his forceful entry.

Her gaze met his—hers glittering with wide-open wonder

and trust to his tarnished, but growing hopeful gaze, glimpsing into his future.

Yeah, they were a perfect fit.

Prudence awoke as the sunlight climbed over the window-sill, and screamed. Jake had left—and he hadn't heard a thing about the bank because she'd fainted dead away the last time they'd made love.

She rolled to her side but was caught in the tangle of her arms. The bastard had tied her to the bed again!

No damn way was he going to walk into a bullet if she had the means to stop it. She rolled her hips, tucking her legs against her chest, then reached up with her feet to shove at the upper rail of the headboard.

The brass didn't budge on the first try, or the second, but went flying when she gave one final, breathless slam, and she was free.

Prudence couldn't get the knots free from her wrists, so she wound them around and around her wrists, tucking in the edges, then scrambled to find a decent dress among the several he'd torn from their hooks last night and tossed on the floor. What did a few wrinkles and footprints mean when your man was facing certain death?

Only she had to remind herself his death wasn't really so certain. She'd left the ending with a delicious ellipsis—three little dots that told the reader they'd learn the hero's fate in the next edition!

Why had she been so greedy? Why hadn't she satisfied her readers with a happy ending? Satisfied herself with the ending she knew she would have written—Jake and Katarina riding off into the sunset together? Or at least the little white church at the end of the main street to be married?

Stuffing her bare feet into her little half-boots, she fled the room, not bothering to lock the door after herself.

As she passed Mr. Pendergast's desk, she yelled, "What time is it?"

"Just a couple minutes to ten," he said, his eyebrows rising as she didn't bother to slow down on her way out the door.

Almost ten! Lord, she was going to be too late. She took off at a run, her feet lifting high, running fast and noticing the wind whistling through the back of her dress.

So she'd forgotten a button or two! Let them gape. She had to get to Jake. Stop him from entering that bank.

She rounded the corner of the main street and saw the bank sitting kitty-corner across the street from the saloon when shots rang out.

Shouts came from inside the bank, but she couldn't stop herself. Katarina wasn't shot. No one but the sheriff fell beneath the hail of bullets.

Prudence ran faster, the pain burning her side not nearly as sharp as the one tightening her chest.

The horses tied to the hitching post at the front of the bank hadn't stopped rearing up on their hind legs or giving their panicked whinnies when she tore open the door of the bank and rushed inside.

A man grabbed her around the waist and pulled her back against his chest.

Prudence jabbed his shin with her heel, turned slightly, and rammed her fist between his legs. Only he'd stepped to the side and her fist hit granite muscle. Pain radiated up to her elbow.

Again, strong arms enfolded her. "It's all right. Shhhh . . . sweetheart. Stop fighting me. It's me. I've got you."

Jake's gentle crooning finally penetrated her panic, and Prudence slumped against his chest. "Jake? You're all right?"

"Not a scratch. Can you stand on your own if I let you go?"

The blood that had drained from her head came back with a rush as she turned. Her fist came up and she punched him straight in the jaw.

Muffled laughter sounded behind her, but she didn't care. "You read my book!"

"Said I would," he said with a lopsided smile, rubbing his reddening jaw.

"You read my book!" she repeated, and stomped her foot. "You let me think you didn't believe me."

"I didn't. Not really. But I read it anyway. So did Billy," he said, nodding to the man standing over two bandits lying on the floor with their hands behind their heads. "We met at the office this morning and decided to set a trap . . . just in case." His eyes narrowed and raked down her body. "How'd you get untied?"

She raised her fists, shaking them, showing him the fabric still tied to her wrists. "I didn't, and I'll punch you a second time if you ever tie me up again."

Jake's slow grin stretched across his face. "You know, everyone in town's gonna know I tied you to your bed now."

She lifted her chin. "Guess you're going to have to make an honest woman of me."

"Guess I will." His gaze softened. "Promise me one thing."

Prudence swallowed, her anger draining away beneath the warmth of his gaze. "What?"

"Promise me you won't ever write about me again."

"Afraid of my talents, Sheriff?"

"Choose someone more deserving of your skill, sweetheart," he said, his tone dry as dust. "Like the James Gang or the Younger Brothers."

She canted her head. "What if I turn my talents to writing a more romantic tale?"

"Then make sure your hero has the kind of wife he has to tip over his knee every once in a while," he drawled.

Prudence's glance slid away for a moment; then she gave him a blazing "Katarina" smile—the kind that knocked her hero sideways and left him breathless every time.

Jake's breath caught. His gaze locked on her lush mouth.

Prudence continued to smile, inwardly, brilliantly, as Jake drew her close for a kiss. She knew exactly the sort of tale she'd tell in the sequels—all with happy-ever-after endings. *After many roller coaster near mishaps . . .*

After all, a good story deserved a hint of danger, a strong hero—and a bold heroine. Katarina wasn't the only woman with a blazing sense of adventure or a lust for a legend.

SECOND WIND

MYLA JACKSON

1

Thunderstruck, Kansas, 1884

Dolly Sherman sat on her trunk, her hands on the edge of the basket, staring out at the miles and miles of prairie below her balloon, or as she liked to refer to it, her air ship. In the vastness of the tall grasses and the gently rolling hills, she could see her future before her. A rush of excitement radiated through her insides. She was finally realizing her dreams. "With that front blowing in behind us, we should be in Dodge City by nightfall."

"I hope we make it to Dodge City before that storm gets to us." Ron Casey stood beside her, his frowning gaze on the rear where storm clouds pushed in behind them. "Don't you think we should put down somewhere before the weather gets bad?"

Ron's words drifted past her like dandelion fluff to be brushed aside. "We'll get there well before the Wild West Show arrives. It gives us a chance to do some repairs to the balloon and maybe put a shiny new coat of lacquer on the basket. I can't wait to meet Mr. Cody in person." Absently, she adjusted the glass vase attached to the inside of the basket. The vase contained a red rose she'd plucked from a garden in Cheyenne.

Eyes narrowed, Ron muttered, "He's just a man. Don't know why you're so all fired up."

"Don't you see? This is the chance of a lifetime." Dolly jumped up from her perch and swung her arms wide. The movement caused the basket to tip violently.

"Hey, watch out!" Ron's hands shot out to grab the ropes anchoring the basket to the balloon. His frown deepened until he looked closely at her face. Then his glower lightened into a smile. "You're the darnedest female, you know that?"

She tipped her head to the side. "Why's that?"

"No matter how hard I try, I can't be mad at you. Especially with your eyes lit up like firecrackers."

"I can't help it. Do you realize, the Wild West Show is about the biggest hit since Barnum & Bailey? And we're going to be in it. We're going to be famous!" She flung her arms around Ron's neck and squealed.

His hands clamped around her waist, his legs spread wide to balance their shifting weight. "Careful there, sweetheart. Can't fall out of the basket now. Not when you're this close to makin' your dreams come true, now can you?"

"I couldn't believe we didn't see him in the crowd at Cheyenne. Buffalo Bill Cody was there and he saw our show." Dolly captured each side of Ron's face between her palms and stared into his eyes. "He wants us. Can you believe it?" She leaned forward and planted a whopping kiss square on Ron's lips. "He wants us."

Ron's hands rested on her hips and pulled her close. "Well, now. If I'd known you'd get so excited about being a part of the Wild West Show, I'd have figured a way to get you in it sooner." He leaned forward and returned the kiss, his hands pulling her hips closer. "I like you like this."

Dolly had laid the groundwork early on in her relationship

with Ron. They were partners, not lovers. As long as he didn't cross the line, they'd get along just fine.

With the excitement of being invited to audition for the Wild West Show in Dodge City three days from now, Dolly couldn't stand still. Her body rippled with energy that no amount of sitting in a basket suspended high above the plains could contain. She had to do something to release some of her pent-up anticipation.

"I know this is against everything I've ever said, but I'm so happy, I can't think straight. I want to kiss you." She wrapped her arms around Ron's neck and kissed him back.

In the back of her mind, she knew she shouldn't lead Ron on. She didn't love him enough to marry him, but . . . well . . . how often did a girl get a chance to have her dreams come true?

Holding her at arm's length, Ron stared down into her eyes. "Are you sure about this?"

A sudden gust of wind bucked the basket. Ron let go of Dolly to grab the edge.

Off balance, Dolly pitched to the side and fell, hitting her head against her trunk. For a moment, blackness engulfed her.

"Dolly, are you all right?" Ron pulled her to her feet and hugged her close. "You had me scared for a moment. Are you sure you're all right?" He stood straight and cocky, and his hands moved upward to trace the sharp indentation of her waist. "Ummm . . . I've wanted to do this for so long." When he reached her breasts, he paused. "What? No corset?"

"Not that it's any of your business, but it was just too darned hot for one today and I fancied breathing for a change." For six months, she'd held this man at arm's length, determined to keep their relationship strictly business, despite Ron's attempts to the contrary. But the heady rush of pending success overruled her normally steadfast commonsense, giving way to the excitement of her future and the looming danger nipping at their heels.

When the pads of Ron's thumbs brushed the underside of her breasts, Dolly didn't slap him aside and give him a thorough tongue-lashing as she should; instead, she leaned into his stroke.

Ron gazed down at her as if trying to read her thoughts. "Aren't you going to toss me over the edge?" He pressed a kiss to her lips, tracing a path from her lips, along her jawline, and to that very sensitive spot beneath her ear.

"Maybe later. Right now, I'm too happy to be angry with you." Despite her initial misgivings, her body responded to his tender attack.

"Good, 'cause I've wanted to do this for a long time." His thumbs grew bolder, daring to circle the tips of her nipples, shaping and forming them into tight distended buds. Then his fingers tugged at the buttons of her shirtwaist blouse, exposing more of her flesh.

"We really shouldn't do this." Dolly pushed against his chest, enjoying the hard planes of his muscles beneath her fingertips.

"Why shouldn't we? You're a widow, for Pete's sake. Who will know?" Having freed all the buttons, he pushed the shirt aside along with the chemise beneath, exposing two aching breasts to the sultry breeze.

Deep inside, Dolly knew she didn't love Ron like a lover should. Perhaps that more than their business relationship had made it easy for her to keep him at arm's length.

But with the breeze kissing the tips of her breasts, all the old longing to be held in a man's arms returned in a heady rush. With a half-hearted attempt to restore reason, she stepped away. The movement tilted the basket, sending Ron crashing against her. Oh hell, she'd been a widow for two long years without the comfort of a man's embrace, why should she deny her natural urges?

She reached up and kissed Ron hard on the lips. Okay, so she didn't feel anything other than desire. No warm, lingering sense of belonging, only the hot flood of unbridled passion. "Don't think everything changes when this is all over." Her fingers made quick work of the buttons on his shirt.

His lips found her breasts. Between kissing and nibbling at one, then the other, he replied, "No, ma'am. Everything will be just as it was."

Deep in her heart, Dolly doubted that, but her body took over where her brain failed to function. "It will be the same," she said fiercely as the ache in her belly transcended to moisture flowing from her pussy. She liked Ron only as a friend. How could she consider fucking her friend?

Her friend lifted her skirts up to her waist and deftly untied her petticoat. The fabric dropped to the floor of the basket, and Dolly kicked her feet free. Next to go were her pantaloons, only a tie string away from nakedness.

The balloon bucked in the rising wind.

Dolly leaned against the basket's edge, her skirts around her ankles, her pussy open to the air and to Ron's view. High in the sky with no one the wiser, the danger of being caught, along with the rising wind, only added to her excitement.

She slid Ron's vest from his shoulders, yanked his shirt from his trousers, and tossed that to the floor as well. When she reached for the button to his trousers, all was lost. Her body was on fire, with only one way to quench the heat.

Beneath his row of buttons, Ron's cock pressed hard against Dolly's fingers. Suddenly, she couldn't get to him fast enough. As if by slaking her thirst, she'd get past this random burst of insanity. Ron's trousers slid to the top of his boots, revealing a rock-hard cock, swollen and throbbing.

Planting his hands on either side of her, Ron pressed his cock into her furry mound. "I've wanted this for so long, I hurt." His lips crushed hers, his hands cupping her ass, kneading her naked flesh.

Yes. She'd been celibate too long. Yes, she wanted him. Yes, she'd pay for it later. None of that mattered now. Only the feel of his hands on her, sliding around to part her cheeks. He fingered a line down her crack to the tight little hole. As he lowered her to the nest of their fallen clothes, she squashed her last twinges of misgivings. Even the pesky one telling her it was a mistake to make love to a man she felt no more for than the love of a friend.

Ron loosened the buttons and ties of her skirt, lifting them over her head and then using them as a pillow. He struggled a little with the ribbon she used to pull her hair back in a loose knot. When she finally lay naked among her skirts, he smiled down at her, his gaze raking in every inch of her. "I've only caught glimpses of you naked."

Dolly gasped. "You weren't supposed to be looking." She should have suspected as much. Traveling across this vast country in nothing more than a balloon, they weren't always privy to a hotel or bathhouse. Many times, they'd camped by streams where she thought she'd gotten far enough away to escape his eager gaze. Apparently not. In many places she hadn't gone far. With the very real threat of Indians and thieves, Dolly didn't stray far from her only protection.

As his gaze slid across her lips, down her neck, to her breasts, and finally to the apex of her thighs, she shivered. The wind was picking up, and they dared not take their minds off navigating their only means of making a living for long, or they'd end up crashed out in the middle of nowhere Kansas and miss their appointment with Buffalo Bill Cody.

Ron tweaked her nipple, rolling it between his thumb and forefinger.

Dolly couldn't hold back the moan that slipped from her lips. She'd gone far too long without a man's touch.

"Like that, do you? You'll like this even better." He bent forward and took the hard little bud between his teeth and nipped at it.

Dolly's back arched off the basket floor. She dug her fingers into his overlong hair and dragged him closer until his mouth fully encompassed her right nipple. "You only knew I'd like it because you do it to all your women." Her words weren't harsh or accusing. She understood Ron perhaps better than he understood himself. He loved women, and they loved him. He was as allergic to commitment as some men were allergic to rattlesnake poison. As long as you knew that going into a relationship with Ron, you'd be all right. Only she wasn't going into a relationship with Ron, she was after only a little celebratory sex, nothing more.

"I'd give up all the other women to have you forever, Dolly Sherman. Marry me." His words whispered against her skin in warm puffs as his mouth moved down her torso. "I could spend the rest of my life getting to know every part of you."

A shiver of alarm rushed over her and she shrugged it off. He probably said that to every woman he made love to before he skipped town. "You'd get bored after one night, Ron Casey." Dolly didn't resist when Ron's knees pressed between her thighs. After all the months of working closely beside him, admiring his well-defined muscles and handsome face, she was ready to let him have his wicked way with her.

"I'd never be bored of you, Dolly. You're one hundred percent gold nugget. All those other women were fool's gold, never around long enough to outlast their shine." His tongue licked a path from her belly button to the curly mound guarding the aching entrance to her pussy.

"Shut up, Ron, and get down to business. The storm will be on us before you know it."

"Oh, no, you don't. I've waited a long time for this." His fingers threaded through her soft, curly hairs to find that wet center, dripping with her desire. "Yeah, that's the way I like it, slick and ready." He dipped in, laving the juices with his tongue. "Ummm . . . sweeter than honey."

The balloon dipped, sending the basket swaying side to side. Another flash of lightning had Dolly counting seconds in her head. One . . . two . . .

Ron parted her folds, exposing her clitoris to the cooling air before his tongue flicked the swollen nub.

"There . . . oh there!" Dolly lost count after two and bucked beneath him. The more he tongued her the less she cared what was happening above the rim of the basket. Delicious, delectable tension built, claiming every nerve and muscle in her body, rising to a screaming pitch. That magical tongue stroked and strummed until her body ignited in an explosion of sensations, cascading in waves as she tumbled back to sated sanity.

Ron climbed back up her body, positioning his cock at the entrance to her moisture-drenched cunt. "Now for the finale." He plunged into her wetness, sliding all the way in until his balls slapped against her buttocks.

Having gone two years without, Dolly's vaginal walls were tight and stretched over his girth. Her husband had been smaller, much smaller, and he'd been less concerned about pleasing her than he was about pleasing himself. Not Ron. Oh, no, not Ron.

As Ron pumped in and out of her, his speed increasing with the strength of the wind, Dolly couldn't help regretting she didn't love Ron. Lust, yes. Love? What was love anyway? She and her husband had had a comfortable relationship of mutual need. Had she loved him? How perfect would it be to love her partner and travel the country by his side, making love along the way?

Burying his face in her neck, Ron grabbed her hips and ground into her one last time. His cock throbbed and strained inside her channel.

A moment of sanity returned, and Dolly shoved his hips back just as his seed spurted out.

Instead of filling her womb, his juices dropped to the floor of the basket.

Several drops of rain slapped against her cheek, shaking her free of the haze of passion, and Dolly sprang to her feet, naked and uncaring of her nudeness. "Oh, sweet Jesus."

Ron stood beside her. "Holy smokes, we're going down!"

"What was I thinking?" Dolly flared the kerosene in a last-ditch effort to pump heat into the struggling balloon. Only thirty feet from the ground, she knew her efforts were wasted. As the ground rushed toward her, regret filled her for her lapse in judgment. "What have I done?"

2

Despite the looming clouds and the scent of rain in the air, Seth Turner rode out on the prairie as far away from the house as possible. His foreman had spotted Kit Jameson riding hard toward the ranch house. That woman never gave up. Her constant badgerin' to marry him and combine the two ranches had Seth turning around in the barnyard ready to ride back out after being on the range all day. Kit was his friend. He could no more marry and bed her than he could his horse, Ranger. That would be like makin' love to a sister. He shuddered.

When Mrs. Hornbuckle hurried out of the house, he knew something more than Kit was about to go wrong with his day. She pressed a letter into his hand and told him to hurry away before Kit arrived.

Before he tore open the letter, he knew what it would say. Glad he'd left the house and Mrs. Hornbuckle's prying eyes, he rode hard until he couldn't see a soul in sight. He couldn't stomach another pitying look as he read his latest rejection letter.

After galloping for over two miles, he brought Ranger, his

black stallion, to a halt. Before he tore open the letter, he steeled himself for the inevitable disappointment. How many times had he thought he'd found a woman to marry and breed heirs to his vast land holdings only to have them cry off before the wedding date arrived?

If he didn't have a full-scale ranching operation to run, he'd go back East, and woo and marry a woman instead of advertising in a damned newspaper. The unfortunate fact remained, he couldn't spare the time. He'd lost his foreman when Jeb's wife insisted they move back East to care for her ailing parents.

Perhaps he was destined to live his life alone with only the local whores to warm his bed on occasion. Mabel and Pearl weren't much to look at. In fact, they looked a lot like a couple of old mares ridden hard and put up wet.

He unfolded the single sheet of paper. As he read the letter, he sighed. Millie Peabody, spinster, had made the decision to remain in Boston. After learning of her decision to become a mail-order bride, the butcher asked her to stay and marry him. As she was much more suited to life in a city, she'd accepted his kind offer.

Crushing the letter in his fist, Seth swore. Was this God's plan for him? Was he to live out his days without a wife? Without a way to spawn the children he craved? "What is it you want me to do? Beg?" He shook his fist at the sky.

Seth swung his leg over the saddle and dropped to the ground. He'd had it with being nice. A man didn't acquire a 5,000-acre spread and a herd of over 1,000 head of cattle by the age of 30 by being nice.

He'd had his share of struggles, shot his share of horse and cattle thieves, and handled just about every problem imaginable. This particular challenge had him stumped. He couldn't argue, fistfight, or shoot his way into a marriage.

Seth paced several yards.

Ranger, his prized black stallion, followed.

When Seth ground to a halt, Ranger bumped into him.

"Why can't a woman apply for the job like a regular ranch hand? A short notice in the newspaper listing my requirements should have them lined up. All a woman has to do is show up with two legs, two breasts, and the ability to bear children. I don't care if she's as ugly as a stump or as wide as a barn. All I want is a woman to give me children.

Ranger nickered.

"Why can't women be more like horses? All you have to do is go out into a pasture and pick one. Why can't people do that?" Grabbing the horse's bridle, Seth glared into soft brown eyes. "Now what? Now where can I turn to find a woman?"

Ranger tossed his head skyward, shaking Seth's grip.

"What, even you can't give a cowboy some advice? Tell me, whom should I turn to?"

Again, the horse lifted his head toward the heavens, whickering softly.

Seth's eyes narrowed, and he looked toward the darkening sky where clouds had built a solid wall to the west. "You mean pray?" Seth ran a hand through his hair and considered the option. "You think He'll help me?"

Nodding, Ranger stomped the ground with his right front hoof.

"Now?" Seth glanced around at the fields of prairie grass littered with cows. "Shouldn't I do something like that in a church?" The nearest church was fifteen miles away. He could go there on Sunday.

Ranger shook his mane.

"You mean here?"

A snort and a nod were his answer.

With a sigh, Seth scraped his hat from his head and dropped to one knee. "I feel stupid."

A nicker sounding suspiciously like laughter erupted from Ranger's full equine lips.

"Can't get no respect. Even from my damned horse." He glared at Ranger. "I'm a desperate man. If praying will help, by God, I'll do it. Despite your snickering."

He dropped his chin and searched his memory for the fancy words he remembered from when he'd attended church as a child. Hell, the last time he was in a church was when he went with his mamma at least twenty-five years ago.

Twenty-five years and none of the words came to him. Nope. Nothing.

Ranger nudged him with his soft muzzle.

"Okay, okay. I'm getting to it." Seth cleared his throat. "Dear Lord—" Lightning flashed, the glow penetrating Seth's eyelids. "I know it's been a while—" Thunder rumbled. "Okay, it's been a long time. Nothin' gets by you, does it?"

Another rumble shook the earth beneath Seth's knee.

Ranger pawed the earth.

"If you could see it in your heart to send me a woman, I'd be much obliged." His words ended in a rush. "There, I prayed." Seth straightened and plunked his hat on his head.

A brilliant flash of lightning ripped through the clouds, skimming across the ground.

Seth jumped back as if the bolt aimed at him.

Ranger pushed Seth with his nose.

"Oh yeah, I forgot." Seth dropped back down to one knee, tipped his hat, and said, "Amen."

When he rose, he glanced toward the east, half hoping . . . For what? A woman to come riding across the prairie and straight into his arms?

Seth snorted. "That'll happen about as soon as it starts raining women from the sky." Thunder added to his harsh laughter.

Ranger reared and backed away.

"What's wrong with you? Never known you to be afraid of a little ol' storm."

Fat drops of rain splashed against his face. "Come on, let's go back to the barn. The good Lord ain't gonna deliver her here in the middle of nowhere."

As Seth swung up into the saddle, another clap of thunder shook the air. "A man could be struck by lightning out here without a tree within miles." A flash struck so close the light blinded him.

Just as he settled into his saddle, something struck him from behind, knocking him clean off his horse. He landed on his chest, the force of the fall knocking the air from his lungs. With his face full of buffalo grass and dust, he couldn't breathe.

What the hell?

As soon as he could suck in enough breath to refill his lungs, Seth rolled to his side, drawing the six-shooter from his holster.

What he saw was unlike anything he'd ever seen in his entire life. A balloon as big as his barn blew over his head dragging what looked like a giant basket along the ground. The basket hit a knoll and tipped over. A door sprang open, spilling some of its contents into the tall prairie grass before moving along, pushed by the strengthening storm. Seth's gaze followed its path until it disappeared over a hill.

Ranger trotted after the monster balloon.

"Whoa, boy. Where do you think you're goin'?"

When the horse reached the small knoll where the basket had tipped, he stopped and nickered.

"Find something?" Rubbing the lump on the back of his head, Seth tromped through the tall grass. As he closed the distance between himself and the horse, a moan rose from the ground. For a moment, Seth thought the wind made the noise. Then another followed the first. Nope. That wasn't wind.

Seth loped to the spot and looked down. He blinked his eyes and looked again.

"No, I'm not believin' this. That ain't what it looks like. No sirree. That bump on my head musta been worse than I thought." He pressed the rising lump, pain shooting down the base of his neck. "Yup, definitely seeing things." Seth grabbed for Ranger's reins.

The horse jerked free and nodded toward the aberration on the ground.

"Don't tell me you're seein' things too." Seth glanced around for his hat before he realized he'd stuck it back on his head. "It can't be real." His gaze returned to the inert form. "But it sure looks like a woman."

His imagination had conjured a woman. She lay on her side with her back to him, naked as the day she was born, but fully growed, judging by her length and the full swell of her hips and thighs. A full mane of golden tresses flowed down over her shoulders to tangle in the buffalo grass.

She moaned and rolled to her back, revealing full, plump breasts prettier than ripe melons, a flat belly, and a triangle of curly blond hair at the juncture of her thighs.

Seth swallowed, his spit lodging at the top of his throat. He inched forward. "If this is a dream"—he shot a glare at Ranger— "don't wake me." Dropping to his knees, he reached out to touch the softest skin he ever laid his hands on. He smoothed his finger over the arm that had moved to drape over her breasts. The arm slid to her side.

Seth's fingers fell to a rosy brown nipple. As if he'd just been kicked in the gut by Ranger, all the air left Seth's lungs, leaving him light-headed and dizzy, while he struggled to breathe. The nipple puckered into a tight bead.

His groin tightened and a flood of longing jerked at Seth's cock.

This beautiful woman was a ray of sunshine. For a moment, Seth swore she held the storm at bay until he could explore every curve, swell, and crevice with his hands. "It can't be," he said in a reverent tone. The silky skin and gentle curves in all the right places, along with the thatch of curly blond hair over her cunt, could only be one thing.

As quiet as a parson in church, Seth spoke, "The Lord answered my prayer." Then he was on his feet whooping and hollering like a young cowboy receiving his first lay from a saloon whore.

A crack of thunder and more raindrops brought him back to earth. He slapped his hat to his chest, bowing his head for a quick, "Thank you kindly, Lord." Then he knelt beside the woman, a grin spreading across his face. No one had ever given him such a gift. Anything he'd gotten in life, he'd had to earn through blood, sweat, and a few bullets. But what he got, he held on to. And he, by God, would hold on to this gift with both hands.

A fat drop of rain slapped against Dolly's eyelid. Her face twitched to shake it loose. Something prickled and jabbed into her side, and her head ached like a train ran through. Was she sick? Had she rolled off her bedroll and onto the grass? If so, why was the grass poking through her nightclothes? Without opening her eyes, she ran a hand over her belly. Her naked belly.

Dolly gasped, her eyes popping open to stare up into the deepest brown eyes she'd ever seen. They didn't belong to Ron; he had green eyes. She'd never seen this man before in her life. Fear shot through her chest and jerked her into an upright position.

The man grinned. "I can't believe my luck." Then he tipped his head to the sky. "Thank you, thank you, Lord."

"Who the hell are you?" A quick glance confirmed it wasn't only her belly that was exposed to the wind and now the steadily falling rain. A drop of rain rolled across her chest and dribbled down between her breasts.

The man's gaze followed its path all the way to her . . .

She reached out and smacked his face, then covered her breasts with one arm and her pussy with her hand. "How rude! Where are my clothes?" Her gaze panned the tall grass around her. No dress, no blouse, nothing. Just a solid black horse that seemed to be enjoying her discomfort.

The man rubbed the red handprint on his cheek, his grin broadening. "I couldn't help staring. You're about the purdiest little filly I've ever seen." He unbuttoned his vest and handed it to her.

"And you think this is going to cover everything important?" She held the vest to her chest, her eyes narrowing.

The cowboy's face turned a bright red. "No, ma'am. Pardon." He slipped his suspenders from his shoulders and let them fall to his waist. Fumbling with one button at a time, he eventually opened his shirt and peeled it off the broadest shoulders Dolly had ever seen. His chest, a plane of hard, defined muscles, was sprinkled with crisp, dark curls, narrowed to a thin line, leading down to disappear below the button of his trousers.

Dolly gulped, almost tempted to tell him to put the shirt back on. Instead, she grabbed for the garment and held it to her chest.

He stood, naked from the waist up, his arms crossed over his chest like a conquering hero.

Her mouth dried, her pussy reacting to his proximity and the direction of his gaze resting on the swells of her breasts. "Do you mind?"

His brow furrowed. "Mind what?"

She stomped her foot in the grass and got jabbed by a prickly buffalo grass stalk. "At least turn your back."

"No, ma'am. I never turn my back on a stranger. Although I don't think we'll be strangers long."

The black stallion nickered as if laughing at his owner.

So the oaf thought to embarrass her by forcing her to dress in front of him? Anger pushed Dolly to her feet. Her vision blurred at the sudden movement. Wanting to cling to her ire, Dolly found herself clinging to the mountain of a man. "What happened? Why am I so dizzy?"

One of his large hands curved around her naked back; the other pressed her face to his bare, damp chest. Yes, indeed, it was as solid as it looked, not a spare ounce of flesh, and every inch tanned. The scent of earth and leather filled her nostrils as a crisp curl tickled her nose.

"You fell from the sky." The man's voice rumbled in his chest, the bass tones and resonance lulling Dolly into a trance until his words sank in.

Sky? She pushed back in his arms and stared up into his eyes. The wind whipped strands of her hair across her cheeks, and raindrops trickled into her eyes. She blinked them away, her heart pounding against her ribs. "My balloon!"

The man's arms, as strong as iron bars, jailed her within his embrace. "It's probably long gone by now. Don't worry, you can stay at my house."

Was he out of his mind or just simple? "Let me go. I have to find my balloon!" Her eyes widened and she gasped. "Ron. Where's Ron?"

A frown creased the man's tanned brow. "Ron?"

"The man I was with. He must be hurt. We have to find him."

3

Man? She had been with a man? Seth shot a glance at Ranger. Had God given him a gift, or only planned to tease him into an early, frustrated grave?

Ranger stepped forward and nudged Seth's back.

Okay, okay, he'd figure it out. "This man Rob, is he your husband?" Seth asked.

"No," she answered. Then her lips clamped shut for a moment. "I mean, yes. Yes, Ron Casey is my husband."

Seth prided himself in reading a man's character, but he didn't have much practice with women, other than the whores in town and his neighbor Kit. And she was more like a man than a woman in his mind.

This golden-haired beauty standing in front of him said one thing, but her cornflower blue eyes said the opposite. Could she want him to think she was married to keep him from claiming what was his God-gifted right? His gut told him she wasn't any more married to this man named Rob, or Ron or whatever his name was, than she was to Ranger.

Until she was legally bound by the church, she was fair game in Seth's eyes.

He shot a look heavenward. Was that it? He had to work for his gift? In his years as a cowboy and rancher he'd never known the good Lord to give him anything for free.

Despite how right she felt in his arms, her skin as soft as newly tanned doe hide, Seth let her go. "All right, then. Let's go find Rob."

"Ron. My . . . husband's name is Rob. I mean Ron." Her cheeks burned a fiery red, making her even more beautiful standing there in his light blue shirt. The tails of the garment hung to her knees, exposing trim calves and the narrowest ankles Seth had ever seen on an adult. "Which way did the balloon go?" she asked.

Tempted to tell her different, the honesty in Seth demanded he help her find the missing balloon and man. "The balloon went that way."

His pretty *gift* turned on her heel and picked her way through the coarse grass, her face screwing into a frown with every tentative step.

He let her go ahead of him for a few moments just to watch her legs—legs he could imagine wrapped around his waist as he plunged into her. No, his woman wasn't married. The good Lord wouldn't be that cruel. All Seth had to do was convince her that she belonged to him. He clapped his hands together, eager to accept the challenge. No time like the present to start.

"You'll never find him at that rate. Allow me." He scooped her up in his arms as if she weighed no more than a newborn kitten. Already, her bare feet were covered in scratches with bright red blood oozing from several deeper wounds.

"Put me down!" She kicked her feet and wiggled a lot, the shirt riding up until her thighs were rubbing against his bare chest.

Seth held tight to what was his. His rock-hard cock twitched behind the buttons of his trousers, eager to claim her. But as with his horses, he knew patience was the key to bringing her around to his way of thinking. Soon, he'd be riding her hard and she'd be screaming for more.

When she reached out and slapped his chest, she did it only once, her hand coming to rest in the dark curls surrounding his hard brown nipple. "Let me down." This time her words were not nearly so convincing. As she stared at her small white hand against his suntanned skin, the hard line of her lips softened and her eyes widened. Beneath the fabric of his shirt, her chest rose and fell in shallow, rapid breaths.

In his horse-soothing voice he whispered against her ear, "You know you can't walk barefooted out here. Let me help you, Angel."

"My name's not Angel, it's Dolly," she said in a breathy voice. Her gaze traveled up his neck to rest on his lips. "You should put me down. I don't even know you."

"Just being friendly, darlin', and we can fix the not knowin' part. I'm Seth Turner. I work this ranch."

She didn't look around at the land; instead, her gaze traveled upward to connect with his. Her hand flexed in the hairs on his chest.

Seth liked the way she felt in his arms. He could carry her all day, but there were better things to do with a willing woman. He just had to show her how willing she could be.

All he needed was a little patience. The cock straining against the confines of his trousers was anything but patient.

"Hey!" a voice sounded from the other side of the hill.

"That's Ron." Dolly pushed against him in an attempt to get down.

Seth's grip tightened; his hand behind her back curled up under her arm where her breast swelled beneath the shirt. Had he ever felt anything so soft, so completely female? Sure, the whores back in Dodge City were women, but they were like tough leather dipped in cheap perfume, not sweet-smelling like the prairie flowers and light as a feather.

"Help!"

Dolly bucked in his arms, bringing him back to the task at hand. "If you must carry me, at least move a little faster. Ron might be hurt."

In no hurry to find the other man, Seth lengthened his stride nonetheless. He topped the hill and they stared out over the rolling prairie. A hand waved at them from the tall grass.

"Help! I think I've broken my leg."

Seth set Dolly down next to a man lying in the grass clutching at his leg, his face gray and strained.

Dolly dropped to her knees, concern pressing a frown between her eyes. "Ron, are you okay?" She stared out above the grass. "Where's the balloon? We have to find the balloon!"

Ron's mouth pressed into a pain-filled line. "The storm blew it away. I need a doctor. I think my leg's busted."

"I'm sorry, Ron. It's just . . . my balloon," she wailed. "We have to find it. We're supposed to be in Dodge City in three days. Without it, we have nothing."

What had her so worried about making it to Dodge City in three days? Seth didn't have all the answers, but he was a patient man, when he needed to be, when the effort was worth the wait. A glance at the woman with the golden blond hair and petite little body reminded him just how worthy of his patience she was.

"Thanks. At least I know where your loyalties lie." Ron shifted, his eyes squeezing shut. "You gotta get me outta here; my leg hurts like hell."

Her face pink and her brows pulled low over her eyes, Dolly straightened and planted her hands on her hips. "Don't just stand there, help him."

Seth scratched his chin. "Seein' as I only have one horse, I can't get you both back to the house right now." He nodded at the man on the ground. "I'll have to leave you here while I go get help."

"I'm staying with my . . . husband." Dolly's hands clasped together in front of her where she wrung them like yesterday's laundry.

Ron's grimace of pain changed briefly into one of surprise. "Husb—"

Dolly nudged the man's wounded leg with her bare toe.

"Ouch! Careful, Dolly, I really think it's broke."

"I'm sorry, darling." She dropped to her knees and smoothed a hand over the man's brow. "Want me to kiss it better?" She leaned across him and planted a chaste kiss on his forehead, not his lips.

Another sign of an unmarried woman, in Seth's mind. Any wife of his would be kissing his lips, not his forehead.

Ron's hands captured her bare thighs and squeezed.

Dolly yelped and slapped his hands away. "Not now, honey," she said through clenched teeth.

"How about later, *wife*?" He smacked her bottom and grinned.

"You have a broken leg, sweetie. We mustn't damage it further."

Dolly shot a glare at Ron when she thought Seth had turned toward his horse. But Seth caught the tight lips and the glare out of the corner of his eye. If she was married to this man, Seth was the President of the United States. Not that Ron hadn't tasted of her honey, which caused a small twinge in Seth's gut. She might have made love with Ron in the past, but once she loved Seth, she'd never look back.

Seth had the advantage of his upbringing on his side. After his mother and father died of scarlet fever, he'd been raised by Madame Rosalee down in Dodge City. He'd had the best education in what it took to make a woman beg for more, and he wasn't afraid to use his knowledge to get what he wanted. Yes, sirree. Just because he couldn't get a woman to move to Kansas, didn't mean he couldn't woo one already in Kansas using his very special skills.

Thunder rumbled, reminding him of the very real danger of his *gift* being struck by lightning. "You'll come with me."

She leaped to her feet, facing him with her hands on her hips. "I'll stay with my husband." Her blue eyes sparked like the hottest fire.

Seth had to shove his hands in his pockets to keep from pulling her into his arms and kissing her soundly on those pretty, thin lips.

A whoop and holler sounded from over the top of the hill, and a whirlwind of motion, girl, and horseflesh crested the hill and skidded to a close stop in the grass next to where Seth and Dolly stood.

"Hey, Turner, you had me worried. I thought you'd been thrown from your horse. Why's Ranger standing up on the rise?"

The voice was feminine, a little rough around the edges, but the person astride the horse in men's trousers, shirt, and vest looked more like a young cowboy than a woman. Kit Jameson had spent too many of her young years in the company of rough and ready men. She didn't know a chemise from a petticoat and didn't want to, as far as Seth could tell. And she was a peskier thorn in his side than any woman had a right to be.

He scowled up at her. "How'd you find me?"

"Oh, don't get your chaps in a twist. Remember, I know where your favorite hiding places are." Her gaze raked the length of Dolly, her brows raising the lower her gaze traveled. "Trespassers? Want me to shoot 'em?" She reached for the revolver in the holster around her waist.

"No, of course not. But since you're here, you can help me get them back to the ranch house." Seth dropped to one knee. "This one's gone and busted his leg."

"Not by choice, believe me." Ron grimaced when Seth ran his hands the length of the injured limb. He stared up at Kit, his eyes narrowing as if he didn't trust her not to shoot him.

"It's busted all right." Seth grabbed the man's boot and pulled the leg out straight.

Ron yelled, "Holy Jesus!" Then he fell over on his back, out cold.

Seth didn't like hurting the man, much, but if he wanted to walk on that leg again, the bone needed to be straightened or he'd have problems later. Being unconscious wasn't such a bad thing either, considering the ride back to the ranch would hurt like hell. He glanced up at Kit. "Mind if I drop him on the back of your horse? I don't think he'll give you any trouble."

"Not like that he won't." Kit chuckled, her gaze running the length of the unconscious man. "He's a looker for a city fella."

"And married." Seth shot a look at Dolly as he hefted Ron up onto his shoulder and tossed him over the back of the horse like a sack of flour. "Ain't that right?"

Dolly swallowed hard. "Yes, that's right." Color climbed up her neck into her cheeks.

"Oh." Kit's lips twisted into a frown. "Seems like all the good ones are taken. Except one." Her brows rose. "What do ya say, Turner?"

"Don't go there, Kit. You know how I feel about you. You're like a kid sister."

"More's the pity." She clucked her tongue. "Can't blame a gal for trying." She cast an appraising glance at Dolly. "Good thing this one's married. She's a bit on the scrawny side. A cull, if you ask me."

Seth wasn't asking her, but he did enjoy the red blooming in Dolly's cheeks and joined Kit in taunting her. "She is a little scrawny. But I don't know that I'd cull her from the herd."

Rage glittered in Dolly's eyes and she crossed her arms over her chest. "In case you hadn't noticed, I'm still standing here, and my hearing is perfectly fine. Now, can we get out of here?"

Without bothering to hide his grin, Seth whistled and Ranger came running. "She might be scrawny, but she's got a lot of sass." He slapped her ass.

Dolly spun, her hands rising into fists. "How dare you!"

Kit's lips twitched. "You have your hands full." She wheeled her horse around, careful not to dump Ron on the ground. "I'll meet you back at the house."

Seth swung up into the saddle. "You're riding with me." He leaned over and held out a hand.

For a moment, Dolly looked as though she'd rather die on the prairie than take his hand. A glance around must have convinced her, because she huffed a loud sigh and reached up to grasp his hand.

"Put your left foot in the stirrup," he instructed.

"I know how to ride a horse. I'm not a complete idiot." Still, she hesitated, biting at her bottom lip. Then she stretched a leg up to place her little white foot into the stirrup. The shirt rode up to expose the fine blond hairs of her pussy. She shot a glance at him and hauled herself up, pushing against the stirrup and clinging to his hand.

Seth swallowed hard and shifted back in his saddle. He positioned Dolly in front of him, practically in his lap, her firm, naked ass resting against the solid ridge of his cock. His eyes rolled to the sky and he prayed for forgiveness for his lusty thoughts. This test was gonna be a lot harder than he originally thought.

Dolly sat ramrod straight, holding herself as far away from him as possible in the limited space. "We'd better hurry if we want to catch the other two. I don't want to leave R—my husband to that woman." Why couldn't she call Ron her husband? Every time she tried to say it, the word stuck in her throat.

A warm breath stirred the loose tendrils behind her ear. "Afraid she'll steal him away from you?"

Closing her eyes, Dolly tried to concentrate. But with the hard line of his penis pressing between the cheeks of her ass, she couldn't think past the moisture easing out of her cunt onto the smooth leather of the saddle. The backs of her legs rested against his trouser-clad thighs, the material a reminder of her near nakedness. Everything she owned was in that balloon, her clothes, her money . . . hell, her life. She had to get it back. The sooner she got Ron settled and found something decent to wear, she'd get back out here to find her balloon. "Can we go?"

Seth flexed his legs beneath her and the horse sprang forward.

The sudden movement rocked Dolly in the saddle, her back slamming against the cowboy's bare chest. He smelled of leather, sweat, and the wide, open prairie. Her senses spun with his overwhelming masculinity. Ron was good-looking in a soft, citified way. This man was as rugged as the Rockies and took her breath away.

Or could she attribute her breathlessness to the arm clamped around her belly like a steel band, the muscles bulging against her ribs and breasts. She tried to pry it loose, but the more she pushed against him, the tighter he squeezed.

Her breaths came in ragged, shallow spurts. With his cock pressed tightly against her buttocks, she couldn't think straight. Blood raced through her veins in a rush outward to her skin. Tingling sensations assailed everywhere her body touched his. And the same blood pushed yearning deep down to the core of her being in a flood of creamy longing. *Please, God, don't let him know the effect he has on me.* Already a pool of musky liquid accumulated on the saddle. Her cunt slid against the hard, smooth leather, the rocking motion similar to that of making love. With the mountain of a cowboy nudging her from behind and her naked pussy skimming through a sea of juices, Dolly had to bite her tongue to hold back the moan.

She gave up on the struggle to put distance between his body and hers. Riding double on a horse, whose natural motion forced them together, was a situation she couldn't avoid or remedy until they reached the ranch house. Near naked and barefoot, she couldn't walk all the way back. Her feet would be bloody stumps within the first mile.

Why the hell had she made love to Ron? None of this would have happened. Her cheeks burned at how she must have looked when Seth found her. How wanton and ... and ... exposed.

Her body shuddered. Unfortunately, not with revulsion or mortification, but more with the image of herself lying among the buffalo grass, as naked as the day she was born and Seth staring down at her.

An ache swelled low in her belly at that special place where men and women were meant to come together. The ache spread throughout her body like a prairie wildfire on a hot summer day.

The arm circling her waist rode up until the rocking motion of the horse caused her breasts to bump against the solid muscles of his forearm. If he didn't deliver her to the ranch owner soon, she'd explode in an uncontrollable ball of flaming orgasm, her lust overruling every last shred of her commonsense.

With the clouds still blocking any view of the sun, dusk crept in, surrounding the horse and the two riders. When they topped a rise, a small oasis of civilization spread before Dolly in the form of a ranch house, a barn, and a few scattered outbuildings.

Oh, thank God. Dolly almost gasped the words aloud. Much more of the rubbing, bumping, and other sensual stimulation, and she'd drag the cowboy off his horse and mount him.

The ranch house, concentrate on the ranch house.

She forced herself to study the two-story structure with its wrap-around porch on all four sides. Light shone from all the windows like welcoming beacons to lost souls—and hers was feeling a little lost about that time.

An overwhelming feeling of home overcame Dolly. She had no home other than the balloon. The house before her belonged to someone else. Maybe a prince in a fairy tale, and she knew fairy tales were for little girls, not disillusioned widows. She'd given up believing in fairy tales a long time ago. If she wanted anything out of life, she had to work for it and rely only on her own industrious nature. She'd relied on a man once before and he'd gotten himself killed by cheating at cards. No sir, she wouldn't rely on anyone but herself ever again.

She didn't belong in that house any more than her cowboy rescuer did. Yet, despite it all, she'd always wished for just such a home—warm, welcoming, and surrounded by the wide, open spaces and a sky you can see for miles and miles. A person could learn to love a place like this. She swallowed hard and straightened, banishing any longing from her system.

As soon as she acquired appropriate clothing and borrowed a horse, she'd find her balloon and move on.

Seth pulled the horse to a halt and stared down at the homestead nestled on the Kansas prairie. "Like it?"

"The owner must be very wealthy to have a home like that."

"Workin' on it," he said.

"It's a nice house. You think the owner will mind us staying until we find my balloon?"

A chuckle rumbled through his broad chest. "He'd be delighted."

"How do you know? Is he a nice man?"

Seth shrugged, a smile pulling at his lips, as if he were in on a secret. "You tell me."

Dolly's eyes narrowed. What secret did he know that he wasn't letting her in on? "I will as soon as you introduce us."

"Already have."

Was the man dense or slow? She hadn't met anyone but him and Kit. Was Kit the owner? Dolly shook her head. Surely not. "I don't understand."

"I'm the owner." He smiled down into her startled eyes, his grin stretching across his face.

4

Dressed in a borrowed nightgown and matching wrap, Dolly paced the floor of the bedroom Seth had given to Ron, determined to keep up the pretense of being a happily married couple. "I can't believe our luck. If I had kept my mind on flying, none of this would have happened."

"You mean, if you hadn't made love to me, none of this would have happened." Ron crossed his arms over his chest. "Excuse me if I'm not as regretful as you are."

She stopped in midstride and snorted. "Was it worth a broken leg?"

Ron leveled his gaze with hers. "Hell yes. Do you know how hard it is to get past your armor? I've been trying for the past year to get you to take me seriously." Dolly had to give him credit. He looked serious.

Still, she didn't love him like she wanted to love a husband. Besides, his reputation as a notorious womanizer ruled him out. "Ron Casey, you flirt with anything in skirts, do you expect me to believe that?"

"Think about it, Dolly. I've tried everything, short of jumping out of the basket at two thousand feet, to get your attention, including trying to make you jealous." He reached out and clasped her hand, staring up into her eyes. "Dolly, when you agreed to make love with me today, it was a dream come true. I'd break both legs if I thought you'd say yes and marry me."

Dolly pulled out of his clutch, strode to the window, and stared out at the night. If she married Ron, she wouldn't have to worry about other men pawing at her, wanting to take her away from her livelihood and ability to support herself. Ron would never be a threat to her emotions either. She loved him like a very good friend. She sighed. And friends should never make love. It ruins the friendship. "We shouldn't have done it."

"I, for one, am glad we did. I've wanted to make love to you for almost as long as Walter's been dead."

Dolly spun to face Ron. "What?"

"You heard me." He pushed himself into a more upright sitting position, grimacing when he jarred his leg. "I've wanted you from the beginning. You just had this wall around you, snapping at any man who dared to call you pretty."

"I did not." As soon as the denial left her lips, she recognized it for the lie it was. She had erected a solid wall around her life and emotions. Having lost one husband, she didn't want to fall into the same trap of relying on another man for her livelihood only to have him up and die on her, leaving her penniless and without a means to take care of herself.

"Yes, you did." Ron shook his head. "Not that I blame you. You are a beautiful woman, and men are bound to find you attractive. I know. I'm one of them."

"Still, as partners, we should have kept the relationship free of emotional encumbrances for both our sakes." She paced across the small room and back.

Ron reached out and snagged her hand again, pulling her closer. "For both our sakes or just for you, Dolly?"

"Anything more would never work."

"Why? Name one good reason." He tugged her arm until her thighs bumped into the bed. "I could be a very good husband to you, if you'd only let me."

"That's just it. I don't want to get married. I have a job waiting for me in Dodge City. Why do I need a husband? I had a partner, and now I've messed that up."

"You still have me." His hand moved from her wrist to her hip. "I could be your partner and your husband. Marry me, Dolly." His hand inched the fabric of her nightgown upward.

Dolly let him do it. Just like she had when he'd made love to her in the balloon. His sexual prowess was worthy, but she hadn't come away longing for more of the same. She'd come away longing for something else.

If she married Ron, she could go on with life as usual. The relationship might be a little more difficult, but she could manage. She liked Ron a great deal, but was it enough of a foundation on which to build a more intimate relationship?

Now, with his hand smoothing the skin of her bare thigh, she tried to picture herself married to him. She'd already crossed the threshold and let him into her body. By all rights, she should marry him.

When Ron's lean, strong fingers touched her center, Dolly closed her eyes and envisioned life as Ron's wife. Making love into the small hours of the morning. Waking with him every morning, in the basket, in a hotel, in a tent, wherever they landed. But Ron's face wasn't the one her mind conjured. And it wasn't Ron's finger dipping between her folds to stroke her clit. Instead of seeing Ron's sandy blond hair and green eyes staring down at her as he plunged into her, Dolly could see only dark hair and deep brown eyes the color of thick molasses.

Dolly's eyes flew open and she stepped out of Ron's reach.

"No, we're partners, not lovers," she said, then ran for the door, her body on fire with longing. The longing was not for her pretend husband, but for the man who'd plucked her from the prairie. A man she couldn't, no, wouldn't have.

With the walls of the house closing in on her, Dolly ran down the stairs and out the side door onto the porch. Her heated skin found little reprieve in the gentle breeze blowing across the rolling hills. Clouds had disappeared, leaving the heavens clean and clear for the stars to shine at their best.

The night was made for lovers. Too bad Dolly wasn't.

After he'd deposited Dolly into Mrs. Hornbuckle's hands, Seth had taken off under the pretext of seeing to the livestock, when he'd actually gone out looking for the missing balloon.

By the desperate look on Dolly's face, it meant a lot to her, and anything that meant a lot to Dolly meant a lot to Seth. He'd show her he was a good choice for a husband.

He'd found the balloon a couple miles from the location where it had dumped its passengers. The trunks filled with Dolly's and Ron's clothing littered the ground nearby. He'd returned to the barn, hitched up the wagon, and gone out to collect it all in the dark.

Once he had loaded the huge balloon and basket on the wagon, he wasn't sure what to do with it. If he told Dolly he'd found her balloon, she'd hurry to repair it and be on her way. How would he get her to fall in love with him if she left so soon?

He needed time. She had to be in Dodge City in three days with her balloon intact. Seth figured she could get there in less than a day. That gave him at least two days to woo and win his bride.

With a silent prayer cast toward the starlit sky, he drove the wagon to the caves in the cliff by the river and stashed the balloon there.

He had returned to the ranch with the trunks and a few of the other items he'd found scattered across the ground.

Draped in a huge robe loaned to her by Mrs. Hornbuckle, Dolly had nodded, accepting his lie with tears in her eyes. The tears ripped through Seth's chest, and he almost spilled the beans about finding her balloon.

She'd saved him the mistake when she'd disappeared up the stairs into the room assigned to Ron, much to Seth's disappointment. He'd insisted it was the better room for recuperating from a broken leg. He'd even helped Ron up the stairs.

The bed was too small for two people to sleep on, which suited Seth just fine. Dolly couldn't play her game of pretend wife with her former lover. Or could she?

Just the thought of Dolly lying naked with Ron made Seth's blood roar through his veins and the heat build beneath his skin. Nothing but a large dose of cold well-water would soothe his irritation and desire, so he headed for the well and drew up a bucket of water.

Having scrubbed his face, neck, and torso, Seth left his shirt and vest hanging on the rail outside his downstairs bedroom. His suspenders hung down around his thighs. He'd removed his boots at the back door and strode along the smooth boards of his bedroom floor in his socked feet, making very little sound.

Knowing Dolly was upstairs in Ron's room made it impossible for Seth to settle down for the night. Instead, he left the confines of the house and strolled out on the porch.

The clock in the parlor struck midnight as he closed the door behind him. Normally, he was in bed and fast asleep by this time. Life on the ranch required him to be up before dawn and working until well after dusk. But tomorrow, after he finished morning chores, he'd set aside his normal routine to take Dolly out looking for the balloon she wouldn't find. That would give him time alone with her. More time to show her his home. Maybe he'd take her down by the lake with a picnic lunch. If he played his cards right, he might even make love to her. His cock twitched, swelling at the thought of seeing Dolly naked again.

When Seth reached the corner of the house, he turned and walked along the south side. With his head down, deep into planning for the following day's courtship, Seth rounded the corner and ran headfirst into someone coming from the opposite direction.

He reached out and grabbed thin, delicate arms clad in a billowy cotton and lace wrap.

"Oh!" Dolly's exclamation burst out in a puff of air and she braced her hands on his naked chest. Then as if realizing the intimacy of her contact, she retracted her fingers, her eyes widening. "I'm sorry. I shouldn't be out here." She made to turn, but Seth's hands held her in place.

He couldn't believe his luck. He'd thought he'd have to wait until the following day to try his hand at wooing his future bride, but here she was, complete with starlight.

The clouds had cleared, leaving a clean wash of stars and a fat yellow moon to shine enough light to see the play of emotions racing across her face.

"I'm glad you're out here," he said, refusing to release her.

"You are?" Her words came out in a breathy whisper.

"Yes, I had a question for you."

"You did?" A shiver shook her slight frame. With the light of the moon glowing behind her, her form was a pale silhouette beneath the thin cotton of her nightgown and wrap. As if she gathered herself around her, she straightened, her mouth tightening. "Well, what is it?"

Raw lust surged beneath the buttons of his trousers as his gaze feasted on the shadowy images of her breasts and hips.

His fingers slid down her arms to her wrists, capturing them between his larger brown fingers. "On the ride to the ranch . . ." He stepped closer until his hips touched hers.

Thankfully, she didn't retreat. She stiffened and her eyes

rounded. Her chest rose and fell in rapid succession beneath the lace-trimmed fabric of her very proper nightgown, tied snuggly at her neck.

How he'd love to pull the bow loose and slide the wrap over her shoulders.

"What about the ride?" She stared up at his mouth, her tongue darting out to trace over her bottom lip.

He pulled her against him, slipping an arm around her waist. Again, she didn't resist; her breasts pressed through the cotton, the beaded tips teasing his naked chest. He reached out and captured her earlobe between his teeth and nipped before whispering, "Were you thinking about me when you creamed my saddle with your juices?"

She gasped, her hand clenching the hairs on his chest, her hips grinding against him. Then, as if she suddenly remembered who she was with, she shoved against him. "How dare you? That's certainly not something you ask a married woman." Her tone was that of an affronted matron, but her body quivered beneath his hands.

He let go suddenly. "And I wouldn't say something like that to a married woman."

Dolly stumbled backward until her bottom connected with the porch rail. "What are you saying?"

Seth stalked her, coming to a halt when his feet stood toe to toe with hers. He leaned down over her, his tall frame towering over her. She tilted so far she would have fallen over the rail backward had he not captured her around the waist.

"You're not really married, are you?" His fingers rose to capture her chin and lift her face to his. "You and *Rob* have never stood in a church and said 'I do,' have you? I may be just a dumb cowboy, but I wasn't raised a fool."

Dolly stood in the man's grip, the smell of clean skin and leather overwhelming her senses. She could very easily fall against him and let him make love to her. If her body had its way, she'd have ridden him on the ride back to the house. "I . . . we . . ." He owned a ranch; clearly, he could have any woman he wanted. Hell, he could buy one, for that matter. The question was what did he want of her? A tumble in the sheets and nothing more? When she left, he'd let her go, no bonds to shackle her to him. Was that his game?

Well, he could keep it. She was safer relying on herself instead of a man. Her face hardened. "*Ron* and I are married, I tell you."

His brows drew downward into a deep V. "I don't believe you."

"Well, it's true, so let me go before I scream." She shoved against his chest.

His arms tightened instead of releasing.

She found herself in the same trap as earlier when she'd ridden in front of him on the saddle. The closer they were, the less she could depend on her willpower to hold him off. Damn it, she didn't want to be drawn to this man. She planted her hands against his chest and pushed.

Her fingers connected with a taut brown nipple, beaded and hard. What would it taste like? Like the man? Warm, hard, and freshly washed?

"You weren't thinking of Ron when you rode in front of me on that saddle." He leaned his body against hers, the hard ridge of his trousers pressing into her belly.

"You have a very large ego." And that wasn't all that was big on this man. Dolly's face flooded with heat, the heat spreading lower to pool in her loins. Damn him.

"Maybe so, but you were thinking of me when you came all over my saddle, weren't you?" He lifted her chin and pierced her with his gaze. "Weren't you?"

Anger blended with lust and welled up in her chest, exploding from her lips. "Yes, damn it. I was thinking of you."

His mouth softened and a smile curved his lips. "Same here. That was the most uncomfortable ride I've ever been on, and you were the cause."

Her lips parted on a gasp. So he'd felt it too. But then he was a man who'd had a near-naked woman draped across his lap. What man wouldn't be thinking of sex?

"Just because I was thinking of you, doesn't mean I'll act on it." Her gaze darted to the side. "After all, I'm a married woman."

"Ha!" His hands captured her hips and pulled her against him. "Married or not, you want me as much as I want you." His fingers dug into the rounded globes of her ass, kneading the flesh, pressing her closer.

Her body responded when her mind failed to bring reason to the madness. Cream coated her pussy, hot, slick, and ready. How could she resist him? Because resist, she must. "Maybe so, but giving into desire would be wrong."

His hands moved up until his thumbs brushed against the swells of her breasts. "How could something that feels so good be wrong?"

Dolly gasped, her eyes rolling to the back of her head, a rush of cream oozing from her cunt. *Lord, help me.*

"Does Rob make you want more?" He leaned forward and kissed the curve of her cheekbone, his lips dragging downward to capture hers in a long, breath-stealing kiss.

She couldn't pull free to save her life. Her traitorous mouth responded despite what her brain was telling her.

When he lifted his mouth from hers, cool air caressed her burning lips and she stood in stunned silence. She wanted him to kiss her again. She wanted more.

"You shouldn't have done that." She closed her eyes and licked her swollen lower lip. "You really shouldn't."

"Shouldn't touch you like this?" His hands rose to the tiny

satin bow at her throat, and with a gentle tug, the bow fell away, the wrap gaping open. "I'm just a man touching a woman."

"A married woman," she said, her breath just a whisper.

Seth's fingers skimmed the swells of her breasts, drifting lower to capture them in the palms of his hands. "If you're married, I'm the King of England."

A moan escaped her lips and she leaned into his hands. "Don't do this, your majesty."

Seth chuckled, one hand toying with the nipple straining through the fabric. He bent to capture the other nipple between his teeth, sucking it into his mouth, fabric and all.

Dolly could do nothing to stop his assault on her senses. Caught up in a lust so strong, her mind blew away with the receding storm.

When his hands reached for the hem of her nightgown, she didn't stop him. Her body craved his touch like a desert craves rain. Up over her head, the nightgown flew. She stood in the moonlight as naked as she'd been when he found her earlier. Cool night air brushed across her skin, ruffling her hair hanging loose down to her waist.

Seth stood back and stared at her in the pale moonlight, heat radiating from his gaze. "You're the most beautiful woman I've ever seen. You really are the answer to my prayers. My gift from the heavens."

"Gift?" She'd never been called a gift before. "I'm not your gift. I'm my own person, and you don't own me." She tried to push against him, but he held firm. He scooped her up and deposited her bottom on the railing.

Dolly clung to Seth's shoulders, her legs swinging open for balance.

Seth stepped into the gap, his arms wrapping around her waist.

Shocks of sensation radiated across her skin where his fingers touched her naked flesh. Her knees automatically clamped around his waist, the action pressing her moist quim against the rigid line of his fly. How she wished he wore fewer clothes. Her longing built into an urgent need to have this cowboy plunge his cock deep inside. The smooth, painted railing against her ass did little to cool the heat swirling inside. As he trailed kisses down the side of her neck, she asked, "What do you mean gift?"

"You're my gift, Dolly. My gift straight from God." He slipped down between her thighs, dropping to one knee. "Let me show you what it's like to go to Heaven." He draped her legs over his shoulders and buried his mouth in her cunt.

Any other words were choked in raging passion so strong Dolly couldn't breathe. If anything, Seth's assault on her pussy was a gift. One she couldn't refuse.

His tongue laved the nubbin of her clit, delving into her cunt to swirl in the juices.

Dolly clung with one hand around the post beside her and the other buried in his hair, urging him closer. Tingling sparks transformed into a firestorm of need.

Seth pressed a finger to her quim, sliding into her moist center, and all the while he flicked her clit with his wicked tongue.

Dolly moaned long and loud. When she remembered where she was, she bit down hard on her lip to keep sound to a minimum. Was she completely wanton to allow Seth to make love to her on the porch? What if Mrs. Hornbuckle stepped out to investigate the cause of the noise?

Then Seth pressed another finger and another inside her pussy, pushing as deep as his long fingers would go. Then he sucked her slit between his teeth and nibbled, tonguing and licking her into a mindless frenzy.

Her legs squeezed around his ears with the effort to keep from crying out. When she rose to the peak and plunged over the edge spiraling out of control, a squeal escaped her lips, with several husky moans following close behind. Her fingers tugged at Seth's dark hair. She had to have him inside her now.

Seth rose to his feet, dropping her legs around his waist. With his cock poised to penetrate, he hesitated. "I want to hear my name on your lips as I fuck you." His hands squeezed her hips in a tight grip, the strength in them like steely bands.

His coarse words and hulking power excited her beyond reason. "Shut up and fuck me." She locked her heels around his back and pulled him into her, his name rising to her lips as she came again. "Seth!"

5

Seth had never been so glad to see Kit riding up on her sorrel gelding the following morning. He needed someone to keep Dolly's supposed husband occupied for the day while he stole his future bride away for a few hours. Kit was just the man . . . er . . . woman to do that.

Kit swung down from her horse, wearing her typical men's trousers, vest, and shirt. The only difference in her usual appearance was that she'd gone to extra effort to ensure the clothing was clean and her auburn hair was combed back into a neat ponytail.

Seth hurried out to greet her before Dolly came out. "You going to church or something?"

Kit frowned, her face coloring beneath her tanned and freckled skin. She pushed her shoulders back and glared at him. "Sometimes I like wearing clean clothes. Is there a law against that?"

"Yeah, since when do you get all cleaned up just to come visit me?"

The color in her cheeks deepened. "Who the hell said I was coming to see you? You've told me time and again you're not interested in marrying me or merging our two ranches. I may be dense, but I'm not a complete idiot. I came to visit your guest . . . guests." She tipped her eyebrows upward, daring him to catch her slip.

Used to Kit's straightforward ways and coarse language, Seth chuckled. "The man who marries you will have more than his hands full."

Kit stepped past him and climbed the steps to the porch. "Well, now, that won't be you, now will it?"

No, it wouldn't be him. Kit was too much like a sister. Oh, he'd considered marrying Kit on more than one occasion, the promise of merging the two ranches tempting. But since she was more like a kid sister to him, Seth couldn't bring himself to marry her. She deserved to find a man who'd love her like a wife, not a sibling. And after making love to Dolly last night, Seth knew without a doubt he couldn't marry Kit. He couldn't turn his back on his gift from Heaven. Nor did he want to.

Thus, his plan for the day. A plan in which Kit could play a vital role. "Kit, before you go inside, I have a favor to ask."

She turned, a deep red brow winging upward. "Seth Turner wants something from me? Now that's a change. You want me to go rope a calf or mend a fence? Seems that's the only thing you've wanted from me in the past."

"No, I have a bigger favor than that." He glanced toward the house. If Dolly heard him making plans with Kit, she'd refuse to go with him. "I need you to distract Mr. Casey while I take Miss Dolly out to find her balloon."

"Isn't she going to go anyway?"

"Yes, but she'll be more likely to stay out longer if she knows Casey is occupied and not in need of her."

"Sounds a bit dishonest, if you ask me. Didn't she say she's married to the man?"

"Yes, but I have reason to believe they aren't married."

"Why would she lie about that?"

"I don't know; maybe because they travel across the country together and it's easier to say they're married to keep the old biddies from flappin' their gums."

Kit's eyes narrowed and she tapped a finger to her chin. "So you think they're lying about being husband and wife?"

"Yup." Seth could almost see the wheels churning behind the gleam in Kit's eyes. His own brows dipped. "I don't like that look."

The gleam disappeared, and Kit was all smiles and innocence. "I don't know what you're talking about. What look?"

"That look you get when you're cookin' up a scheme I'm not going to like."

"Oh, quit your bellyachin'. I'd be happy as a pig in the mud to sit with Mr. Casey. I'm sure we'll find *something* in common." A sly grin slid up the sides of her face.

Now that he had Kit's agreement to help out, Seth wasn't so sure he wanted her anywhere near Ron or Dolly. "Whatever you're plannin', don't do it."

"Look, you have your own plan with your Dolly, leave me be with Mr. Casey. We'll get along just fine." She stepped through the door before he could delve into her statement.

Seth had a bad feeling about leaving Kit with Ron, but when Dolly descended from the stairs dressed in a split skirt and boots, any other words of warning dried with all his spit.

"Are you taking me out to find my balloon today, Mr. Turner?" Dolly slid her fingers into doeskin gloves and pushed a stray strand of her hair beneath the brim of her straw hat. She was a vision in female curves.

Kit stared from her to Seth and back. "If you'll excuse me, I'll check in on Mr. Casey."

Seth didn't acknowledge her leaving. His gaze drank in every inch of Dolly, imagining her as she'd looked last night, naked and kissed by the moonlight.

"The horses are ready." And so was he. If he could just skip to his planned lunch by the lake, he would. He had a saddlebag loaded with a blanket and all the fixings for a picnic. The blanket weighed prominently in his mind, and all he could do to her on that little scrap of wool.

His cock thickened and he dropped his hat to cover the bulge. "Kit's offered to stay and entertain Mr. Casey while we're out searching."

A snort sounded from halfway up the stairs. "Offered, huh! Stampeded, more like," she muttered.

Dolly's eyes widened and she glanced back at the red-haired woman nearing the top landing. "Are you sure you won't come with us? Ron will be fine on his own."

Was that desperation in Dolly's voice? Was she afraid of being alone with him? A smile twitched the corners of Seth's mouth. Oh yes, she was afraid, and well she should be. He would be relentless in his attack on her defenses.

Last night only proved she was the woman for him. Despite her protests that they shouldn't make love, her body's reaction was proof positive they were meant for each other.

"I wouldn't dream of leaving your *husband* alone while you're out with Seth. Just be careful of snakes in the grass." Kit stared at Seth, clearly indicating he was the snake to whom she referred.

Color rose in Dolly's cheeks. "Do you have a foreman or ranch hand who could take me out to find the balloon? I don't want to take you away from important ranching business." Her hands wrung together, the leather gloves making a soft swishing sound.

Seth almost laughed out loud. He really had her nervous. Good. He wanted her to be on edge. When they finally came together, she'd be wound so tight, she'd explode in his arms.

He could hardly wait.

"Take your time," Kit said airily. "I'll stay with your *husband* until your return."

* * *

Dolly's knees shook and her pussy was tender from Seth's lovemaking the previous night. If she weren't desperate to find her balloon, she'd cry off and tell him she wasn't up to searching today. Which she really wasn't. The thought of sitting on a saddle made her cream all over again. Every time she rubbed her crotch against the smooth leather, she'd think of sitting astride Seth on the ride to the ranch.

Holy Jesus, what was she going to do? Even fully clothed and wearing the appropriate undergarments, her body was on fire with lust.

Thank goodness riding alone was more demanding and there'd be distance between them. She could do this, she coached herself.

When she found her balloon, she'd get it up and flying, and leave this ranch and its very handsome owner behind. Her dreams began in Dodge City. Everything she'd worked for would be waiting for her there. The Wild West Show would guarantee her livelihood for as long as she needed to save enough money to buy a little house in a small town. She'd always liked the idea of living close to a river, and maybe she'd get a cat or a dog to keep her company.

When had the dream of owning her own home lost its luster? Was it when she'd realized she'd be living that dream alone. Hadn't she told Ron she didn't want to marry? Wasn't she afraid of investing her heart in another man? Losing the one you loved was never easy. She'd decided a long time ago that never falling in love again would eliminate the pain of loss. You couldn't miss what you didn't have to begin with.

Dolly squared her shoulders and stepped through the door. "Let's get going. I need to find that balloon as soon as possible."

Hell, she might decide to continue ballooning even after she'd purchased her house. Surrounded by people at the county fairs or in the crowds attending the Wild West Show, she'd never lack for company.

Dolly sighed. Fitting in had never been one of her strong suits. That's why ballooning from place to place hadn't bothered her until now.

Seth's hand cupped her elbow, and he walked her down the steps. His warm, strong fingers reassured her in a small way. "Come on. I have a horse picked out just for you. Her name's Angel."

Tied to the hitching post, Angel was as white as Seth's massive stallion was dark. Her pale blue eyes gazed down at Dolly as if to say she didn't like the idea of a ride on the prairie any more than Dolly did, but that she'd tolerate it with grace. Which made Dolly feel all the better.

In a balloon high over the Earth, she felt far safer than on the back of a living, breathing animal as big and heavy as a horse. She didn't bother to tell Seth she'd been thrown from a horse at the age of ten and hadn't liked riding since. Wouldn't he laugh at the notion?

Thank goodness Angel wasn't equipped with a sidesaddle. Dolly wore a split skirt so that she could ride astride. Sidesaddles were too precarious. After a silent prayer and a tentative pat on the animal's neck, Dolly gathered the reins, climbed the wooden block positioned next to Angel, and placed her foot in the stirrup.

At the exact moment she shifted her weight from the box to the stirrup, a cat raced around the side of the house, a rangy mutt in hot pursuit, barking at the top of his lungs.

Angel whinnied and danced to the side.

Dolly's fingers slipped on the saddle horn, and she would have fallen back if Seth's hands hadn't been there to capture her around the waist. With the ease of a man used to hard work and heavy loads, he tossed her up into the saddle, his hand resting on her thigh long after she needed it to gain her balance.

Clutching the saddle horn, Dolly fought to school the abject fear from her face. Not that Seth's opinion of her meant a hill of beans, but she didn't like making a fool of herself in front of an accomplished rider. Nor did she like to admit she was inept on a horse. If forced to admit, she'd probably confess to preferring riding double with Seth than riding alone.

However, riding double with Seth unleashed an entirely different set of problems. Number one being her body's traitorous reaction to him. Last night had been a really enormous mistake in her book.

Seth lifted Dolly's ankle, his fingers firm and gentle as he guided her boot into the stirrup. "I'd venture to guess you're regretting last night about now." His words were spoken softly, meant to be heard by her alone.

Heat suffused her neck, rising up into her cheeks. "It was wrong. I'm a mar—"

"I know, you keep saying you're a married woman." Seth looked up into her eyes, his gaze steady, unyielding. "What's your last name?" His question shot out fast, demanding an answer equally as swift.

"Sherm—" Dolly clamped her mouth shut. "I used to go by Sherman. Ron and I were recently married. Before that I was widowed. Not that it's any of your business."

"I'll make it my business to get to know the woman I make love to." He turned the horse around and slapped her rump.

Angel hopped a few steps forward.

The sudden movement had Dolly grasping for the saddle horn, her heart in her throat. She had to bite down hard on her lip to keep from crying out.

A soft chuckle sounded from the window above the porch.

Kit sat in the open window of Ron's room. "Ride much?"

Dolly's back stiffened and she sat up straight, attempting to look as though she knew what the hell she was doing even if she lacked confidence in her abilities. She smiled sweetly at Kit. "Give my husband my love and tell him not to worry. I'll be back when I find our balloon."

"Oh, don't worry about Mr. Casey. We'll entertain each other just fine while you're gone." Her lips curled in what appeared to be a devilish grin. "You be sure to take care of my sweetie. Mr. Turner and I go back a long way. Don't we, Seth?"

Dolly knew that look as one female to another.

Seth glared up at the redhead in the window. "Behave, Kit."

"I'm only saying we've *known* each other for a very long time. And you've known *Mrs.* Casey how long?" Kit's emphasis on the word "known" could only mean one thing. She and Seth had had a love affair.

"Enough." Seth swung up into his saddle and reined the black stallion in a half circle. "Come on, Dolly. We have a balloon to find."

With a last calculating glance at the tough redhead in the window, Dolly nudged her horse into a light canter, hoping that the animal knew how to follow the leader, and that the leader, Seth, knew where to look for her balloon.

The fact she wasn't much good on a horse, along with Kit's words of warning, made Dolly all the more aware of how she didn't fit in on this ranch. Despite the fact the house was straight out of her fairy-tale dreams, the life was not. She didn't know anything about ranching.

As they ventured out on the prairie, Dolly could think of one good thing about following behind Seth. She didn't have to be on guard, hiding her feelings all the time.

Seth sat his horse like he'd been born to ride. The gentle swaying motion was as natural as making love and reminded Dolly of last night with each step the horse took.

Dolly had enough to deal with staying seated on the horse and reining in her mounting desire. If she didn't find her balloon soon, she didn't know what she'd do. Any more time with Seth was bound to lead to more of what happened last night. Her pussy creamed at the thought.

While her gaze panned the horizon, searching for her missing balloon, her thoughts returned to the porch rail and the wicked things Seth had done to her.

Hell, she'd been married, but Walter never licked her pussy like Seth had. Walter had made love the only way Dolly ever knew, like most people did, as far as she was aware. Holy Jesus, what Seth had done . . .

Heavy cream soaked through her clothing and she squirmed in the saddle.

"Ready to stop for a while?"

"No, we should keep looking. I'm sure the balloon won't be far." She didn't want to stop because stopping meant conversation and standing next to Seth. Dolly didn't trust him not to try something again. If she were honest, she couldn't trust herself to resist his persuasive assaults.

Seth reined in next to her. "The horses need water. There's a lake ahead where we can stop for a few minutes."

When he put it in the guise of the horses' well-being, how could Dolly argue? She was doomed. And saddle sore. And pussy sore from the thorough fucking she'd gotten last night.

She inhaled and let out a long breath. *Get last night out of your mind.*

Seth urged his horse to the edge of a rise and stopped, turning back with a smile on his face. "Did you say something?"

"No, no. Nothing." As her horse moved abreast of his, she stared out at a glittering lake straight from an artist's painting of paradise. Water glistened in the sunlight, and trees dotted the shoreline, spreading little patches of shade in the grass. A picture-perfect setting in every way. Dolly sighed. How often had she longed for such a place to call home?

Seth dismounted and held out his arms for her. "Let's give the horses a rest."

Ignoring his hands, Dolly determined to dismount on her own. With a firm hold on the saddle horn, she swung her right leg free of the stirrup and around to the other side of the horse. Angel danced to the side as Dolly glanced over her shoulder to gauge the distance to the ground. She was a lot higher up than she'd remembered. Perhaps the wooden step had given her a false sense of security. Where was a log, a rock, or anything when you needed a step to get down?

Her problem was solved when large hands spanned her narrow waist and gently set her on the ground.

"I could have gotten down by myself," she muttered, less than grateful when she should have been thanking him. That she was out of her element was clear, but he didn't have to emphasize it by constantly coming to her rescue.

"I know you could, but I'm hungry and didn't want to wait all day." He smacked her bottom, grabbed the reins, and led the horses to one of the shade trees where he tied them.

Dolly followed. She hadn't realized just how much work riding for several hours was until Seth mentioned food. Her stomach made a loud, rumbling noise. "Should we go back to the house for lunch?"

"No need. Mrs. Hornbuckle packed a lunch for us." He opened the saddlebag on the back of his horse and pulled a brightly colored Indian blanket from its depths.

After he spread the blanket on the grass, he glanced up.

Dolly's breath caught in her throat at the very hungry look in his eyes. A look that made her feel like she was the main course for lunch.

Forcing air past her vocal chords, she broke eye contact with the swarthy cowboy and stared out over the lake. The day was hot and sticky; how she'd love to dip her feet in the water to cool the rising heat spreading through her body.

"If you don't mind, I'd like to walk along the lake for a few minutes."

"Go right ahead. I'll lay out the food."

Dolly strode to the lake's edge and stared into the clear, clean water. Her toes tingled inside her boots. Before she could think through her actions, Dolly dropped to the ground and pulled her boots and stockings off, dropping them to the sandy shoreline. Her split skirt allowed her to wade in up to her ankles without lifting the hem. Dolly waded along the edge of the lake, letting the mud and silt of the lake bottom squish between her toes.

With no one around for miles, a person could swim naked in the water without a care for propriety or anything else. Dolly longed to shed her clinging clothing and do just that.

"I like to swim here on hot days like today."

Dolly spun to find Seth shed of his boots and socks, wading into the water behind her. He stood so close his chest filled her vision and her heart hammered against her ribs.

Dolly combed a strand of hair behind her ears. "I thought you were laying out the food."

"I did." He smiled down at her. "Lunch is served."

"Oh, then let me get my socks and boots on."

"No need." He scooped her up and carried her back to the blanket, depositing her beside the spread of last night's fried chicken and slabs of bread baked fresh that morning.

After they finished their meal, Dolly managed a yawn and leaned back on the blanket, replete and feigning exhaustion, which was not far from the truth, having gone to bed after midnight the night before. She forced the reason she'd gone to bed so late to the back of her mind, determined to keep their balloon-finding expedition on a purely hands-off basis. "Why Kansas?"

Perhaps if she kept him talking, she'd forget how badly her body craved his touch and how badly she wanted him to do what he'd done to her the night before. Just the image of his mouth claiming her pussy had moisture coating her channel. How in Heaven's name would she ward off any advances the cowboy might attempt when her body reacted in such a manner? And would he attempt an advance? She risked a glance in his direction, a flare of hope filling her.

6

Seth tossed the crumbs and chicken bones into the grass and stretched out next to Dolly, leaning on his elbow. How soon could he kiss her and not have his face slapped? How soon could he plunge his cock inside her and have her calling out his name for more? This wooing game was tiresome and took entirely too long. He had only one more day before he had to let her go on to Dodge City. He bit back his impatience and answered her question. "I've lived in Kansas most of my life, except for time I spent as a bounty hunter."

Dolly turned to face him, resting her cheek on her hand. "Bounty hunter? Isn't that dangerous?"

"If you don't know how to handle a gun, maybe." He liked the way her hand cupped her cheek. He wanted to do just that.

"What made you come back here?" Her words brought him back.

"I had enough money to do what I wanted and I missed the wide-open spaces."

"Don't they have wide-open spaces in other states?"

"Yeah, I suppose. But not like they do here. I wanted a place

I could raise a few cows and ki—" He sat up, cursing himself inside for jumping the gun. Was her sweet-smellin' skin turning his mind to mush? He was actin' like some greenhorn cowboy who never talked to women. If he didn't handle this right, he was afraid she'd bolt. If there was one thing he'd learned from the ladies at Madame Rosalee's, women could be skittish like young colts. Come on too strong, and they'd run scared.

First things first. Get Dolly to like him, get her to like his place, and then get her to agree to marry him. After he accomplished all that, they could talk about children. And Seth wanted at least half a dozen of them. Having grown up an only child, he didn't want any kid of his to go without the benefit of brothers and sisters.

"Did your parents leave you this ranch?" Dolly's eyelids were closed. Apparently she hadn't picked up on his slip about kids.

Seth breathed a sigh and leaned back on his elbow, admiring the paleness of her skin and the way her breasts rose and fell with each breath she took. "No, I bought this place and the cattle on it a couple years ago with the money I earned bounty huntin'. I built the house last year." All he needed now was a wife to make it complete.

The woman lying on the blanket before him was the one he wanted, and he'd do his damnedest to win her. He reached out and pushed a strand of her hair behind her ear.

"Ummm. That's nice, but you shouldn't. I'm married."

"I think you're lying." He bent to kiss her exposed earlobe, sucking it between his teeth to nibble the soft petal. "If you were happily married, you wouldn't have let me do what I did last night."

"I shouldn't have."

"Nor would you let me do what I'm about to do now." His hand slid over the curve of her hip, pulling her closer until her pussy rubbed against the ridge beneath his trousers.

"Who said I was going to let you do anything?" Her eyes opened, all sleepiness disappearing from their pale-blue depths.

"You will. Just as soon as I do this." He leaned forward and crushed her lips with his. His hand moved up her sides until his thumbs skimmed over her puckered nipples straining through the crisp white blouse.

Dolly's back arched off the blanket, pushing her breast into his palm. "You're not playing fair."

"And you're not married. Besides, I wasn't thinking about fair, just about playing." His lips traveled from hers to her chin and down to the top button of her blouse. He flicked it open and pressed a kiss to her neck. He flicked several more buttons open until he exposed the swell of those luscious breasts.

One at a time, he kissed each rounded rise, her skin twitching against his lips. When he freed the last button and pulled her blouse from the waistline of her skirt, she didn't utter a protest. In fact, she helped divest herself of the offending garment, leaving only her camisole in place. Then she guided his hands to the button closure on her skirt.

A slow chuckle rose in his chest. "I thought this was a bad idea."

"Oh, it's a very bad idea, I fear." She dug her fingers into his hair and pulled him down for a long kiss. "Make love to me, Seth." She pulled him closer, her hands reaching for the buttons on his shirt, making short work of releasing them and peeling the garment from his shoulders.

"Am I hearing you right? You want me to make love to you in the open, in the daylight? Aren't you afraid something will get back to your husband?" He could have kicked himself as soon as the words were out of his mouth.

Dolly's hands paused on the button clasp at his waist, her eyes going round. "Husband? Oh, yes." She clamped a hand to her mouth. "What was I thinking?"

"You weren't thinking. Which, in this case, was a good

thing. You were in the middle of feeling." He closed his hand around her wrist and guided her to the buttons on his trousers. "Go on feeling." He reached out and cupped her breast beneath the fine cotton of her camisole, rolling a beaded nipple between his thumb and forefinger.

Her back arched off the ground, and she moaned. "What about Ron?"

Seth replaced his fingers with his tongue, laving the nipple through the thin fabric until it was cool and wet. Then he blew a warm, steady stream of air across the damp surface and watched the dark brown areola pucker even more. "What about Ron? You aren't married, are you?"

"Would you believe we're engaged?" Dolly's leg slid up Seth's thigh. "He loves me."

"But you haven't given me a chance to love you." He bent over her, until his mouth hovered above her breast, reveling in her admission to the lie. She wasn't married. He'd known it all along, or he wouldn't have poached on another man's territory. Now all he had to do was convince her she would make a huge mistake in marrying Ron. "Give me a chance to show you how much."

A moan escaped her lips and she pushed upward, tugging the camisole downward, revealing her naked breast.

He accepted her offering, the nipple sliding into his mouth.

Seth found the buttons for her riding skirt and worked them free; all the while his tongue dueled with hers. When all the buttons hung open, he yanked her skirt down over her thighs and ankles and tossed it to the corner of the blanket. Beneath the skirt were her cotton drawers—clean, white, and in his way. He found the bow to the drawstring and jerked it loose. The drawers went the way of the skirt. Finally, he had her in nothing more than a thin camisole pulled low exposing one voluptuous orb.

He lay beside her and trailed his finger from her belly button downward.

Her stomach muscles clenched; her skin quivered. When he stopped short of her mound of light blond curls, she grabbed his hand and guided it the rest of the way.

Seth chuckled. "Eager, now? Is it that you like making love in the wide-open spaces?"

"Did anyone ever tell you that you talk a lot for a cowboy?" Her small fingers captured each side of his face and pulled him close for a searing kiss that stirred his blood and sent it south. "Shut up and fuck me."

His cock swelled and stiffened, finding its way through the opening of his trousers to press against her hip. "I want to show you more than just a good fuck. Do you trust me?" His palm rested against her cheek and he stared down into her eyes, hesitant to do anything until he had her full agreement. What he was about to show her wasn't something a gentlewoman would normally do with a man. But Madame Rosalee had assured him it would make a woman follow him to the ends of the earth for more.

Seth had no business trotting off to the ends of the earth, but having Dolly follow him anywhere would be a very good thing. Mostly he wanted her to follow him home and stay.

Her blue eyes widened and her breath came in shallow pants. "If you're talking about more of what you showed me last night, I'll risk it." Her words ended on a whisper, her thighs falling open in anticipation of what was to come.

His hand dipped between her legs and tested her core. Oh, yes, she wanted him. Her pussy dripped with her juices, stirring fire inside his groin. "You're so wet."

"You are so vocal. I wish you'd fill your mouth with something other than words."

He slapped the inside of her thigh, a wicked smile curving

his lips. "You should be careful what you wish for. You might not be capable of handling everything I can give."

Her chest heaved faster, her eyes glazed. "We shall see."

Seth ran his hands over her naked skin, upward to caress her breasts and toy with the turgid peaks of her nipples. He lifted the camisole over her head. As his fingers traced a path down to her hips, he smiled. "Yes, indeed. We shall see." Then he grasped her hips and flipped her over to lie on her stomach.

She landed with an oomph. "What the hell?"

"This is all part of my plan to fuck you."

"I'm not a dog or horse."

"I'm told it inspires the animal in a woman."

"Not in this woman." She tried to turn over onto her back, but his hand stopped her. "Let me face you. This can't be right."

"Didn't you say you'd trust me?"

"No, I did not."

Warm hands descended on her shoulder blades and slid down her spine to her hips. "Are you afraid?"

"No, of course not."

Yet her body quivered deliciously beneath his hands. "Then let me love you."

Let me love you. Despite the animalistic position, Dolly's quim quivered in anticipation. *Let me love you.*

Was he after more than a romp in the grass? Or was this what he did with all his women? Whatever his motive, Dolly gave in, eagerly awaiting his next move. On her hands and knees with her naked ass exposed to the air, a cool breeze feathered across her moist opening, the sensation titillating, causing her breasts to tighten.

Seth leaned over her, his chest hairs rubbing against her back, his stubbled chin tickling the side of her throat. "Ready for some fun?" With one hand, he pressed his cock to the lips of her pussy.

Ready? Her body tightened at just the thought of his cock entering her from behind. Ready? Oh yes! She leaned back, anxious for the fucking to begin.

Calloused hands reached beneath her and grasped her breasts, palming the dangling mounds. Then he eased into her, his cock stretching and filling her channel.

Dolly rocked back, taking more of him into her until his balls bumped against her.

His hands traveled down her torso, skimming the curve of her waist. He grasped her hips and pushed her away.

A cry of disappointment rose in her throat only to exit in a rush of air.

Seth slammed his cock into her, driving deep. On his knees and holding her ass, he pumped in and out.

The motion, the position, the wilderness surrounding her combined to catapult Dolly higher than any balloon could ever take her. As she shot over the edge and into a calliope of stark and beautiful sensations, she realized Seth had ground to a halt, holding her firmly against him and filling her with the length of his magnificent cock. His shaft twitched, pumping his seed into her womb.

The joy of being controlled and mastered like an animal was a new experience to Dolly.

When they finally collapsed to the blanket, Seth curled around her backside, maintaining the intimate connection. Dolly had never felt so complete and protected. Odd in contrast to the previous mastery. Exhaustion claimed her in a huge yawn, and she pressed back against Seth, pulling his arm underneath her breasts, the warmth and support comforting at the same time as it made her tingle. She could get used to this kind of lovemaking. Maybe being in charge wasn't always the way to go. Giving up a little of the control could yield wondrous results.

Dolly yawned again, her eyelids drifting closed.

* * *

How long she slept, she didn't know, but the sun tipped toward the western sky when she opened her eyes. A tongue tickled the back of her ear, pulling her out of a nice dream about her and Seth floating above the sea of prairie grass on a cloud. The tonguing turned into light nips, and Dolly became fully alert to the realization that a thick rod pressed against her buttocks. Walter had never been ready again after such a brief respite.

Dolly's body quickened. How could she crave his so soon? Her pussy was deliciously sore from their previous foray into animal sex. Was she becoming addicted to making love with this man? When the time came to leave, would she be able to?

Seth's right hand spanned across her flat belly, sliding lower to cup her sex.

"Seth." Her fingers captured his wrist and held him still for a moment, though her juices flowed inside, slicking the walls of her cunt, preparing for his entrance.

"Yes, my love." Seth flicked her earlobe with the tip of his tongue and blew on the dampness.

A shiver of desire trickled down her neck. She had to remain firm, set aside his expectations and follow her own dreams. Her life was her vessel to command. With his cock nudging against her ass, Dolly found it hard to focus, but she managed to say, "Just because we made love doesn't change a thing. I'm still going to Dodge City as soon as I find my balloon."

His left hand curled around her back and claimed her left breast, tweaking the nipple into a hardened bead. "If you want." The other hand slipped lower to delve between her legs.

"I mean it. I won't let another man control my life." Her words wobbled when he found her clit and stroked it with his forefinger. "I'm in charge of my destiny."

"And marrying Ron won't interfere?"

"Ron lets me do what I want. I make the decisions."

Pushing up to one elbow, Seth stared down at her, his finger dipping into her moist center. "And you don't think I will let you take charge?"

Would he? Dolly stared up into deep brown eyes so dark they were almost black in their intensity. "No, you didn't get this ranch by letting others make the decisions. You're used to taking charge. I won't let another man take charge of my life. I did that once and I was left a penniless widow. I won't do it again."

"I won't leave you penniless, Dolly." That finger swirled around her opening, ducking in to scrape inside her channel.

Her body responded by arching off the blanket. "See? You're doing it now? I don't have any control over my body or what you do to it."

Seth's hand froze, a frown bringing his brows together. "Is that so?"

He dropped to his back on the blanket. "Then *you* take control, Dolly. Take control and show me you can handle it."

For a moment, Dolly lay still, her heart hammering against her chest. How could he stop so suddenly when her pussy cried out for more? She had half a mind to leave him lying there naked and ride back to the ranch.

His cock stood at attention, pointing to the clear blue sky above, a proud flag waving at her, challenging her to take control as she claimed she wanted.

And she could.

A sinking feeling settled in the pit of her belly.

She could if she knew how.

"What's wrong? Don't you want to take charge?" Seth stretched, his lean, muscular thigh bumping against hers. Every muscle in his chest and abdomen flexed, his penis twitching as he moved.

Dolly ran her tongue across her bottom lip. She'd always wondered what it would taste like to suck on a man's cock. She'd heard of such things when men thought she wasn't listening. Apparently, men liked it enough to pay good money for a whore to perform the deed.

Seth's brows rose. "Well?"

"I'm thinking." Dolly rose to her knees and ran her gaze from his head to his toes.

A chuckle rumbled from deep in his chest. "Are all the parts in the right places?"

Were all the parts . . . Boy, were they! She'd never taken the opportunity to fully study the male anatomy, at least not like she did now. Walter hadn't been anything like Seth. He was short, thinner, and less muscled. And his cock was half the size, even fully erect.

Breathing rasped in her chest as she gazed at the full thickness of Seth's penis. Purple lines laced the length to the velvety tip. The man rivaled his own stallion—a veritable stud.

Dolly's fingers twitched with the need to touch his steely firmness, to feel it in her hands, not just her cunt. Tentatively, she reached out and grasped his shaft with one hand, then the other.

His sharp intake of breath sounded almost like Seth was in pain. One look at his expression dispelled that thought. His eyes drooped, and his breathing grew more rapid. "Don't stop now," he said through gritted teeth.

As she realized her hands on his cock had caused him that intense look of ecstasy, a surge of power washed over Dolly. Easing her hands up the length of his cock, she marveled at the velvety smooth skin casing the rock-hard firmness. When her fingers reached the crown, she swirled her fingernail across the opening, and a drop of come eased out.

Dolly leaned over and touched her tongue to the drop. It tasted salty and musky, a heady combination that made her pussy slick. She licked him again, her tongue laving the tip and sliding down the length to his balls.

Seth's ass clenched and he rose off the ground.

"You like that?" she whispered against his cock.

"More than you can even begin to imagine."

"I have a very good imagination." She ran her tongue up the length to the tip and captured him in her mouth.

When he surged upward, Dolly leaned back, her mouth releasing his shaft. "Oh, no, you said I could be in control."

Gathering a ragged breath, Seth settled back against the blanket, his jaw clenching so tightly it twitched. "Have your way with me."

With a secret smile, Dolly did. This time, when she closed her mouth over him, she moved over him and swallowed his cock until it bumped against the back of her throat.

He groaned, his buttocks tightening.

Dolly leaned back until his penis slipped out all the way to the tip.

Her hands braced on either of his hips and she lifted his ass from the ground, shoving him deep inside her mouth and letting him go, his cock swinging free.

"It works even better if you get something out of it. Mind if I show you? You're still in charge and you can tell me to stop if you want. But I guarantee you'll like it."

Eager to learn and grateful he would continue to let her be in charge, Dolly captured his gaze. "What do I do?"

Seth clasped one of her legs and lifted it over his chest, planting her knee on the ground. She faced away from him, her ass close to his chin. The position was excellent for sucking his cock, and she leaned forward to take him into her mouth again. "Mmmm . . . much better."

"Honey, you haven't even begun to know better." His arms hooked around her thighs and he pushed her legs open wider until she lowered to his face, her pussy hovering over his lips. "I'll get you started; then you can tell me what you like." Seth leaned up and flicked her clit with his tongue. "How's that?"

Dolly almost bit into his cock, the sensations rampaging through her made her want to scream. Heat seared a path from her cunt all the way through her body. With his cock in her mouth and his mouth on her pussy, she was overwhelmed with the powerful sensations shooting through her like fireworks on the Fourth of July.

When he didn't do it again, she lowered more until she was in his face with her most private parts.

Still, he didn't continue with the torturous pleasure. "Uh-uh. You have to tell me what you want. You're in charge."

She almost growled her frustration, embarrassed at being forced to vocalize her needs. "More please, do it again."

"Do what?" He blew a cool stream of air on her pussy. "I'm just a dumb cowboy; you'll have to tell me what it is you want me to do."

Dolly wanted to kick him in the head for teasing her so. "Lick me like you did."

"Where?" He blew again on her moist opening, the cool air only making her hotter.

"Lick my clit, for Pete's sake." She sank lower until she could feel his nose pressing into her buttocks. Then a warm, wet tongue snaked out and flicked her clit, and she almost leaped off him with the force of her body's reaction. "There! Oh God, right there. Lick it again," she cried. Then she sucked his cock into her mouth, wrapping her hands around the base.

Up and down, her mouth mimicked the motion of him pumping in and out of her pussy, the way she wanted him now. If the steely hardness of his cock and the lusty groans he breathed against her moist center were any indication, he liked what she was doing to him. That feeling of power made her all the more intoxicated.

When Seth reached up, parted the twin globes of her ass, and poked a finger into the tight lips of her anus, she burst over the edge and plummeted into the sea of pure lusty sensations threatening to consume her. She pulled free of his cock and tried to breathe, her chest constricted with the force of her orgasm. Finally, she plummeted to earth, her body quivering and shaking. Despite her weakened state, she still wanted more. Instead of collapsing on the blanket beside him, Dolly climbed over Seth until she faced him; then she eased her pussy down over his cock, fitting him snugly inside her where she felt he belonged.

He filled her to full and his eyes closed, a satisfied smile lifting the corners of his mouth. "I think you will take charge more often, witch."

"Shut up and kiss me." She leaned forward and pressed her lips to his, her tongue reaching out to part his lips. The taste of her sex was still in his mouth, and it fired up her juices all over.

She rose up on her knees and lowered herself down over him, and did it again, until she was moving in a steady rhythm.

Seth's face tensed, his jaw tightening.

Beneath her, she felt his groin rise up to meet her thrust for thrust until he impaled her with his thick cock. Their bodies came together in savage need.

Seth thrust upward one last time and grabbed her hips to stop her motion.

Inside she felt the jerking, spurting sensation as he cast his seed inside her. When Seth released her hips, Dolly collapsed against his chest, her body limp and satiated.

If that was what it felt like to be in charge . . . oh my.

His calloused fingers smoothed over her naked shoulder and he pressed a kiss to her temple. "Do you still want to go to Dodge City?"

Her body screamed *Hell no,* but when Dolly opened her mouth, she said, "Yes."

7

Seth took the lead for the next two hours, guiding Dolly into ravines and over hilltops in search of her beloved balloon. With all his heart he wished he hadn't found the confounded contraption. How could he let her have it when he wanted to keep her there?

The more she searched, the quieter she became, her face lined in a deep frown, worry making her blue eyes gray.

If her balloon meant that much to her, he'd give it to her tomorrow. Hell, he'd give her anything to see her smile again.

Nearing dusk, Seth had to convince her that searching after dark would accomplish nothing. When she'd insisted, he'd made up a story about how bandits and horse thieves were known to roam the prairie at night. The deeper the pack of lies he spread, the worse he felt. Then again, he couldn't blurt out that he'd found her balloon the day before, or she'd likely skin him alive.

She drooped in the saddle, and if Seth wasn't mistaken, she was saddle sore from more than just riding the horse all day. Dolly needed rest.

As they approached the ranch house, the sun dropped below the horizon, cloaking the yard and porch in gray.

"About time you two returned," Ron called out from a rocking chair on the porch.

Dolly frowned and swung out of the saddle onto the step stool. With her legs still shaking, she clung to the stirrup to stay on her feet. "How did you get down the stairs?"

"Had a little help from the two women. We've been waiting dinner for you."

"You should have gone on without us. We still have to take care of the horses." Dolly gathered the reins and turned the horse toward the barn.

"Don't worry about the horses," Seth said, relieving her of Angel's reins. "I'll take care of them."

"Good, then go wash up." Ron clapped his hands together. "Kit and I have a surprise for you."

Seth didn't like the devilish quirk at the corner of Ron's mouth or the way he smiled like the cat that ate the pet mouse. "I'll be back in a few minutes. You can start supper without me."

"We'll wait." Ron reached out and grabbed Dolly's hand. "Miss me, wife?" He pulled her onto his lap, grunting when she bumped his injured leg. As he nuzzled her neck, he cast a challenging glance at Seth.

Seth clenched the reins between his fingers, grinding a quarter inch off his back teeth in his effort not to say anything about Ron's proprietary hold on Dolly. She wanted to be in charge of her destiny. But if she didn't take charge of it and get out of Ron's lap soon, he'd have to move her himself.

Dolly pushed against Ron's chest and stood. "He knows we're not married."

Ron's brows dipped and he glared at Seth. "Not from lack of trying on my part."

Seth hesitated. The horses needed to be brushed and fed, but he hated leaving Dolly alone with Ron for even a minute. The man clearly wanted her as his own. But not as much as Seth did.

"You shouldn't have moved from the room upstairs." Dolly frowned down at Ron. "How's the leg?"

"Hurts like hell, but I'll live. I needed air and sunlight, and I wasn't getting much on the second floor. And I missed you." He reached out and captured her hand. "What about the balloon? Did you find it?"

Dolly's shoulders sagged. "No, but I'm sure we will tomorrow. We have to; without it we have nothing."

Seth wanted to say that she had anything she wanted from him, but that independent streak in Dolly wouldn't let her accept anything, unless it was on her terms. "I'll be back." Seth spun on his heel, fighting the urge to break Ron's other leg. If he continued to touch Dolly, he might have to shoot him.

When he reached the barn, his anger and frustration hadn't lessened. With more speed than patience, he tossed saddles onto the stall rails, blankets followed. "Why can't she let me take care of her? That balloon is dangerous. Too dangerous for a woman."

Ranger tossed his head.

"I'm glad someone agrees with me." Seth ran a brush across Ranger's back. "She's determined to go on to Dodge City whether she finds her balloon or not."

The stallion's head dipped low and he snorted.

"I know. I don't understand how God could gift me with a woman and take her away. It's as if he's testing me and I'm failing miserably. I don't suppose I could tie her to the bed and make her stay."

Ranger turned a level stare at him, his big brown eyes narrowing.

"No?" Seth's hand paused in midstroke with the brush. "I suppose she wouldn't be too happy about that. But what else can I do? She's a stubborn woman."

The horse's shoulder shook as if he shrugged.

"Thanks, I was counting on you to come up with a good plan. I'm fresh out of ideas." Seth finished brushing Ranger and moved to Angel. "What about you?"

The white mare had stood by patiently listening to Seth's one-sided conversation. Unlike Ranger, she'd kept her opinions to herself and stood quietly.

He smoothed the brush over her neck. "Do you have an opinion?"

The horse stared at him, her soft eyes accusing and sad.

"You think I should give her the balloon, don't you?"

Ranger shook his head and whinnied beside him.

"Shut up, you're not helping. Maybe Angel knows better what to do. After all, you're a male too." Seth turned back to Angel and brushed behind her ears. "If I give her back the balloon, she'll leave."

Angel turned her head to stare at him. Her gaze bore into his soul.

"You're right. If I don't let her make her own decision, she'll hate me. She wants to be in charge of her destiny. Whatever that means." Seth sighed, his heart squeezing at the thought of losing Dolly. His body still hummed from the exciting way she'd made love to him by the lake. An image of her naked body riding him like a bucking bronco made his cock twitch and strain for another ride. More than that, he liked her determination and bravery. Despite her fear of horses, she'd gone out riding to find the balloon.

Angel nudged his chest.

"Yeah, it'll hurt. But it's the only way to win her. She has to want to come to me or I will never have her." Seth patted Angel's neck and scratched her behind the ears. "I'll give her the balloon tomorrow."

Ranger whinnied and turned his back on Seth.

"We'll just have to get over it, Ranger. Angel's right." Seth flung the brush on the shelf, led both horses out to the corral, and turned them loose. He tossed some hay into the manger and stood staring out at the stars lighting the heavens one at a time as darkness cloaked the Kansas sky. The prairie seemed even bigger at the thought of Dolly leaving.

Why did he need all this land and cattle? All he'd accomplished was to tie himself down. If he didn't have anyone to share it with, it wasn't worth staying.

How long had it been since he'd been to Dodge City and visited the "girls," his family, at Madame Rosalee's? A long time. Well, it was time he went, and maybe he'd stay a while and try to win Dolly on her own turf. But first, he had to own up to his little pack of lies.

Dolly stripped from her riding clothes and washed her face, hands, and body. As she trailed the washrag over her skin, she could feel the touch of Seth's hands all over again.

A moan escaped her lips and her hand traveled downward to the juncture of her thighs where her pussy creamed at just the thought of what they'd done that day. She'd been a complete, brazen hussy lying naked in the open, making love to a virtual stranger.

Her fingers flicked against her clit, and Seth's tongue was there in her memory, laving her to distraction until she cried out his name to the sky. Oh the things he could do to her.

She'd never had a lover quite like Seth. Her husband had loved her in his own quiet way, and Ron was good in his way. Although, now Ron was too possessive when she'd already told him it was a mistake. She didn't love Ron.

But Seth . . .

The potential for happiness with Seth was huge. The man was good with animals, and he obviously loved where he lived. He was a man who could provide for a wife and any family that came along, no doubt. And the things he'd shown her, the way he'd brought her to orgasm, and the different ways to make love he'd shown her . . . well. Her breath caught in her throat and heat welled low in her belly. A body could get used to that really fast.

Was she crazy to move on to Dodge City and leave Seth behind? Without a balloon, she didn't have a way to make a living. Then again, she didn't belong on a ranch. Hell, she didn't even like to ride or shoot or do whatever it was you did with cows.

Besides, she refused to stay with Seth strictly because he could provide for her. She'd worked hard to make it on her own, she couldn't give that up. No, she wouldn't.

She shook out her best dress, a sapphire blue gown that showed off her tiny waist to perfection. She'd spent money she could ill afford for this eye-catcher, and she wore the dress only for performances. Was that what she was about to give, the greatest performance of her life? Would she lie about her growing feelings for Seth, telling him he didn't mean anything to her? *Thank you for putting up me and my fiancé and helping me look for my balloon, but if it's all the same to you, I'll be on my way if you'd be so good as to lend me a horse and a wagon.*

Halfway down the stairs, she paused. If she was so determined to move on to Dodge City, why was she dressing in her best dress? She almost turned around and raced back to her room to change when she spotted Ron sitting in the parlor and, conversely, he spotted her.

"You are a vision, Dolly. Come, sit with me." He patted the silk cushion of a Victorian sofa.

Dolly shook her head and wandered around the parlor, admiring the delicate furniture and woven rugs. How did a coarse cowboy acquire such beautiful things? She fingered the edge of the lace curtains hanging at a window.

"Are you getting anxious about the scheduled meeting in Dodge City?"

"Yes." She was getting even more anxious about leaving this

ranch and Seth, but she couldn't admit that to Ron when she couldn't admit it to herself.

"I can't wait, although I'm not sure how I'll manage getting into a balloon basket with this leg." He tapped his finger to the wooden splits tied to each side of his injured limb. "All I know is that I want you to myself again. You don't know how frustrating it was to watch you ride off with that brute of a cowboy."

When she wandered by him again, he captured her hand and pulled her against his good leg. "I'm serious, Dolly. I love you, and I want to marry you."

Ron wouldn't have been this insistent if they hadn't made love in the sky. He'd have happily remained her partner and she wouldn't have to feel guilty for making love to Seth. Now, she felt responsible for Ron's happiness when she couldn't even make room in her life for her own. Dolly shook her hand free. "Don't love me, Ron. There's a woman somewhere who will love you more than I ever could. You just have to wait for her."

His mouth curved into a frown. "There's no one I could love more than you, Dolly."

"Where is everyone?" Kit called out from the staircase.

Ron's frown transformed into a grin. "Wait until you see what we've been up to."

About that time, Seth walked through the front door, his face and shirt damp, probably from a dousing at the pump outside.

Dolly's heart skipped a beat when his gaze met hers. A flush of heat rose from her core all the way up into her cheeks. Damn the man, he made her hot.

"About time you came inside. I thought I was going to have to lasso you and drag you in." Kit chuckled, still out of sight at the top of the stairs. "Wait, I like the sound of that."

Seth's glance turned to the other woman, his eyes widening, then narrowing. "Kit?" Then he grinned.

That grin made a knot of something that felt very much like jealousy rise up in Dolly's throat. What had Kit done to put such a look on Seth's face? Dolly moved to the doorway and looked up.

Poised at the top of the stairs was a woman Dolly didn't recognize. Dressed in a ruby red dress, cut low over her bosoms and cinched tightly around an impossibly tiny waist, she descended the stairs one step at a time, a smile lifting the corners of her pretty lips. "Gosh, Seth, you'd think I was a circus attraction by the way your jaw is hanging open."

Not until the woman opened her mouth did it dawn on Dolly that this beauty was Kit. The cowgirl was anything but a girl, her womanly curves exposed in the gown designed to grace the ballrooms of New York or Boston, not the parlor of a simple house out in the middle of the Kansas prairie.

As fast as Seth's grin appeared, it disappeared. "Holy Jesus, Kit! Put some clothes on." Seth grabbed a knitted throw from a chair in the corner and wrapped it around Kit's shoulders. "I don't know what's got into you, runnin' around like a whore in a saloon. And what are you doing in Madame Rosalee's dress, anyway?"

Kit's mouth pressed into a mutinous line. "Well, ain't that a helluva note." She glared at Ron. "Told you it wouldn't make a bit of a difference." She yanked the wrap from around her shoulders and tossed it back on the chair. Then she planted her hands on her hips and looked Seth square in the eye. "What's it take to get through to you? Do I have to tie a rope around you to make you notice me as other than another cowboy?"

Seth shook his head, his lips twisting into a wry grimace. "No, Kit. I know who you are, and that you're a beautiful woman."

"Boy is she." Ron sat on the sofa, loosening the top button of his shirt. "I knew that dress would look good, but just not how good. Come here, let me look at you."

Kit's face flushed crimson and she tugged at the low neckline of her gown. "You don't think it shows off too much of my . . . well . . . too much of me?" She moved across the floor and stood in front of Ron.

"No." Ron grasped her hands, his gaze drinking in her beauty.

"Yes!" Seth pointed to the door. "Take that dress off this minute."

Dolly glanced from Seth to Kit and back to Seth. His anger was real. Real like a man who loved this woman.

Kit knew how to ride, rope, and wrangle cattle, or whatever you did with cows. When she dressed like a woman, she was lovely, if a little on the graceless side. Nevertheless, she was everything Seth needed and she had a ranch next to his.

How could Dolly compete? Not that she had any intention of competing. She had a balloon to find and a job waiting for her in Dodge City.

While Seth berated Ron for dressing Kit up like a floozy, Dolly slipped out the front door and onto the porch.

The temperature had dropped, lending a chill to the late summer air. The earthy scent of barn animals textured the clean fresh air; Dolly inhaled and let out a long sigh.

If she didn't find her balloon tomorrow, she'd ask Seth to take her to Dodge City in a wagon. One way or another, she'd get to the Wild West Show. She'd have another balloon made, even if she had to beg, borrow, or steal the funds to finance it. Above all, she had to make it on her own. She couldn't rely on anyone but herself, certainly not a man with eyes the color of maple syrup or a smile that could melt the coldest heart. Besides, she didn't belong in a fairy-tale house in the middle of the prairie. Kit did. Not Dolly.

"Aren't you coming in for dinner?" Seth's arms circled her from behind and he pulled her against the length of his body.

"I'm not hungry," she lied. She was hungry, all right, but not for food. Frankly, she was hungry for him and something more she refused to put a name to.

When Seth leaned forward and kissed the side of her neck, Dolly tipped her head to give him full access to her throat. This would be the last time she'd let him kiss her, the last time his hands would rove over her body. She savored the flood of sensations like a starving man savors a cracker.

When he turned her in his arms, she didn't dare look up into his eyes. Wasn't it already hard enough to focus on her goals and purpose? Instead, she studied the full line of his lips and the hard angles of his jaw.

"Why are you so quiet? When you aren't talking, I know you're thinking. And something tells me I'm not going to like what you're thinking."

"I'm leaving tomorrow, whether or not I have the balloon. I have to meet up with Buffalo Bill Cody the following day and discuss what I can do without a balloon. Hell, I don't know what I'm going to do about the balloon. I just don't know." She leaned her forehead against his chest.

"I know where your balloon is."

Dolly rattled on, discombobulated by Seth's nearness and the hard ridge of his cock pressing against her belly. "Bill won't want us in the show if our act blew away."

"Did you hear me? I said I know where your balloon is."

This time the gist of his words sank into her head and she gasped, grabbing his shirt. "You do?" Happiness filled her chest. That balloon meant freedom. As soon as the happiness rose, it disappeared. It also meant she'd be leaving. In a more subdued tone, she asked, "Where is it? When did you find it?"

Now was the time of reckoning. Seth drew in a deep breath. "I found it not far from where you and Ron landed. Just over the hill."

"I don't understand." She shook her head. "We were all over that area today."

His head dropped and he inhaled again before he explained. "I found it yesterday right after I left you and Ron at the house. I went back out and found it in the dark." He wasn't proud of the lie, but he'd do it all over again for the one day he had with Dolly.

"You knew all along? Why didn't you tell me?" Then her eyes widened. "You lied to me."

Seth stood straighter. "I wanted a day with you." He grabbed her shoulders. "Don't you see? When you fell out of the sky, you were a gift from God, the answer to my prayers. I just had to have time to convince you to stay with me."

Her brow furrowed into a hurt frown. "So far all I'm convinced of is that I can't trust you. I want my balloon now."

"It's in a cave down by the river. I'll have it to you tomorrow morning as soon as the sun comes up. I give you my word." He stared down into her eyes.

Her blue eyes swam with tears, and she pulled free of his hands. "And I'm supposed to trust your word? After you dragged me around all day, making a complete fool of myself on a horse? I'll find it myself." She stomped toward the door and yanked it open.

Seth followed and caught her arm before she stepped down off the porch. He'd known she'd be mad, but not this mad. "You can't. It's dark out there, and you'll need a wagon. We'll get it in the morning."

Her back was stiff and she refused to meet his eyes. "Very well. At the crack of dawn, I expect to see a wagon out here, ready to go."

"There will be." His fingers curved around her cheek. "I'm sorry, Dolly. I just wanted a chance to be with you."

"Well you got that, didn't you?" Her head shot up and she glared at him. "And I thought for once I'd met a decent man. A man who wouldn't lie to or take advantage of a woman." She brushed his hands aside. "I guess I was wrong. Now, if you'll excuse me. I'd like to go for a short walk, that is, if I have your permission to wander around your property." Her blue-eyed gaze flashed in the muted light streaming from the window.

"Of course, you can walk. My home is yours." Or so he'd hoped. The more anger she displayed, the further away his dream grew. He'd surely loused up any chances he had to be with Dolly. Maybe after she slept on it, she'd come around to see his intentions had been honorable. His hands dropped to his sides and he stood on the top step as she descended and walked into the darkness. He felt his chance for happiness slip away as she disappeared into the darkness. The good Lord had sent him a gift and a test.

Damned if he didn't fail the test. Now he'd lose his gift.

8

After Dolly had checked all the lines and made a thorough inspection of the balloon, she couldn't believe her luck. Nothing was missing and everything appeared to be in working order, except the broken glass of her vase. A small price to pay for having survived a terrible crash. Within an hour, she had the balloon filled and her trunks stowed.

Ron was a bit more of a hassle than the trunks. It took Seth and one of his ranch hands to heft him through the basket door. By the time he was seated on one of the trunks, his face was ashen.

Guilt stabbed at Dolly's gut. If she wasn't in such a hurry to get to Dodge City, she'd have given Ron a bit more time to recover from the broken leg. If she searched a little deeper, she'd admit she wasn't so intent about getting to Dodge City as she was about getting away from Seth and all he stood for.

He'd lied, a fault she shouldn't forgive, but the earnest way he'd held her and told her she was his gift from God had melted her anger. She'd had to work hard to restore her righteous indignation by the next morning. Had she not, she'd have thrown herself into his arms and stayed on the ranch with him, giving up her independence to become a rancher's wife, dependent on him for her livelihood.

And hadn't she sworn never to become dependent on anyone? Even if he had eyes the color of maple syrup and arms as solid as tree trunks.

Dolly hurried through her preparations, forcing back any lingering feelings for the man she'd spent a magical day with, reminding herself that one day did not make a relationship. There was no truth to the myth of love at first sight.

Then why was her chest squeezing in on her and her eyes blurring with tears every time she bumped into the man? She shook her head and kept going until the time came to set sail in her balloon. A glance at the western sky struck a note of concern in her chest. The storm clouds that had been brewing on the horizon had crept across the prairie. If she didn't get a move on, she'd be caught up in the turbulence. But turbulence or not, she'd rather face rough weather than the storm building inside her chest.

When she stepped through the gate of the basket and closed it behind her, she felt as though she were closing the door on her heart. A foolish notion, she chided herself. Her dreams lay in Dodge City where she'd join up with the Wild West Show.

Seth stood next to the basket, his hands holding firmly to the ropes. "You sure this thing is safe?" His furrowed brows showed his doubt and concern.

Dolly bit back her immediate response of *safer than staying with you*. "Very. If you'll let go of the ropes, we'll be on our way."

He held tight, a sigh escaping his lips. "I've only known you a day, but that doesn't change how I feel. I love you, Dolly Sherman, and I want to marry you. If you change your mind, you know where to find me."

A lump rose in her throat and she fought the tears welling in her eyes. She forced words past her lips. "Let go of the rope, please."

Slowly, as though it hurt to do it, Seth let go of the ropes.

Dolly applied more heat and the balloon ascended into the air.

Seth stood in the field, alone but for his horse, Ranger.

The higher the balloon drifted, the more Dolly realized the mistake she was making.

"I can't believe you're leaving him." Other than a few expletives over the pain he was feeling, Ron hadn't spoken much until now.

"He's a stranger. Why would I stay?" Dolly stared down at the man who was slowly becoming a speck on the prairie.

"He clearly loves you, and if I'm not mistaken, you have feelings for him as well." He glanced at the darkening sky. "And the weather is looking pretty wicked. If you ask me, we're in for a helluva ride."

"I had to leave. Don't you see?"

"Why? Because you didn't want to take a chance on trusting someone to take care of you?" Ron shook his head. "I love you, too, Dolly, and I'd rather see you go back and marry the cowboy and be happy the rest of your life than go on pretending to be so brave."

"I am brave."

"Liar. If you were so brave, you'd have given Seth a chance."

The wind twirled the basket around and Dolly grabbed hold of the edge to remain on her feet. Maybe she had been a bit hasty to take off with a storm so close.

"Better hold on, we're in for a rough ride," Ron called out.

Just as he spoke the words, a gust buffeted the balloon and basket, knocking Dolly off her feet. Her head struck the side of her trunk and her vision blurred. Oh no! She couldn't black out now, not with Ron incapacitated with his leg. The harder she fought the encroaching blackness, the faster it overcame her.

"Dolly, are you all right?" Ron pulled her to her feet and hugged her close. "You had me scared for a moment." He stood straight, holding her against him.

It took a moment for Dolly to realize he didn't have a splint on his leg. "What the hell, Ron? You shouldn't have taken off the splint. What about your leg?"

He stared into her eyes and laughed. "You must have hit your head harder than I thought. My leg's fine." His hands moved upward, tracing the indentation of her waist. "What? No corset?"

Dolly slapped his hands away, a strange sense that she'd done this all before. "Don't touch me like that, Ron."

"Why not, you were all for it just a moment ago." He reached for her hips and pulled her snuggly against his, the hard ridge of his cock pressing into her belly.

Panic seized her and she shoved him away. "I was a fool to make love with you once, but I told you, it was a mistake."

"What do you mean, you made love to me?" Ron shook his head, the smile slipping from his lips. "Did I miss something?"

What was happening? Why was Ron being so obtuse, and where were his splints? He acted as though he'd never broken his leg.

When he reached for her again, she slapped his hands away. "Don't, Ron. I love Seth." She clapped a hand to her mouth, the words having escaped of their own accord. But once she'd admitted it, she couldn't go back. She loved Seth.

Ron crossed his arms over his chest. "Who is Seth? Is he someone you met back in Cheyenne?"

"What are you talking about? Seth is the man whose ranch we just left."

With a frown, Ron shook his head. "I think you hit your head harder than you thought. Maybe you should sit down. We should be in Dodge City with three days to spare. You'll have time to rest and recuperate from your fall."

"Three days? We only have today and tomorrow to get there. And you know Seth and Kit. And you broke your leg when our balloon crashed. Why are you acting so strangely?"

"I've never met anyone by the name of Seth or Kit." Ron placed a hand around her shoulders. "Sit down, Dolly. You must be suffering from your fall."

She perched on the edge of her trunk and stared at the thin glass vase in the corner of the basket. The glass was completely intact and a rose still rested inside. What the hell?

Dolly stared around at the darkening sky.

Had the balloon crash been a dream? Had she imagined falling in love with Seth and spending a wonderful day on the ranch with him?

She stood and stared out over the prairie. The balloon was losing altitude and she should do something soon, or they'd crash.

Then she spotted a dot in the distance. It was black and tan. Like a black horse and a cowboy sitting astride. Could it be Seth? Could it be she was being given a chance to start over?

"Are you sure you're all right?" Ron asked, grasping her shoulders and spinning her to face him.

"I think so." The more she thought about it, the lighter her heart grew. "Yes, I know I am."

Hadn't Seth said God had given her as a gift? When her balloon had crashed, he'd rescued her. Was God giving her a second chance at a life with Seth?

Yes!

Dolly reached for the buttons on her shirt and fumbled with them until she had them completely undone. Then she yanked her blouse from the waistband of her skirt.

"Change your mind?" Ron reached out and captured her waist, bending to kiss her throat.

"No! Don't do that." She pushed him aside and fought to loosen the button on her skirt. He'd found her naked on the prairie. She wanted him to find her just so.

"Here, let me help." Ron freed the button and pulled the skirt down over her legs.

"Hurry. We only have a few moments." She glanced over the side of the basket, and a thrill of fear raced through her. They were getting dangerously close to the ground, the balloon practically dropping from the sky.

When Ron dove for the burner, Dolly yelled, "Don't touch that!"

"But we'll crash."

"I know." She loosened her petticoat and stepped out of it, then lifted her camisole over her head.

Ron reached for the burner, his eyes wide with worry. "We have to gain altitude."

"No!" She dove for Ron, knocking him away from the burner. He couldn't change a thing or they wouldn't crash and be rescued by Seth. Dolly didn't know how this could happen, or how they'd gone back in time, she just knew. This was her chance to start over, to make it right and stay with Seth.

When she climbed back to her feet, she saw him sitting on Ranger, his back to them. Then the basket hit him in the head and continued on across the prairie.

Holy Jesus, what had she done? The ground raced up to meet them, and the basket bumped against a rise; the door flew open and dumped Dolly onto the prairie grass. Her head hit hard and grayness crept in on the sides.

She let the blackness consume her.

When her eyes opened again, she was immediately aware of grass poking into her bare skin. When she rolled to her back, a man with wavy brown hair and deep brown eyes stared down at her.

He grinned. "I can't believe my luck." Then he tipped his head to the sky. "Thank you, thank you, Lord."

"Seth?" Dolly stared up into the face she'd grown to love in less than two days.

His eyes widened. "You know my name?"

She smiled and wrapped her arms around his neck. "Of course I know your name."

He straightened, pulling her into his lap. "How?"

She nestled against his chest, rubbing her breasts against him. "I'm your gift, Seth. Didn't you just pray for me?"

Tentatively, his hands ran over her body as if he might be dreaming. "My gift?" Then his arms circled her and he stood, bringing her with him. "Woooweee!" he shouted to the sky. "I never thought the good Lord would answer me so fast."

"Well, now that you have your gift, what are you going to do with me?" She smiled at him, thinking of a lot of things she'd like to do to him.

Seth stood her on her feet and scratched his head. "I don't know. This is all kind of sudden."

The black stallion behind him nudged him, throwing him against Dolly.

Happiness filled her to overflowing. Any second thoughts were blown away in her second wind. She'd been given her own gift from God. A chance to do it all over, and this time, she'd do it right.

Dolly wrapped her arms around Seth's neck again and leaned close to whisper in his ear. "If you don't have any ideas, I have a few of my own." Her leg climbed his, circling behind, her warm, wet pussy rubbing against his thigh. That should get him started. She'd show him more later. She had plenty of time, now that she'd come home.

CINNAMON AND SPARKS

LAYLA CHASE

1

Colorado Territory, 1876

Sheriff Kent Wyman stood in the office of the Montrose Metal mine and watched a petite figure scale the wooden scaffolding being erected not thirty feet away. His friend John Terrill was intent on this dangerous pyrotechnic show for his mine's celebration.

At the sight of her rounded ass stretching the limits of work denims, he stiffened, wondering how, the week before, he'd mistaken her for a young man. Granted, her dark hair had been covered by a cap as she'd worked side by side with another man unloading boxes from a rail car.

When he first saw her, he would have walked his horse right by the depot if he hadn't caught sight of the Henderson boys running from the rail tracks like their breeches were on fire. A breeze wafted the scent of sulfur, and he'd spotted a burning fuse on a string of firecrackers not fifteen feet away.

At the sudden popping sound, his horse merely shied, but two others tied to the depot's hitching rail reared, broke their reins, and galloped away—right toward the youth unloading cargo.

"Hey, look out! Runaway horses!" Kent kicked Blaze's sides and galloped toward the ramp.

The youth turned but seemed frozen in place, hands gripping a burlap bag.

"Run." Kent skidded Blaze to a stop, vaulted off, and tackled the youth, landing on the rocky ground and rolling out of the path of the frantic horses. When the rolling stopped, Kent found his hand cupped over the soft mound of a woman's breast. And that was just one feature of a curvy female that felt wonderful pressed on top of him.

For an instant, his mind flashed to their bodies in more intimate circumstances. Private, and with less clothing.

The head resting on his shoulder shook. "Hey." Her body stiffened and she struggled against his grasp, planting her hands on his chest.

A curtain of black hair loosened from her cap, the scent of roses surrounding his head. Silky tendrils grazed his cheek, and he commanded his body not to react.

Her flashing brown eyes narrowed. "Let me go." The woman moved her legs, straddling his thigh, and scrambled to get leverage.

Her movements only pressed her leg harder against his groin, and he stifled a groan. Too much time had passed since he'd had a woman, but he wasn't about to embarrass himself in the middle of Buckskin. He threw his arms out to the sides to release her but peered through the fall of wavy hair for glimpses of her face.

She pushed off and leaned back on her heels, shoving the curly mass of hair over one shoulder. "Well!"

"Oriana! Are you all right?" A young man rushed to her side and grabbed her arm, helping her stand.

Oriana—the name sounded like a princess in a storybook.

Kent's gaze narrowed at the pair obviously on familiar terms. This princess looked like she already had a prince. Disappointment ran through his thoughts.

Kent shook away that odd thought and scrambled to his feet, patting his clothes to shake off the dust. "Sorry, ma'am. Didn't want a new arrival in town getting trampled by runaway horses." A short glance down the street confirmed the horses were being tended. He straightened his vest that had flapped open in the tussle. The arousing tussle.

"I thank you for that, sir." Her gaze centered on his vest and the tin star. "Um, Sheriff." She darted a frowning glance at the man next to her, then turned and extended her hand. "Sheriff, my name is Oriana Donato Ignacio. I represent the Donato Pyrotechnic Company, and we've been hired by—"

He held tight to her small, oddly strong hand dwarfed in his, but the rest of his body stilled. She would have to be connected to this reckless folly. "I know who hired you."

Her eyes rounded then clouded, but her gaze never dropped. "Oh?"

With his hand extended, the other man stepped forward, a wide smile on his lips. "Sir, my name is Dante Donato, and I am pleased to meet you. Later in the week, we will be visiting your office—to discuss the business permit. I'm glad we've gotten the basic introductions behind us." His gaze dropped to their still-clasped hands.

Kent released the lady's hand and shook Dante's, noticing the similarity in their dark eyes and wavy hair. "You're right about the permit. As sheriff, my responsibility is to keep watch for the town's safety."

"I can see that." Dante clapped a hand on Kent's shoulder. "You're a helpful man to have standing by in an emergency." He nudged an elbow at Oriana's side.

She blinked in confusion, looking sideways, then her eyes widened. "Oh, yes. Sheriff, I must thank you for your quick thinking in my rescue." A smile slowly spread across her lips. "Years have passed since my last wrestling match."

Every day since that incident, Kent had contemplated the possible meanings of her last statement. Had she simply been making light of the situation? Or had she been hinting at something more?

The doorknob clattered behind him, and heavy boot steps scraped on the office flooring. "Kent? You're here again?"

Without turning, Kent knew an avidly curious expression would be on his best friend's face. He'd heard it in John's tone. "Need to keep an eye on the construction of this"—he waved an impatient hand toward the structure—"thing."

"That's what you told me yesterday." John walked to his desk, chuckling. "And the day before. And the day before that."

"You don't take these pyrotechnics seriously enough."

"I don't have to because you're being too serious. I've told you over and over—the accident that happened our first year wasn't anyone's fault. We've taken better precautions since then."

Kent turned and stared at his friend. "I'm not concerned about your abilities, John."

"Besides, you weren't even sheriff at the time."

"Doesn't mean I don't care about the welfare of the miners." His jaw tightened and his hands drew into fists.

Papers rattled and a pen tapped on the desktop. "Why does this sound personal?"

Kent turned back to the window, wondering if his tumultuous feelings showed on his face. Ever since he'd tangled with the petite lady with the wavy black hair, he'd felt like he'd been enchanted.

His sleep was filled with dreams of their tussle in various

stages of undress. One night, he'd woken rock hard, tangled in the bed sheets, and had to finish off what the erotic dream started.

An act he hadn't performed in a long time. One that had stopped the ache for only a short spell.

"Not personal. That's my job." Kent felt the familiar tightness in his chest and fought against the memory. He'd never told his friend how much being near mines of any type bothered him. Ever since the accident in the Montana gold mines claimed his father's life. After the funeral, Kent swore to find a different line of work.

"Okay, buddy, you keep telling yourself that." The wooden chair creaked as John spoke. "Want more coffee?"

Kent held his tin mug to the side. "Sure."

Outside, the sun shone and glinted off the head of the hammer in Oriana's hand. Kent let his gaze wander, watching the sure movements of her feet as she moved agilely over the scaffold, testing crosspieces, hammering in extra nails here and there. The breeze brought only an occasional word of her conversation with the other workers. Part of him wanted to step outside just to hear her voice again.

An action that would prove his interest was much more than professional.

Her denims pulled tight with each stretch she made, and he couldn't keep his gaze way. The woman's ass was plump and rounded, and his hands itched to feel the weight of—

A crack sounded and her body abruptly swung to the right side.

"Ahh. Help!"

Damn! Kent dropped his mug and sprinted for the door. "John, get a ladder." The image of her body crumpled at the base of the structure flashed across his mind.

He vaulted down the office steps and crossed the open

ground with long strides. Oriana hung about twenty feet above him. He caught a glimpse of another body moving toward her but judged that person was too far away.

"Oriana, I'm right below you. Hang on."

She glanced over her shoulder, her feet swinging in the air, reaching for the next piece of wood.

Within seconds, he'd scaled ten feet, but she was still out of reach.

"Ow, I can't hold on."

"Wrap your arm around the post. I'll climb to you." He waited to make sure she moved in that direction, then positioned himself under her before climbing. If she fell, at least his body could deflect her descent. When he reached her, he kept climbing until his body surrounded hers and he pressed her against the post. "Let your left hand go."

At that moment, Dante appeared at their side. "Ori, the sheriff has you. Let go." He tapped his hand on her white-knuckled grip on the wood.

Kent couldn't see her face, but he felt her body lean against his, and he welcomed the weight. She trusted him not to let her fall. That gesture meant the world. "Grab my forearms and lower your feet to rest on my boots. I'll climb us down together."

Her hands grabbed his arms. She inhaled a quick breath and stiffened, then adjusted her shoes over his. "I'm ready."

Kent heard pain in her words but needed to get them back to ground level. "Left, first." He shifted his weight to his right foot and lowered his left. Her ass nestled against his groin, and he felt himself hardening. Damn, this was not the time to be having randy reactions.

Focus on getting the lady to safety.

"Now, right." His voice came out more gruffly than he intended.

Within only a few such movements, they were both on firm ground.

The minute their feet hit the ground, she turned in his arms and grabbed him around the waist, her body shaking. "Thank you."

Kent reached a hand to her chin and tipped up her head until he could see her eyes.

She blinked quickly and the moisture lining her lashes glinted.

Relief at her safety flooded him and he leaned over, the thought of providing comfort uppermost in his mind.

A thump sounded and Dante jumped down nearby.

The moment was broken. Kent stepped back.

The man rushed to his sister's side, enveloping her in a tight hug. He spoke in rapid Italian, stopping only when she nodded. "Let me see your hands."

"Only a few splinters." Her dark gaze went to his, warming. "Again, Sheriff, I find myself needing to thank you."

"Since rescuing you has become a habit, call me Kent." He glanced at her hands, reddened from work and stained with chemicals. A jagged piece of wood stuck from her palm.

John ran up, dropping a ladder and striding to where they stood. "Are you all right, Mrs. Ignacio?"

Kent jerked every time he heard her name. Through a bit of questioning, he'd learned she was a widow, but he preferred to think of her only as Oriana. With no other man having made a prior claim.

"I'll be fine."

"No, you need help." Dante turned to the mine owner. "Mr. Terrill, her hand needs tending."

A gasp sounded.

Kent turned to see Oriana staring at her hand, and noticed for the first time her pale skin and quick breathing. "Do you feel faint?"

She turned and blinked slowly, her wounded hand thrust from her side.

"Ah hell." He scooped her into his arms and headed toward the mine's office. "John, get the mine doctor."

Oriana's mind wheeled at what had just happened. She'd nearly fallen off the top of a thirty-foot platform. Then she'd climbed down from that height with a hard male body touching every inch of her back, rump, and legs. Between fear and excitement, she'd barely taken a full breath. Now she'd been rescued again by the formidable, brown-haired sheriff, the one man in this territory who set her blood blazing.

Carrying her, his strong arms cradled her tight against his hard body. Each stride he took jostled her right breast against his chest, abrading her nipple against the chemise. When she worked, she never wore a corset, and the heat from his large hand on her ribcage seeped through the thin layers of her clothing. His other hand clamped her hip, a place no man had touched in the three years since she'd become a widow.

When they reached the base of the stairs, she straightened her arm and leaned slightly away. "I can walk from here."

"Steady." Kent shifted his grip and, for a moment, his hand cupped her rump, then slid back to her thigh. "No, ma'am. I didn't rescue you just to have you tumble down these steps. I'm not letting you go until I put you on the sofa in John's office."

Masterful. His words sent a thrill through her. She relaxed and rested her forehead against his warm neck. For now, she'd let someone else be in control. But only for a little while. Then she had something important to figure out.

He moved with such ease as he mounted the stairs to the office. Even though they'd barely met, Oriana trusted him. She inhaled and sighed. He smelled of sunshine and coffee mixed with male sweat. And a bit of bay rum.

Masculine smells that sent her female thoughts racing.

Thoughts she hadn't dared entertain for such a long time. What if—

With a sharp bang, he kicked at the base of the office door and it swung wider. "Here we are." He maneuvered them through the door and across the room, leaning to place her on the sofa.

The shift in contact with his solid body felt like a loss, and she gripped his neck tighter. She glanced up to thank him and saw his blue-gray eyes turn smoky. The man was interested . . . and staring at her lips as if he'd devour them.

His large hands cupped hers, rough fingers trailing along the outside of her injured hand. With a quick twist, he pulled out the wooden spike and tossed it to the floor.

Again, the feeling of him commanding the situation ran through her body. Tension coiled between her thighs, the delicious sensation that had been ignored too long. Her mouth immediately dried, and she had to lick her lips before speaking.

His gaze dropped to her mouth, flared, and then slowly rose to connect with hers.

"Thanks for your help." She gave him a grateful smile.

"That's one way to say thanks." A brown eyebrow raised in challenge. "Know any others?"

"You're absolutely right." She tensed her arms to pull his head lower and brushed her lips across his firm ones. The brief contact left her hungry for more. She opened her eyelids enough to see his reaction.

A grin quirked the corner of his mouth. "I did rescue you twice."

Desire bolted through her, hot and quick. She fingered the hair behind his ear and stretched to press a demanding kiss against his mouth. This time, she sucked and nibbled at his lower lip, hungry for his response.

But he straightened, breaking her hold.

At his abrupt move, she fell back against the cushion, confusion scrambling her thoughts, until she heard the stomp of boots on the wooden stairs outside.

The mine owner strode across the floor, a stooped man right behind him. "Here's the doc. Show him your hand."

Kent moved to one side, a hand rubbing at the back of his neck.

She knew her cheeks were flushed and her heartbeat raced. Symptoms she hoped the doctor would attribute to her recent fright. Her fingers curled into a fist, and she pulled away her hand. "If you have a needle, doctor, I can get the rest of this out myself."

"Name's Sutton, ma'am." The gray-haired man set down a weathered wooden box and rummaged inside until he found a packet of steel needles. "I'm not really a doctor. Being around mines most of my life gave me lots of practice at patching people up."

"Don't be stubborn, Ori." Dante walked across the room and knelt at her side. "Let the man help you."

Using only gentle pressure, Sutton's hands cupped hers.

Oriana relaxed her fingers. His first jab at the splinter's remains made her wince; then she steeled herself. She'd had enough trouble convincing her brothers she could do this job. She was not going to return home and listen to Dante relay stories about how she'd fussed over a sliver of wood.

"Here, drink this."

A tumbler with an inch of amber liquid hung in front of her. She glanced up to meet Kent's concerned blue-gray gaze, grabbed the glass, and tossed back the contents, pressing her lips together at the sting of whiskey on her throat. The alcohol warmed her already heated insides, but Kent's gesture warmed her heart.

Cool liquid splashed on her hand, and the skin around the sliver stung. She sucked in a breath and glanced at who held the bottle.

"To clean it." Kent pulled away the bottle and turned.

"Ori, this is nothing." Dante ran a comforting hand along the arm not being tended. "Remember when we were kids and were playing pirates at Popo's house? Matteo fell down the stairs, shattered his wooden sword, and a piece of the handle stuck in his thigh. Now that was a splinter!"

"I remember." Oriana knew what her brother was doing and she loved him for trying to distract her.

"And remember how much he yelled when you cut it out so Mama and Papa wouldn't learn about it?"

What Dante didn't know was she had all the distraction she needed in the form of the tall, brown-haired man staring out the window. She pulled her gaze back to her brother's worried face and smiled. "What I remember is how you turned green when I had to stitch his wound closed."

He grinned, then his gaze turned serious.

"That's it." Sutton held up the jagged splinter clamped in a pair of tweezers. "A bit of salve and a bandage, and you'll be right as rain."

Oriana looked at her reddened palm and flexed her hand, grateful the wound hadn't bled much. "Just a small bandage. I need to fix that broken support and check the others."

Dante shook his head. "Maybe I should."

"Why? This injury won't keep me down." She glimpsed worry in her brother's gaze and sat up, her uninjured hand gripping his arm. "What's wrong?"

Dante's eyebrows clamped into a tight wrinkle. "*Silenzio,* Oriana."

At his command spoken in their native language, she battled not to remind Dante who was the elder Donato here.

Kent shoved his hands in his front pockets and stepped close, his gaze narrowed. "Why aren't you speaking in English?"

Forcing a smile, Oriana tore her gaze from her brother's

worried expression. "I apologize for my brother's impetuous-ness. He doesn't intend to be rude."

With an impatient gesture, Dante shook off her hand. "This isn't about rudeness. Ori, we have private matters to discuss."

"Are you discussing that structure out there? Or the accident? If so, you'd better start talking. And in English." Kent pointed a finger in Dante's face. "Because that involves the people under my jurisdiction, and I need to know."

With a shrug, Dante gave her one last look and turned toward the mine owner and the sheriff.

The moment she spotted that look, she knew what he would say was serious and would jeopardize everything she'd worked so hard for. She jumped to her feet, swaying a bit, and moved between the two men squared off in the middle of the office.

"Perhaps Dante only wants to express his brotherly concerns in private." She couldn't ignore the sick feeling in the pit of her stomach. Something was very wrong. She looped her arm through Dante's and pulled him toward the door. "We'll just leave you gentlemen and get back to work now."

Dante didn't move. "No, maybe this shouldn't be private."

Oriana jerked his arm and, breaking into rapid-fire Italian, told him to respect her authority and remain quiet until they reached a private location.

His answer was long and animated, his hands moving through the air almost as fast as his lips spat out the information.

He'd discovered the board hadn't broken on its own. The wood was sawed three quarters of the width through. Anyone who touched that support, put any weight on it, was meant to have a nasty fall. *Sabotaggio.*

"Whoa!" Kent held up both hands. "I understood that last word. You just said sabotage. You telling us this act was deliberate?"

For Oriana, everything moved in slow motion. Words

sounded guttural, and gestures moved as if through cold molasses. In the past, her family had discussed cases like this, but none had ever been aimed at the Donatos.

Dante walked to the doorway and picked up a length of lumber resting against the wall. He carried it back to the sheriff and held it out, pointing a finger at one end. "See for yourself. Looks like a saw cut to me."

Kent accepted the piece of wood and examined the end, his brows dropping lower over his eyes.

John moved beside him and took the wood, turning it as he stared. "I agree. This isn't a break." He tapped the end into his open palm. "But maybe this was present when you bought the lumber."

Dante stiffened and squared his shoulders.

Oriana battled her own immediate denial and pressed a restraining hand to her brother's chest. "Calm down, Dante. Let me take care of this." Rumors might spread from this room that could prove damaging to the family's reputation. She would not let that happen.

Resolved to remain calm, with a weak smile, she turned to the mine owner. "Mr. Terrill, I assure you my brother and I check and recheck all of our equipment and our supplies. The Donatos pride themselves on safe working practices."

John looked to Kent and then back to Oriana with a shake of his head. "I didn't mean to insinuate anything. I'm looking for a more logical answer here."

"Let my brother and I go back outside. We will check every board, nail, and brace on the structure."

"No need." Kent's deep, authoritative voice rumbled over her assurances. "This project is shut down."

Impossible. How could she explain this to her family? She whirled to face him. "No!"

Kent narrowed his gaze and spoke through clenched teeth. "Nobody goes near that scaffold."

Oriana quelled at the fierce look in Kent's eyes. Oops, maybe that was too strong. "Please reconsider." She stepped close and reached out a hand, then quickly drew it back. "Someone has to check the construction." She searched his stony expression, her thoughts racing at what she could say to change his mind. Earlier, the man had mentioned safety.

Maybe if she acted like she needed his help . . . At this point, she would say anything to keep him from stopping this exhibition. "I'll need advice on hiring guards to prevent a reoccurrence."

He gave her a short nod. "In my office. After supper."

2

The clock behind him struck seven times and he tossed down the stack of wrinkled wanted posters he'd been studying. Some of them were so old he wondered whether the men remained on the loose or were even still alive.

The scuffling of shoes on the wooden planking sounded outside the office door. "Come on, little lady. Let me help you."

What the hell? Kent scooted back his chair and started for the door.

A surprised exhalation of air sounded, followed by a moan and a dull thud.

The office door opened and a well-dressed woman stepped over a man's body crumpled on the boardwalk. "Evening, Sheriff." She moved into the room and stood near his desk, straightening the sleeves on her jacket.

Kent glanced between her and the fallen figure groaning as he clutched his chest. What the hell had happened here? He squatted down next to the man and rolled him to his back.

Whiskey and stale tobacco fumes stung his nose. Lester Olson, drunk as usual.

Balancing on the balls of his feet, Kent debated about hauling Lester into a jail cell and letting him sleep off the booze again. Not tonight. Not if the man could clear the boardwalk on his own volition. He shoved a hand at Lester's shoulder. "Get yourself on home, Lester. Go sleep it off."

"My chest burns like wildfire." Lester struggled to balance his weight on his elbows. "What did she hit me with? Never saw it coming."

Kent grabbed an arm, hoisted Lester to his feet, and sent him in the direction of his house. For several seconds, he watched to make sure Lester wasn't too far gone to stumble home. With a satisfied nod, he squared his shoulders, straightened his vest, and walked back into the office.

The short woman shifted through the posters on his desk, a gloved hand moving the papers from one pile to another. A dark red jacket and skirt hugged her curves, and a black hat with ribbons trailing off the back sat on dark hair pulled into a twist. A lady with some class. "Now, ma'am. Can you explain what happened out there?"

She turned at the sound of his voice, a smile teasing her lips. "Ma'am?"

Her smile gave him the feeling she knew something he didn't. A feeling he didn't like. "Well, I find a man floundering on the ground at the same time you're walking through my door. Lester's wobbling his way home, so you'd be the one to provide the particulars."

"The man tried to escort me and I didn't need help." A gloved hand waved in the air. "He wouldn't release my arm, so I subdued him."

Thoughts of how a woman her size could have done that ran through his head. "I'm grateful you're all right and I apologize for that drunk's behavior. Will you trust me to see you safely to your destination?"

"This is my destination. I came to see you." Her smile widened.

"I don't understand." He walked closer. The minute he smelled violets, he knew. His gaze swept her body again and he didn't know how he could have been so blind. "Oriana? I apologize for not recognizing you."

The brim of her hat bobbed as she dipped her chin. "I do look different than the other times."

Different was an understatement. He positioned a chair next to his desk and waved a hand. "Please, sit."

She moved to the chair and sat, arranging her skirts.

Realizing he stared, Kent shook his head and walked around her to his chair. "I didn't forget the appointment, but the"—he cleared his throat and shot another glance at this woman. Not good to accuse a sophisticated lady like her of coldcocking a man—"incident with Lester took it right out of my mind."

Oriana moved forward in her chair and rested a black-gloved hand on the desk. "Sheriff . . . Kent, I need this anniversary exhibition to go on as planned."

He rocked back on two chair legs and looked at her earnest expression, her tense body. Her soft, rounded body. His mind drifted to a few things he could do that might relax her. And him.

"Kent?"

The chair landed with a thud. To regain his composure, he shoved at the papers in front of him. "Uh, sorry." One was covered with his broad scrawl and he pulled it in front of him. "I made a list."

"A list?" She stood and leaned over his side. "Did you find something wrong after we left?"

Her scent wrapped around his senses, and he knew if he

turned his head he'd get a glimpse of her rounded bosom. Tension gripped his groin and he shifted in the chair. If she continued standing there, he couldn't proceed in a business-like manner.

"Sit and we'll discuss this." His voice was gruffer than he intended, but something about this woman got to him on a primal level.

She scooted her chair so she was perched at the edge of the desk, knees facing him. "May I read the list?"

He passed her the paper, then watched as her brown eyes scanned what he'd written.

When she looked up, her brows were wrinkled and her lips pressed into a thin line. "Are you trying to close down this event?"

"I don't know what you mean."

"These safety precautions are too stringent."

Irritation flashed through him, and he shifted in his chair before forcing himself to meet her curious gaze. "My responsibility is looking out for the public safety."

"Pails of water *and* buckets of dirt at every source of ignition?" She leaned forward to set the list on the edge of the desk and pointed at the written words. "Two wagons filled with dirt?"

"Nothing wrong with that." He hated being on the defensive. Who was this bit of a woman to question his authority? He glanced sideways and inwardly groaned at the hint of rounded breasts over the neckline of her dress.

"You're absolutely right, Sheriff. If you'd read the contract between our company and Mr. Terrill, you'd see we have outlined similar precautionary measures." Her gaze flicked back to the list and her mouth turned down. "Just not to the extent you demand."

He shrugged. "So this time you do."

"But these are prohibitive." She shook the paper.

He noticed a glint in her eyes and a blush in her cheeks. Probably with irritation, but his imagination went in another direction. "Sorry, those are my conditions."

"In addition, having this many pails on the platform creates potential hazards for the workers."

"I don't see that."

"I'll sketch it." She pulled her chair right next to his and stretched for the pen and inkwell.

Her breast rubbed the length of his arm, and he inhaled through clenched teeth. He flashed a glance at her face but saw no change in her expression.

Within moments, she'd drawn several blocks with various shapes on top. "Here are the displays. We need room to walk along and between these to ignite the fuses." She turned to look at him. "See?"

Their faces were only inches apart.

Her eyes rounded and she blinked; then she cleared her throat. "You need to look at the drawing, Kent."

"Sorry." He shifted his gaze and focused on her sketch. "These are the places where you'll set off the fireworks?"

"Right. So if we have to put pails here, here, and here"—the pen scribbled groups of circles—"we won't have any room to walk. Our plan calls for pails of dirt, not water, at the edges of the platform. In almost ten years," she paused a moment before continuing, "our firm hasn't had an injury or accident." She leaned an elbow on the desk and turned to him. "I'd say our established procedures are successful."

He wondered about the cause of her hesitation. "How about today?" The image of her hanging from that loose board went through his mind and he shoved to his feet. "You can't be claiming that was only an accident."

A gloved hand waved in dismissal and she shook her head. "My brother is young and likes to hear himself talk. Plus, he's Italian, so the more dramatic the story, the better."

"I saw the board. The cut was deliberate." He paced away from the desk and back. "We all talked about the possibility of sabotage."

"In your inspection, did you find others?"

"No, the structure is solid. I checked it. Twice."

"You checked it again after I left?" A smile touched her lips and she looked at her hands. When her head rose, her expression was composed. "Then, you can issue the permit."

He shook his head. "Not so fast."

"What?" She jumped to her feet and walked around the chair. "Is there another list? Are there other concerns?"

Kent steeled himself not to react to her upturned face, to her eyes flashing dark warnings. "The same list. Same concerns." He couldn't shake the idea that the firecrackers at the train depot and the sawed board were connected. For six months, the town of Buckskin had been peaceful. Nothing more exciting than an occasional fistfight over a card game or housing a drunk on a Saturday night.

This woman arrives in town and all hell breaks loose. Or maybe that was just because he couldn't forget the memory of her soft body pressing down on his. Was his reaction based on personal feelings?

He rubbed a hand over the back of his neck. "Safety is my biggest concern."

"And it's mine too." She stepped closer. "I assure you the Donato Pyrotechnic Company puts safety first. I can't let this . . . incident cause the pyrotechnic celebration to be cancelled. Sheriff, such an act would adversely affect my family's business, possibly besmirching our name."

Hearing her use his job title made him mad. He grabbed her arms. "Damn it, lady. Don't you see that I'm worried about your safety?" For a long moment, he stared into her eyes, waiting for a sign of censure, a sign that would tell him he'd gotten their earlier kiss all wrong.

When her eyes warmed like hot cocoa and she let out a little sigh, he couldn't hold back. His mouth crashed down on hers, his lips pressing for a response.

She wrapped her arms around his waist and ran her hands over his back. Her lips eased open and her tongue slipped out, touching his lower lip, then retreating.

Heat rose in his chest, and he wrapped his arms around her shoulders, stroking his tongue over her lips in answer to her hesitant foray. He lifted a hand to caress her cheek and tilted her head to get a better angle on her mouth.

Her hand squeezed along the muscles of his back, moving lower; then she grabbed his ass and squeezed.

Without thinking, he rocked his hips and pressed his stiff cock against her abdomen. For an instant, he relished the sweet pleasure; then he stilled. Whoa. This was getting out of hand for being in the middle of his office.

A moan hummed on her lips. She responded by nestling her body against his, rubbing her breasts across his chest and wiggling her hips against his groin.

Kent broke the kiss and blew out a frustrated breath. "Wait."

"No." Her plea whooshed out on a sigh.

"Look around." He loosened his hold and rested his hands on her shoulders. "We're in the middle of my office. Anyone could walk in."

"You're too practical." She spun away and stomped to the door, turning the key in its lock and tossing it into the far corner of the room. With quick movements, she yanked down the shade on the large window facing the street. "Problem solved."

The key thudded with a hollow clunk. Kent chuckled. "That it is." He ran a hand through his hair, wondering where they went from here. He decided to let her lead the way. "Now back to business."

If the man thought they were getting back to discussing the

exhibition, he was mistaken. She'd had a taste of what delights this handsome man offered, and it hadn't been enough. Shaping her lips into a wide, inviting grin, she sashayed toward him, watching his gray eyes darken at her movements. "Oh, is that what you call it?" She stopped only inches away and rested a hand on his chest, rubbing a circle and peeking at him from under her eyelashes. "I call it pleasure. And I want more."

Under her hand, Kent's body stilled.

So, he still wasn't getting her message?

With her hand still on his chest, she pushed.

He eased backward, one step at a time, until his thighs met the desk and he sat on the edge. A grin played at his lips, but he remained quiet. And watchful.

"Oh, this is definitely better." She moved into the space between his legs, the petticoats pressing against his thighs. While keeping her gaze locked with his, she raised her arms to pull out the pearl-tipped hatpin and removed her hat. With a sideways twist, she laid the hat on the desk near his hip.

His gaze dropped to the plump flesh straining the top of her blouse, eyelids widening and nostrils flaring.

The heated look in his eyes did her in. She wrapped a hand around the back of his neck and pulled him close, close enough to feel his hot breath huff against her chin. Her mouth sought his, angling first one way, then the other. She opened her lips enough to nibble his lower lip, then soothed the spot with a lapping of her tongue.

His hands cupped her jaw and his tongue invaded her mouth, probing, searching.

Oriana's excitement built; her nipples tingled and heaviness settled in her womb. The bold strokes of his tongue conjured thoughts of other parts of his body invading hers. Moisture seeped into her feminine curls. Although she'd never admit it aloud, she loved being mastered.

A hand moved along her jaw to her neck and up to cradle the back of her head, strong fingers pressing against her scalp. His hands moved over the bulk of her hair with hesitant movements.

"Take them out." His voice was gruff, his stare intent. "I want to feel your hair."

With quick movements, she reached for the hairpins and drew them out. Pings of metal hitting the wood floor sounded.

At the release of the pins' pressure, she sighed. Shaking her head unbound the tight twist, and her heavy hair fell over her shoulders and down her back.

Kent wrapped his hands in her waves and groaned with pleasure. "Soft, like I remembered."

Just hearing his pleasure in touching it boosted her excitement. She anchored her hands at his waist and closed her eyes, loving the feel of his hands running through her hair.

His lips kissed down her neck, nipping just a little at her collarbone.

Her nipples pulsed in reaction, aching to be touched.

When his mouth touched the hollow of her throat, she gasped and straightened until she could see his beautiful gray eyes. "Where's your bed?"

"Upstairs."

Her blood raced, and her breath whooshed out on a sigh. "Show me."

"You sure?" His brows drew together. "We don't have to."

Dropping a hand below his belt, she cupped his cock. "This is what I want."

After one last look into her eyes, he grabbed her hand and tugged her behind him.

Finally. Oriana grinned as she followed his long strides to the door. Oh. The door to the street. She scanned the office, looking for an alternate location.

He grabbed the knob and twisted. "Damn, it's locked." He started to the corner where she'd tossed the key, scraping his boot along the floor.

Reality hit hard. What would people say if they saw the sheriff hauling the new arrival up the stairs to his rooms?

The scraping sounds stopped; then he rested a hand on the wall, lowering his head with a shake. "We can't go to my room."

No! He couldn't be having second thoughts. Her blood raced even faster at the idea that her body might not get its needed release. She tore off her gloves, letting them drop to the floor. Her fingers moved to the buttons at the neckline of her blouse and eased them open, exposing the lace of her thin chemise. "I know."

"You do?" Kent looked over his shoulder and slowly straightened.

"The back room will have to do. I hope there's a cot." She tugged the blouse from the waistband of her skirt and shrugged it off her shoulders. With a saucy wink, she turned and sauntered toward the door where she'd spotted a coat hanging. A quick look around confirmed that a cot lined one wall and some storage crates sat in another corner under a low table.

Kent appeared in the doorway, hands braced on the wood. His gaze was narrowed and serious.

For an instant, she debated about stopping, grabbing her things and fleeing into the dark night. But she wasn't going to let his sense of decency stop her from enjoying what she knew would be a wonderful experience. "Don't say it."

"What? That we shouldn't be doing this? That—"

Before he said something final, she crossed the floor and pressed a hand to his mouth, her gaze searching his. "Tell me you don't want me, and I'll leave."

His shoulders sagged. "Hard to deny the evidence."

"I want you, Kent." Her hands dropped to his belt and

worked at freeing the strip of leather from the metal buckle. "And I won't hold you to anything in the morning."

Not that she planned on being here.

When she'd worked the belt free, she started on the buttons at the front of his trousers. Her fingers grazed his engorged cock, and for a moment, she hesitated. His girth was so big, and she hadn't been with anyone in a very long time.

Kent's hands cupped her breasts, his thumbs flicking her nipples to stiff points.

Awareness shot to her pussy and she leaned forward, rubbing her breasts against his palms.

He hissed a breath between his teeth and bent his head to take her nipple into his mouth, laving her through the thin cotton, sucking more of her breast into his warm mouth.

She arched her back and fumbled with the buttons at the back of her skirt. They released and the skirt fell into a heap at her feet. She stepped out, kicking the skirts and petticoats aside.

His hand kneaded her other breast, rolling the tip between two fingers. The sensations his mouth created were heavenly, making her breasts heavy and the rest of her body zing with excitement.

With a yank, she pulled open his trousers and shoved them and his flannel underdrawers down his slim hips. Her hands explored the hard muscle of his flanks and circled around to his tight ass. Deliciously taut, his thighs were furred with coarse hair that tickled her palms.

He leaned back and his hands worked at the buttons of her chemise, using his pinky fingers to keep her nipples budded.

Her hands circled to the front until they wrapped around his thick cock and stroked from the curly hairs at the base to the rounded tip. Too long had passed since she'd held the hard proof of the difference between a man and a woman.

Since she'd seen pulsing evidence of a man's desire for her.

Since she'd felt the silkiness over steel of a man's warm shaft.

"Lady, you're driving me close to the edge." His words were rough and filled with need. After speaking, he dipped his head and flicked a tongue over her sensitive nipple. His hand traced the curve of her breast, skimmed over her ribs and waist, and reached for the slit in her pantalets. A finger dipped into her moist curls, sliding along her folds.

She threw back her head and closed her eyes, savoring the tickle of his warm tongue. Her senses whirled like a Texas twister, leaving her breathless, and her knees buckled.

His arm encircled her back and he wedged a leg between hers. "Back up."

To get her balance, she reached under his shirttails to grab his muscled sides and held tight as he walked her backward. The friction of his skin on her pussy almost spun her out of control. Her butt encountered the cool, hard edge of the table, and she sucked in a breath, grabbing hold of his shirt.

Strong hands lifted her to sit on the wooden table, then trailed down the sides of her breasts, her waist, and her hips to her thighs. "Better brace yourself."

Her fingers went to the first button. "Not until I get your shirt off."

"Not this time." Then he lifted her legs and wrapped them around his waist. One step forward and his cock nudged at her damp opening. He rocked his hips to ease inside, bracing one hand on the wall past her shoulder, the other on her hip.

Oriana grabbed the end of the table with one hand and locked the other around Kent's neck. She tilted her hips to get friction on her female bud and bit her lip at the tug of stretching on her moist channel as his cock stroked inside. By arching her back, she brushed her nipples along his chest with each slow stroke. The tingles went straight to her core, releasing her dewy juices, and she gasped.

Kent groaned, a sound that crawled from deep in his throat,

and thrust all the way inside, circling his hips. Then he withdrew his length almost to the tip and plunged back inside.

The heaviness in her belly settled lower and she felt the first pulses of her release grab his cock and coax him along. Locking both hands around his neck, she pulled with her legs and moved herself against each of his strokes. Her release exploded, showering her entire body with sparks and drawing out a satisfied wail.

His thrusts intensified, and both hands cradled her hips, pulling her toward him when he moved.

Oriana tried to pull with her legs, but she still gasped for air from the intensity of her release. Pulling one hand from his neck, she reached under his shirt and caressed his abdomen, climbing upward for her target. Crisp hair surrounded a round disk with a rock-hard pebble in the center. She rolled the nub between her fingers, pinching it.

Kent threw back his head, pumped once more, then growled his satisfaction. His damp forehead dropped to her shoulder, and his huffing breath blew between her breasts.

Her fingers ran through his thick hair that hung below his shirt collar.

"Give me a minute. I'll move us to the cot."

Lying entwined, his arms holding her close, their legs tangled. The image ran through her mind, and she savored the idea. What wouldn't she give for that to occur? But she'd stayed too long as it was. Dante would be looking for her, and she couldn't have him tracking her here. "That's not necessary."

His head lifted enough for his narrowed gaze to connect with hers. "Why not?"

Uh-oh. "Because I can walk on my own." At least, she hoped her legs would hold her up.

In one movement, he stepped back and scooped her into his arms.

"Twice in one day." She barely had time to grab hold around his neck. "A lady could get used to this."

With two strides, he crossed the room and laid her on the bed, grabbing a blanket from a nearby shelf. "Scoot over." He yanked off his shirt and tossed it behind him.

For an instant, she wished for enough light to truly see what looked like a perfect chest. Then his words registered and she moved to the edge closest to the room, making sure she wouldn't get trapped against the wall. Her reward was the gentle bump of his cock on her hip as he climbed over her. "Sorry, I always have this side of the bed. Ever since I was a little girl."

"Shh." Warm arms wrapped around her, and the blanket was tossed over their legs. His hand ran up and down her arm. "Just want to touch you."

She nestled her head on his firm chest and ran a hand over his stomach. A tight, flat stomach with just enough hair to tickle her palm. The urge to return to her room at the camp tugged at her awareness. She knew she shouldn't be here, but her chest tightened with the intimacy of the moment. Being in Kent's embrace felt so good, so safe.

Kent's breathing deepened, and his hand dropped from her arm to the mattress.

Oriana shifted, easing a leg over the edge, and the iron bed frame creaked. She chanced a glance back over her shoulder, but he lay peaceful, his chest rising with each breath. As gently as she could, she inched toward the foot of the mattress. Slowly, she lowered her feet to the floor, grabbed her clothes, and tiptoed out of the room.

Kent intended to count to fifty before opening an eyelid, but when he heard the click of the office door lock, he sprang out of bed and scrambled to pull on his clothes. What was she up to at this time of night?

More important, why had she left his bed?

3

The cart bounced along the rutted road in the morning sun, hitting a big hole.

Oriana jostled and gripped the edge of the seat, wincing at the pinch of her injury. "I told you, Mr. Terrill, I could have driven myself into town this morning."

"I don't mind. Didn't have much to do in the office this morning." He shrugged and leaned his elbows on his thighs. "If I didn't need to check at the depot for a shipment I've been expecting, we could have ridden on horseback."

A laugh escaped before she could suppress it. "Sorry if that sounded rude. As much as I enjoy reading about western women who push the plow or rope cattle, riding this close to a horse is about as primitive as I prefer." With a gasp, she turned sideways on the seat.

A shot rang out and a dull thud sounded behind them. A second shot spat up dirt near the horse's hooves.

"Hold on." John Terrill slapped the reins with a loud crack against the horse's rump. "Run, Star, run."

Oriana braced her feet on the floor and grabbed the wooden

seat tight. The rattle and jerk of the wagon shook them against one another, but propriety couldn't be observed in such a circumstance. She looked over her shoulder at the nearby rocks, but the rocky terrain whizzed by too fast to see anything. Not that she would have known what to look for.

A knot grabbed her stomach and twisted. Someone had shot at them.

Just like in a dime novel.

The rattling and jostling seemed to go on forever. Twice she bit her tongue before she clenched her jaw tight.

When they rounded a curve and the roofs of the town's buildings appeared in view, she finally took a deep breath. Almost there.

Once they passed the livery stable, John slowed the horse to a walk and guided them straight for the sheriff's office.

The cart came to a halt, and the horse blew out a shuddering neigh, its sides heaving with each breath.

Oriana closed her eyes and let her chin sag down.

"Mrs. Ignacio, are you hurt?"

She shook her head and swallowed hard against a parched throat. "No, just need to catch my breath."

"John! What's wrong?" Boot steps moving in quick succession resounded along the boardwalk.

Kent. Oriana jerked up her head and turned toward the building to look into his worried expression.

He narrowed his gaze and glanced at her body from head to toe while speaking, "I saw that turn you made just outside of town. You had two wheels off the ground."

"Two shots. Up near Miller's Notch." He jerked a thumb over his shoulder. "One hit the wagon."

"The wagon?" Kent jumped off the boardwalk and circled toward the back.

"Kent, help the lady down first and into a chair." John

dropped into the street. "That was a hard ride, especially for a city gal."

"Don't pamper me." Oriana unclenched her grip and shook her hands to ease the stiffness. "I can climb down myself. I do navigate the streets of New York City on a regular basis. Now that's a hard ride."

Kent stood at the side of the wagon and raised his arms to grab her around the waist. "Allow me the pleasure."

One look into his teasing eyes and she relented, placing her hands on his broad shoulders. Any excuse to touch him again. As she studied his gaze, she looked for any trace of animosity at her desertion the previous night but saw only concern. When her feet hit the dirt, she wanted to melt against his chest and feel the strength of his embrace.

That freedom wasn't hers. Their night together was enjoyed with no promises, no thought of any future actions.

His hands stayed on her waist a moment longer. "You steady on your feet?"

On her feet? Yes. About her emotions? She wasn't so sure. She tugged at the front of her jacket and smoothed the folds of her skirt. "I'm fine." She walked to the step in front of his office and looked over a shoulder. "Thank you for your concern. May I wait for you inside your office?"

"We have business inside?"

The memory of the activities inside that office the previous evening flashed through her body, making her skin flush. She pressed her lips together to keep a moan from escaping. "Finalizing the business permit?"

A glint flashed in his eyes and he nodded before joining John at the back of the wagon.

Something in his expression told her that wouldn't be the only topic for discussion.

* * *

Kent's chest burned, and he kept flexing and relaxing his hands. Someone had shot at them. Someone had shot at Oriana.

Add this to the fact that the board had been deliberately cut through—after the platform was built. After their inspection, he and John agreed that from the stability of the rest of the structure, the Donatos did quality work. Neither of them would have knowingly used a piece of damaged lumber.

At the back of the wagon, he spotted one of the upright boards with an angry gash of splintered wood. Kent ran his finger inside the hole but felt only jagged fragments. "You find a bullet?"

"Nah, must have rattled out on the crazy ride."

"Think it was an accident?"

"With one shot, maybe someone's out hunting and a shot goes wide of the prey. That's logical." He drew a hand down his face, then stepped close and lowered his head. "The second one was too close to Star's feet to be accidental. Someone meant to give us a scare."

Although he'd suspected that very truth, hearing John's statement still boiled his blood. "You mean her?"

"Didn't exactly say that."

"Admit it, John. Someone could have gotten to you anytime." He clapped a hand on his friend's shoulder. "Don't mean disrespect, but you're here, available, all the time. A walking target." He jerked a thumb over his shoulder toward the building, his throat drawing tight around the words as he spoke them. "The lady in there is the new ingredient in the mix."

"That was my conclusion too. What do you make of this?"

"I'm still figuring on the matter. Got any troubles at the mine I need to know about?"

"Nope, haven't heard anything from either foreman."

Kent cut a glance at the office door to make sure it was still closed. "Did more than one company bid on the project?"

"Yeah, three."

"A disgruntled competitor?" The moment he spoke the words, he realized the incidents had suddenly taken on more weight. If a competitor was angry about not receiving the commission, then the acts would continue. Future attempts would be made to stop the exhibition.

These threats would continue.

John ran a hand through his red hair. "I suppose."

Kent's plan of action was now clear. Not to let that woman out of his sight.

The door behind him rattled. "Excuse me, gentlemen."

At the sound of her voice, Kent scanned the street, looking for anything out of the ordinary. Then he turned.

Oriana stepped through the doorway. "If this conversation will be lengthy, I have errands to run and I can return. The sheriff and I have a business matter to discuss." Her gaze met his.

"Go back inside." Irritation at the situation tightened his chest. He vaulted onto the boardwalk and stepped close, using his body to shield hers.

She stiffened, her jaw tight. "Why?"

He rested a hand on hers and squeezed. "Please. I'll explain inside." When she stepped backward, he crossed the threshold, then glanced over his shoulder. "Go about your business, John. I'll see her safely back to the mine later."

"Will do."

"And, John, keep an eye out."

"That I will do, buddy." With a wave of farewell, John snapped the reins and the horse trotted down the dirt street.

Kent shut the door and leaned back against it, bracing himself for the coming conversation. How would a city woman take the news that she'd been in someone's gun sights? Their acquaintance was too short for him to predict. Somehow, he doubted she'd take the news quietly.

She stood not three feet away, watching him with dark, expressive eyes. "Should I be worried?"

Did he scare her with the totality of his suspicions or just enough to keep her close? "I'll bet you've been too busy to take a tour of Buckskin. Why don't I accompany you on your errands?"

Her gaze narrowed, and she edged a step closer. "That shot wasn't an accident."

So much for sparing her. "Figured that out, did you?" With a shove, he pushed off the door and started across the room, careful not to walk too close. One whiff of her violet scent would scatter his thoughts, and he needed to stay focused.

"Wasn't hard. Kent, I watched you and John through the window." Her steps echoed with light tip-taps. "I sure hope you don't ever bet big at a poker table."

Getting through the next couple of days without the town's population being decreased was all he hoped for. His leather gun belt hung from a wall hook; he lifted it down and placed the gun and holster on top of the desk. From the bottom drawer of his desk, he pulled out a box of bullets. "Give me a couple minutes to get ready."

"You need a loaded gun to do this?" She jammed her hands on her hips.

Her voice held a tone he couldn't identify, and he didn't want to upset her more. "Appears so." He lowered himself into the chair and flipped open the box lid. The gun was fully loaded—he checked it every morning. With precise movements, he filled the empty loops along the gun belt's back strap with bullets. When it was full, he looked up.

"Oh, this is so exciting." Her eyes glinted with anticipation, and her hands waved in front of her as she talked. "I'm going to be escorted down the street of a western town with a sheriff wearing a sidearm. That's the right word, isn't it?"

The dark flash of her eyes reminded him of another type of flash that had been there the previous night. "Could be called that. It's a Colt .45 peacemaker."

"An authentic Colt? This is wonderful."

Not exactly his choice of description. "Oriana, this is for protection." He laid his hand on top of the weapon.

"I know. This is just like in the novels I read back home. I was telling John about them right before the first shot." She stopped her pacing and leaned her hands on the edge of his desk. "Put it on."

The sudden change in conversation topic added to the view of her rounded breasts straining against the neckline of her dress muddled his thoughts. Frowning, he shook his head. "Pardon?"

"Model them." Her hands waved upward. "I want to see you wearing the belt and holster."

Had the woman lost her wits? The Sheriff of Buckskin was not about to parade around like some dandy. He stood, scooped up the gun belt, and stomped to the door, resting a hand on the knob. "Where are we headed first?"

"To the mercantile, I guess." Her mouth turned down at the edges, and her gaze flicked between his face and his hand. "And I need to check for a telegram from my family. Where would I pick that up?"

"Same place. Langston Mercantile." He opened the door and cast a brief glance at the activity exposed in the doorway. Jake Morris rumbled by in a delivery wagon loaded with lumber. The young Carstairs family walked on the boardwalk across the street. Nothing out of the ordinary. Kent turned back toward the office, waiting.

"Just one minute. I feel horribly disheveled." Her hands rose to pat the twist at the back of her head, tuck in a few stray hairs, and adjust her hat.

The sight of her hands touching her hat reminded him of a similar action from the night before. Although at the time, she'd been removing her hat. An action that led to further undressing and their bodies in close, intimate contact. He steeled himself against the temptation to pull her into his arms. The timing was all wrong.

"I'm ready." A smile flashed and she walked past him and onto the boardwalk. "Which way?"

The sweet scent of violets tickled his nose, and heaviness settled in his groin. He pulled the door harder than he intended and it closed with a slam. "Langston's is across the street and north two blocks." As he spoke, he wrapped the gun belt around his hips and adjusted the buckle.

"North?" She turned, her eyes widening as they centered on the gun belt. Her lips quirked up on one side, but she pressed them into a straight line before raising her brown gaze to meet his. "Which way is that?"

With an effort, he reined in his reaction at having her gaze focused on his groin. Kent stepped to the far side of the boardwalk and, for a few seconds, scanned the street and nearby buildings. Smoke from the blacksmith's forge swirled from the open doors. In the livery's corral, Hiram worked a horse on the end of a rope. The doors of Murphy's Tavern were still closed. The Langston youth swept the boards in front of the mercantile.

Seeing nothing out of the ordinary, Kent extended his left elbow in her direction. "We'll cross the street first." His right hand hung loose but ready at his side.

The next hour or so was spent in a similar manner. From a spot near the front window of each shop, Kent studied the street and the shops for the sight of strangers or for unexpected movements from anyone.

Oriana chatted easily with those she encountered and shopped as if this were a normal day, looking through the entire inventory before making her purchases. Imported soap and Swiss chocolates from the mercantile, a pair of handkerchiefs from the dressmaker, and socks for Dante from the haberdashery.

As the morning wore on, Kent struggled to keep his gaze on the street when he felt pulled to watch the lively woman go about her business. Her outgoing manner and inquisitive nature encouraged the shopkeepers of this territorial town to show off their best items for the new arrival. From the bits of conversation he overheard, Kent knew they were as eager for information about life in the East as Oriana was to learn about the West.

Kent's thoughts registered the fact that her home was in New York. Women from the East didn't relocate well to the frontier. A liaison four years earlier with the daughter of the previous mine owner had proved that. Kent shook his head and repositioned his shoulder against the wall.

He hadn't thought about Annabelle in years. Her aristocratic blonde beauty was only a blurred memory, but her cutting words were branded on his heart. "You're only a poor sheriff. You'll never give me what I need."

"Kent? My, what a scowl."

Oriana's teasing tone brought him from his dark thoughts, and he shifted his weight to turn toward her. "Does this mean you're finished?"

"With this side of the street." With a saucy wink, she strolled close and peered out the window. "What shops are over on the other side? Oh, a café." She turned and touched his forearm with the tips of her fingers. "Let's get a meal. My reward for your patience."

Café? In Buckskin? Let the lady call it what she liked. Kent's mind turned over the layout of Ethel's dining hall and figured the location of a couple of tables that were the safest. "I could eat."

An hour later, Oriana set down her empty cup of coffee and wished for the freedom to loosen her corset ties. Ethel's apple pie was one of the best she'd tasted, and she'd eaten every crumb. She eyed Kent as he worked on his second helping, wondering if he was going to refer to their interlude the previous evening.

Their conversation during the meal had surprised her. Kent was as well-read as most of the men in her family's circle of acquaintances. Although they differed over preference for Dickens or Hawthorne, she admired any man who admitted to reading Jane Austen.

She hoped the morning spent chatting with the local merchants and spending a bit of money on items she didn't really need would promote good will toward Donato Pyrotechnics. Support from a local community could assist an application for the firm's next project—the statehood celebration. Mama always said a smile and a little bit of conversation helped with any endeavor.

Kent's fork clattered against his plate. "If you're done, shall we leave?"

Her thoughts went to what would come next—a drive back to the mine, another inspection of the already-checked rockets and equipment, and an evening spent in her room at the small foreman's house, playing cards with her brother.

Not the most exciting evening she could imagine.

On this trip away from her family's prying eyes, she wanted to fill every minute with new sights and experiences. "Have I seen all of Buckskin? You did offer to give me a tour."

"More coffee, folks?" Ethel stood at the edge of the table with a speckled coffeepot.

The coffee may not be the best she'd tasted, but at this point, Oriana would accept anything to keep the handsome man close. She turned a wide smile toward Ethel. "That would be lovely. And I have to compliment you on the pie. Absolutely delicious." As she spoke, she uncrossed her legs, nudging the tip of her shoe along Kent's boot. She watched his nostrils flare and his gray gaze cut sideways, but he didn't say a word.

Now she knew for a fact she wasn't the only one affected by this attraction. What fun to tease him!

She raised her cup, inhaled its rich fragrance, and blew across its surface, making sure to purse her lips. "Tell me, Kent, why you're resistant to Donato's presentation of the fireworks your friend ordered."

Shaking his head, he leaned his elbows on the table, his gaze dragging upward from her mouth. "When did I say that?"

Her gaze met his and held, secretly wondering how bold she dared be in public. Her heart beating wildly in her chest, she looked from under her eyelashes. "Communication doesn't only happen with words." She grazed her shoe up his pants leg and stopped just above his knee, drawing slow circles on the inside of his thigh.

His chair jerked and he grabbed hold of the table's edge with one hand, his knuckles whitening. "Is that right?" His breath huffed out.

With a slow movement, she set her cup on the table and slid her hand over the tablecloth to run a finger over the back of his hand. Coarse hairs tickled her fingertips. "I watched your face yesterday when the mishap was being discussed."

For several moments, his heated gaze followed the movement of her hand; then he shot to his feet. "I'll take you on that tour now." He started to dig into a front pocket.

So he didn't want to flirt in the town's café. With a sigh, Oriana reached for her reticule. "This is my treat. Please let me pay."

"Maybe another time." Several coins thudded onto the table

and he clasped her elbow, easing her to her feet. "I need some fresh air."

They walked through the door and along the boardwalk for several feet before his grip tightened and he leaned close. "What the hell are you doing?"

Had she gone too far? Her mouth went dry. "Just explaining my point."

"Like—"

Boot steps resounded on the boards. A tall woman holding the hand of a small girl wearing a red bonnet approached. Her head was bent as if she watched where each foot was placed.

Straightening, Kent touched the brim of his hat and nodded. "Mrs. Wilson."

"Afternoon, Sheriff." The woman slowed, shot furtive glances between them, but held her head averted and at an odd angle.

They had reached the street when the woman called out, "Sheriff?"

With a flash of the special insight shared by women in her family, Oriana knew the woman wished to speak with Kent privately. "I'll just wait here." She moved next to the boardwalk and pretended interest in the goings and comings of strangers in the street.

Kent climbed the stairs again. Voices murmured behind her, Kent's deep tones and the woman's softer ones.

"I have ball. See?" The little girl held out a hand with a dusty blue rubber ball. "Play wif me?" She tossed the ball into the street and it rolled toward the center.

"Oh, you might lose it." Oriana scurried after the disappearing toy and scooped it into her gloved hand. Holding it high, she turned and waved it at the child. "Here, I've got your ball."

Pounding hoof beats sounded from nearby, and Oriana turned with a gasp. A riderless horse charged, kicking up clouds of dust as it galloped down the street. Straight for her. Indecision about which way to move rooted her feet to the ground.

"Look out!" Kent's warning sounded. He jumped over the railing and covered the distance in a few strides. His arm went around her waist, and he tugged her back toward the safety of the building.

Oriana leaned against his strength and sucked in deep breaths.

He held her at arm's length and bent his knees so he could meet her gaze. "You okay?"

Barely able to catch her breath, she nodded and blinked, fighting the scared tears that threatened.

"Lady, you've got to move when something is coming your way." His lips spread into a grin.

"Runaway horses are not something I encounter in New York." She shuddered. "Happens here a lot, does it?"

"Actually, no. These two instances are the only ones I recall."

"Is the lady okay, Sheriff?"

His hold loosened and he turned. "A bit shaken is all."

On legs that wobbled a bit, Oriana stepped to the boardwalk and held out her hand. "Here's your toy, sweetie." Gathering her confidence, she turned to Kent. "What else is there to see?"

A dark scowl drew together his brows and he shook his head. "Your tour is over." His hand rested at the small of her back and pressed her forward.

At his urging, she walked, allowing his masterful behavior to seep into her awareness. Sheriff Wyman was a protective man. For a few moments, she let herself believe his actions were personal, maybe springing from the intimacies they'd shared the previous night. Her nipples hardened and pressed against the stiffness of her corset.

Being out here in the frontier was more primal than anything she'd experienced. Ever.

"We're going back to the office." His words were clipped. "If I have to lock you in a cell, I'm keeping you safe."

"Oh, will you use manacles?"

4

Manacles! Kent couldn't believe what he'd just heard. While walking out in the street, he couldn't react. What he wanted to do was push her against the wall of the closest building and kiss her silly. But practicality won out. He guided her across the dirt street, up the wooden steps, and hurried her down the boardwalk to his office. If he didn't feel her in his arms within a few moments, he'd break something. With the closed door at his back, he steeled himself to reveal his suspicions. "I think it was intentional."

"Like the gunfire?" Her voice rose in surprise.

"Yep, that's why you are officially in protective custody. Don't even think about going anywhere without me."

She pulled back and looked up, dark eyes shining. "This could be fun."

When he spotted the mischief in her gaze, he groaned and bent his head to capture her tantalizing lips. Maybe he should keep his worries about the seriousness of the matter to himself. Right now, he wanted to forget about the outside world and just enjoy this willing lady's curves. He reached behind him and turned the key in the door's lock, creating their own private world.

His lips tasted her eager ones in nibbling bites, then sucked her lower lip between his, swirling his tongue along the line of her teeth. She tasted of rich coffee and sweet spices, and something else. A taste that stirred feelings deep inside him, a taste he couldn't identify but knew he had to have more of.

She tugged at the hair behind his ears and ran her fingers along the back of his neck, her touch delicate.

His arms tightened around her curves, and he walked them toward the back of the office. His thigh moved between her legs, and he just barely restrained himself from grinding his lengthening cock against her soft belly.

Her full skirts enveloped him. With a whimper, she grasped his shoulders, clamped her thighs around his, and angled her hips down.

He pressed harder, his tongue stroking in rhythm with moving his leg higher. His reward was a delighted gasp and a whoosh of air across his lips.

Oriana pulled back her head to connect with his gaze and smiled. "Being the strong man, huh?"

His steps stopped, and he gazed at her puffy lips and the dreamy look in her eyes. Damn, just looking at her made him hot. His hand traced from her back to her ribs, his thumb rubbing the underside of her breast. "Only if you want me to."

"How protective is your custody?" She tilted her head, batted her eyelashes, and glanced from the side of one eye. "Do you have to lock me up?"

They'd reached the wooden door that led to the jail cells. He pulled open the door and pressed her back against the doorjamb, aligning his body against hers. Somewhere in his heated thoughts he registered how well they fit together and that he'd missed the feel of a woman in his hands. "Now, what fun would that be? You inside the cell and me outside?"

"But you're forgetting the manacles." One eyelid dropped in a lazy wink.

His blood surged. She'd been serious about that? He nuzzled kisses along her neck and pressed his hips against her belly, enjoying the sweet pleasure-pain of his trousers constraining his rigid erection.

Her tongue traced the seam of his lips, forcing its way inside, and lining the inside of his lips before pushing deeper with quick jabs.

His tongue met hers and dueled, angling, swirling, caressing, first fast and then slow. Until now, he'd never been with a woman who demanded her equal share of control. The fact she did was exciting as hell.

Her lips moved along his jaw and down to his chin.

The sensation of her warm lips on his skin made his chest burn. "I was joking about the wrist irons."

"I wasn't." She lapped a trail along his neck and kissed the skin exposed by his open collar. "I've often wondered about giving control to my partner."

"That's a hell of a lot of trust, lady."

"And who better to trust than a sheriff?" She leaned forward and rubbed her breasts against his chest. "I've heard bondage can make the experience better. Want to be my master?"

His mouth went dry and his chest tightened at the heated look in her gaze. In that moment, he wanted to do anything she asked.

He ran a finger along the edge of her dress's neckline, dipping a finger into the deep valley between her plump breasts. Easing along her rounded curves, he stretched his finger closer to the nipple, but her dress was too tight.

"I'll get the irons. You get into the far cell and wait."

With long strides, he crossed the room to his desk and yanked open the top drawer, pulling out his wrist irons. On his return to the cell, he grabbed an extra pillow and blanket from the storeroom. When he rounded the corner, his boots skidded as his steps faltered.

Oriana stood facing the opposite direction, with her hands flat on the wall and her legs spread wide.

In one of his favorite positions.

Once inside the cell, he tossed the blanket and pillow on a nearby cot and shoved the irons into his back pocket. He walked behind her, grasping her hips and aligning his thighs along her ass, but her petticoats were in the way.

"I thought you might have to frisk me first." She looked over her shoulder and grinned. "Or at least, I hoped you would."

At least one of them was thinking with their brain. He leaned his body over her back and wrapped his left arm around her waist, anchoring her in one spot. He stretched his other arm until his hand lay atop hers, then traced zigzag trails along her arm from wrist to shoulder.

She shivered, arched her back, and tossed her head. "Ahh, I like that."

The warmth of her body seeped into his, and the scent of violets filled his nose. Suddenly, he knew what he wanted, and that was to run his fingers through her hair. He circled her waist with his hands and spun her to face him. To carry out the image of a master, he forced a rasp into his voice. "Loosen your hair."

With a devilish sparkle in her dark eyes, she pressed her arms against the sides of her breasts, plumping her cleavage, and sighed before reaching her arms high to the back of her head. When the pins came out, she shook her head to fan dark waves around her shoulders. A few tendrils draped her forehead and she peeked through them.

A seductive image. Like a picture of the sirens he'd seen once. His cock hardened and he widened his stance. "Unbutton your blouse."

Keeping her gaze locked with his, her fingers rose to the top of her neckline and slid the top button through the loop. With each button's release, the front of her blouse gaped farther open, exposing the lace and tucks of her camisole and pale breasts over the top.

After the last button was released, she shimmied her shoulders and the fabric fell away, exposing pale arms.

Her seductive moves pumped his blood higher. To keep from grabbing her and hauling her curves tight to his body, he tightened his hands into fists. "Shake off the blouse."

When she'd done as he commanded, he anchored one hand on her hip, skimmed the other up the side of her corset, and tried cupping a breast. The stiffness of the covering kept him from feeling her curvaceous body, and he turned her around and ripped at the laces.

Her head fell back and she gasped, her breath whooshing out in quick pants. As soon as the corset loosened, she pulled it over her head and let it drop to the floor.

The afternoon sun coming through the barred window opening cast light shafts across her skin, showing off pebbled nipples pushing against the thin cloth of her camisole.

Her body's natural reaction to their sex play.

A reaction that sent waves of powerful wanting through him. Finally, he could fill his hands with the ample weight of her breasts and squeeze, feeling her pearled nubs against his palms. His fingers caressed along the sides of her breasts, drawing together at the tips, thumbs flicking the nipples.

Her breath sucked in sharply and she stiffened; then she leaned into his touch.

Before he let his baser nature surface, he ran his hands roughly over her hips and ass, fingers spread wide, pretending to search for a weapon. Dropping into a crouch, he ran his hand down the full length of her skirts, over the stiff petticoats to the tops of her boots. Working quickly, he unhooked and loosened the laces, then lifted out each foot before peeling off her stockings and garters. Ah, soft skin. On the inside of her warm thighs, he caressed the smooth cotton fabric of her pantalets, regretting the thin barrier of the cloth.

He wanted to feel skin on skin, and his thumbs traced the slit of her pantalets, dipping inside and tickling her feminine curls. Her damp feminine curls. Deep inside his chest, his breath caught, and he fought the tightness that registered how much he cared about this petite but feisty woman.

Impossible. He'd been down this road before and he wasn't going to give his heart to a woman from the East. Not to one who would enjoy his time, but then move back home. That was a dose of heartache he didn't need.

"Don't forget, I was serious about being your prisoner."

With her words, his restraint weakened, and he grabbed the wrist irons from his hip pocket. He stood slowly, brushing his thighs along hers and trailing his hand up her sides. His left hand entwined with hers and, in a big circle, pulled her hand up, over her head, and clicked her wrist to the horizontal bar.

She shivered, her lids heavy over her eyes. "Oh, what are you going to do next?"

Maintaining eye contact, he stroked her other arm, caressing the skin with slow circles, moving up to the tips of her fingers. "Put you completely under my control."

"Oh." She inhaled with a gasp and shuddered.

Watching her eyes shine with a dreamy expression, he wrapped the cool metal around her delicate wrist and looped it over an upright bar. Then he stepped back, crossed his arms over his chest, and widened his stance. The picture of her standing, immobile—the shadowy circles of her areolae through the thin fabric of her chemise, the triangle of darkness at the juncture of her thighs—made him rock hard, and he forced himself to breathe with slow, even breaths.

She waited, watching with dark, curious eyes. Her gaze

traced down his body, widening when she looked at the long bulge straining the fly of his trousers.

He studied her eyes, knowing if he spotted only one flash of uneasiness, he'd immediately unlock the manacles. Power was not his goal—he wanted trust.

With a toss of her wavy hair, she raised her gaze to his and smiled, then nibbled on her lower lip.

Her body was ripe with curves a man could really get his hands on. As he watched, her nipples peaked and tented the bodice of her chemise. An invitation if he ever saw one. He stepped forward and filled his hands with her heavy breasts, flicking his thumbs across the tips, feeling them tighten even more.

Oriana let out her breath with a sigh that ended with a little moan. Her knee nudged his and ran up along the inside of his thigh.

Anchoring his right hand on her hip, Kent bent his head and circled the end of his tongue around her pearled nub before taking the tip of one breast into his mouth, sucking it deeper. The scent of violets and warm woman filled his nostrils, making his cock throb with wanting.

Wanting this woman.

Her body arched, pressing her breast deeper, and she let out a squeaky cry of delight.

Encouraged by her satisfied sounds, he sucked harder, pressing the flat of his tongue against her breast in a rhythmic motion. The fingers of his left hand rolled and pinched the nipple of her other breast. He ran his fingers around the waist of her pantalets, searching for the way to strip it off her body. He had to touch her skin. His chest ached with the need to have her naked and vulnerable before his gaze.

For a moment, the button resisted and he yanked. When it finally gave way, the thin fabric slid over her hips and fell into a pool at her feet. The moment his hands touched bare skin, he stilled, heart racing wildly, then raised his head and covered her mouth with a hard kiss. This kiss demanded, his tongue pressing past her lips and teeth to confront her quick jabs of her warm tongue. They mated, swirling and stroking.

He pressed his aching groin against her belly, the contact creating a burn in his cock and balls. In the same moment, he resented and was glad that the restraints of his trousers kept him from acting like a savage. His body responded to hers like to no other woman before.

He moved his hand to cup her pussy and felt damp curls and womanly heat. A heat he needed to taste. Easing away from their kiss, he pressed his lips down the column of her neck and flicked his tongue into the valley of her cleavage. The deep, warm valley between her plump, rounded breasts.

A shudder ran through her body and she wiggled under his touch.

The clanking of the irons against the cell bars reminded him she was at his mercy, kicking up his desire to pleasure her before seeking his own release. Lowering himself to his knees, he trailed kisses down the fabric covering her stomach until he reached her navel.

And bare skin.

His tongue circled the opening and darted inside with quick jabs, an imitation of the act his body ached to perform.

The musky scent of her arousal tickled his nose. With swirling moves of his tongue, he kissed a path across her abdomen, savoring the texture of soft skin as he approached the dark curls covering her feminine treasure.

Her body moved beneath his touch, hips swaying and a leg rubbing sinuously along his arm and shoulder. Breathy sighs and moans accompanied her movements.

Her sounds of rising excitement fueled his movements. With long strokes, he ran his hands down the outside of her thighs, circling them around to the front of her knees. Hands spread into a V, he inched them back up her shapely leg, his thumbs drawing circles along her inner thigh.

With a whimper, she pressed her legs together.

"Move them apart." His words rasped from his dry throat.

Her legs eased open, releasing more of her musky scent, showing her readiness.

He inched his thumbs higher, watching her skin pebble with goose flesh. Anticipation tightened his chest as he ran his thumbs along the velvety folds of her pussy. Her honeyed juices moistened his path, and he pressed deeper, rubbing along her sweet feminine opening. The knowledge he was in control of her body, of her release, shot through him, and his cock throbbed against his trousers. Sweet agony. With his thumbnails surrounding her clit, he stroked it back and forth.

Above him, she drew in a quick inhalation and let out a low, throaty sigh. Her body sagged.

Unable to resist any longer, he leaned close and ran his tongue along the path his thumbs had blazed. He tasted her— sweet and musky. His tongue circled her tight clit and stroked along her folds.

She let out a gasp that staccatoed into a high-pitched cry, and her thighs squeezed the sides of his head.

His tongue probed her pussy, pushing deep into her honeyed channel and swirling his tongue around her clit. As her excitement grew, he lapped at her tangy juices and tickled her bud, prolonging the pulses of her release.

When her body finally relaxed, he sat back on his heels and let his gaze travel up her body until he met her eyes, dazed with satiation.

"I want to touch you." Her words came out on a throaty whisper.

"Not yet."

He rose and reached for the buttons of his trousers, pushing each through its hole with an impatient jab. When the last one was freed, he hooked his thumbs inside the waistband and shoved the cloth down his thighs, his belt buckle landing with a thud on the wooden floor.

Her gaze lowered to the bulge in the front of his underdrawers. A smile twitched at the corner of her mouth. "At least let me see." Her body shuddered, a metallic clink sounding with each move.

He trailed his fingers along his sides and pushed the flannel drawers over his hips, then stepped out of his clothes and kicked them to the side.

Her eyes widened and her pink tongue moistened her swollen lower lip. "Ooo."

The sound of awe in her sigh shot male pride through his body. He stepped forward, pressing his cock against her belly. He'd held himself back long enough and his body burned for release.

She arched and rubbed her breasts against his chest. "I want to see all of you."

"Later." He filled his hands with the skin of her rounded ass and lifted her legs around his own hips. The head of his cock nestled against the heat of her opening, inching inside with each slow roll of his hips.

"More." Her head nudged his cheek, and her lips grazed his neck.

The rounded curves pressed against his body, the brush of tight nipples against his chest, the violet scent of her hair invaded his nose. No longer could he hold back. He plunged his cock deep inside and felt her tight, welcoming heat surround him.

She let out a gasp. Her legs tightened, easing her along his length, then relaxed, slamming her pussy against him. The circling of her hips pressed her mons against the base of his cock.

A woman who sought her own enjoyment. He liked that.

Bracing his legs, he stroked hard and fast, his breath rasping out in harsh bursts.

She pressed her forehead to his shoulder, breathy grunts sounding with each of his movements.

Two more long thrusts and the fire ignited. His balls tingled and his cock shot his seed deep inside, the muscles of her channel milking every last drop. He circled his arms tighter around her back and held her close, their hearts hammering against their clasped chests and their breaths rasping loud in the small space.

When he finally caught his breath from that amazing act, he slid his hands down her legs, enjoying the slide over her soft skin. Fingers clasped around her ankles, he lowered her feet to the cell floor at the same time he pulled out. The loss of warmth was instantaneous, and disconcerting. "You all right?"

"Fine." She sighed, the air skimming his chest.

With quick moves, he pulled the key from his trouser pocket and unlocked the manacles. Slipping an arm around her delicate waist, he guided her to the cot and climbed on beside her.

The warmth of her soft curves snuggled tight to his body, and she circled her fingers on his chest.

Lingering after intimacy had never been his style, but he couldn't tear himself away from her arms. He caressed her arm, from fingertips to shoulder, then ran his fingers through the length of her long waves. Soft waves that seemed to go on forever. Waves that a man could get lost in.

To clear away that errant thought, he jerked his head and pressed deeper into the pillow.

With slowing moves, her hand rested on his belly and her body sagged against his.

After several minutes of listening to her shallow breaths, he slipped out from under the sheets. He needed to leave before his feelings got any more tangled.

5

The nerves in Oriana's stomach jumped and sputtered like a sparkler. She surveyed the exhibit's platform with its multiple setups and safety precautions. Every item on her checklist had been inspected three times. Preparations were complete, but for some reason, she still didn't feel ready. Knowing that someone might be trying to stop this display weighed on her thoughts.

Dante, who seemed to be adapting quite well to the less-civilized ways of the West, had scoffed at her concerns. He put the incidents off to life on the frontier.

Below her, the celebration had been in full swing for a couple hours. Those in attendance had enjoyed the potluck dinner and cleared away the dirty dishes. Only a table groaning under the weight of layer cakes and a variety of fruit pies remained.

Oriana lowered herself to the platform and scanned the crowd for signs of Kent. She hadn't seen him since he'd dropped her at the foreman's house the previous night. During the ride from Buckskin, they'd both been enjoying the afterglow of what they'd shared, and conversation had been light. Once she was alone in her bed, she'd worried about her behavior.

After their intimacies had taken on a fantasy aspect, she wanted to see him in the daylight and know that she hadn't demanded too much. Just because she'd always wanted to be subdued didn't mean he wanted that. Although he'd certainly seemed to be a willing enough participant.

The boards on the ladder creaked. Her heart jumped into her throat, and she turned, hoping to see Kent.

Dante's head rose into sight, and he jumped with a thud. "Hey, did you know the sheriff was bringing a security force to the event? He says you discussed this and that we're bearing the cost."

"I authorized it." She schooled her features not to show the disappointment weighing on her heart. "I know you don't think those incidents are important, but I've got to consider the publicity aspects. We can't have any rumors being circulated about our company's practices or our exhibits' safety." Her hand cut through the air with a sharp jab. "Especially not since Primo wants us to lay the groundwork for this territory's statehood celebration."

His dark head nodded. "Yeah, I forgot about that."

"Plus, the mine owner has to be concerned about protecting his people."

"This is more serious than I thought." He fingered the shadowy beginnings of a moustache he'd started to grow since their arrival. "Sorry, Ori, I should have listened to you the first time you mentioned this matter."

Pasting on a smile to reassure him, she ran a consoling hand up and down his arm and smiled. Dante was smart and would make a good businessman in a few years. Now, he loved action and excitement more. "That's why Primo sent you. To see how the business runs in the field and to learn about all the aspects." She cast another look over the crowd, hungry for a glimpse of a tall man with a confident stride. "So, you talked with Kent recently?"

"About fifteen minutes ago. Why?"

With an offhanded wave, she forced her voice to sound non-chalant. "He asked to review the safety list before the exhibition starts."

"That your only reason?"

At his question, she turned and narrowed her gaze, glaring at her brother's too-innocent expression. Had he discovered her interest in the sheriff? "Why do you ask?"

He raised his hands and took one step back, a wide grin on his lips. "Thought you might have a thing for the lawman. But excuse me for asking."

Across the platform, the boards of the ladder creaked again. "Oriana?"

A thrill ran through her at the sound of Kent's voice. She turned toward his deep tone that soothed her senses. But her manner had to appear perfectly business-like. No reasons existed for Dante to learn the added elements of her relationship with the sheriff. "I'm here. I have the list ready for you to check."

Kent stepped onto the platform, his gaze taking in Oriana and Dante. "Good, you're both here. I'm reporting I've stationed five armed guards around the perimeter of the crowd." His serious gaze pinned Oriana. "Shouldn't have a problem with runaway horses tonight."

She handed him the folded paper and scanned the waiting crowd below, looking to spot the men he'd hired. Lordy, she hoped they weren't burly goons who might scare away some of the celebration's audience. This exhibit contained enough elements to keep her nerves at the flash point. If one more thing went wrong, she didn't know if she'd retain her composure.

While Kent scanned the list, she took a moment to study his expression. Brows drawn together and eyes serious as he read. Proud nose with a bump along the ridge that balanced a firm jaw. Well-defined lips—her heart rate sped as she remembered the delicious response his lips and tongue had evoked. All day, she'd wondered what she would say to him when they met again.

Last night had been magical for her—a truly unique experience—and she'd hoped to be able to tell him so. More importantly, she'd hoped to hear him speak similar sentiments. But with her brother present, that wouldn't be possible.

"The extra dirt we discussed is where?" Kent looked around the wooden platform, then pinned her with a hard stare.

Dante stepped forward and gestured with a sweep of his arm. "The cart at the base of the ladder has a load of dirt. I rigged a pulley so buckets could be hauled up if needed."

"Be sure to report to John about how that works. He has a crew of miners standing by."

A smile meant to reassure covered Dante's mouth. "If all goes well, we won't need it."

The sharpness of Kent's tone stung and she hesitated before responding. "Of course, we'll wait until the crowd clears before running a test." He might try to act like he wasn't remembering their play the night before, but she knew his expression well enough to see he was agitated. She recognized the signs—he was remembering the previous night but trying not to.

"You have a pencil?" He held out his hand.

Dante pulled one from his shirt pocket and passed it to him. While Kent signed at the bottom of the list, Dante winked at Oriana.

When he finished, she let out her breath in a whoosh of relief. All their efforts would be recognized. And her work—the special rockets with metallic salts for sparkly effects, the secret scent—would finally be on display.

"Tell me where I can sit so I won't be in your way."

She whirled, her mouth open. "You're really staying up here? During the exhibit?"

His brows drew low, and his lips pressed into a straight line. "I told you—I'm not leaving your side."

"This is where I leave." Dante saluted and headed toward the edge of the platform.

Oriana shifted her attention to her departing brother. "Do you have the flag?"

"Yep, it's near the first setup." His dark eyes glanced at Kent, then back. "*Buono fortuna.*"

Maybe she would need good luck. Oriana watched her brother descend the ladder, suddenly aware that this was the moment she'd been dreading all day. All during the last-minute insertion of her signature element and fuses. While she'd lowered the shells into their slots and readied the buckets of water and sand. The gentle evening breeze wasn't the reason for the goose flesh rising on her arms and the back of her neck. This delicious sensation invaded her body whenever Kent was near. Like her body knew when his was close.

Nonna Violetta, Zia Donella, and Zia Christiana had told her about this sensation, but she'd never experienced it when she was married to her Anthony.

"You look nice tonight."

Was he joking? She glanced over her shoulder. This was her oldest dress, but it had been tailored to allow her movement while still being safe. Two panels at the front and back covered the split skirt underneath. "This was a compromise between the clothes you've seen me work in and the dress my mama thought was appropriate for a representative of the family. My aunts came up with the design."

"I like how it fits." His gaze slowly traveled up from the hem that hit her midcalf and stopped on her ass. "Never thought I'd be jealous of a stretch of fabric."

With a spiral of anticipation stirring in her belly, she turned and met his gaze, placing a hand on a hip. "Nobody here stopping you."

"You forgetting where we are?" He turned his head and swept his arm in a wide arc to encompass the crowd below.

A sly grin slid across her lips, and she stepped closer, putting a swing into her hips. "A public setting is just another one of my fantasies. . . ."

He shook his head and chuckled. "You are the damnedest woman I've ever met."

"I hope so." Her fingers itched to touch him, and she sauntered a step closer, then halted. Kent was right. They were in full view of the gathered crowd. Even if she was only passing through, she had to remember he had a reputation in this community. He'd still be here and facing these people after she and Dante were on the train headed east.

That thought weighed heavy on her heart, but she didn't want to think about leaving right now. Every time she did, her throat tightened and her thoughts grew confused.

"Oriana, about last night . . ." His voice was close and deep. Although she listened hard, she didn't hear a note of regret. "I can only say—"

"Last night's done." She pressed a hand to his mouth, too aware of the warm skin beneath her fingers. "Let's talk about tonight. I've always loved this—sparkly colors and lights bursting against the sky."

"Always?" His eyebrows rose and his blue-gray eyes lit with amusement.

Her hand dropped away when she shrugged. "Since age three when my father showed me how to put protective caps on the end of fuses. Everyone in the family worked. As we grew, we learned more tasks." Again, nerves attacked her stomach and she wondered if she should reveal the truth about her role. She turned and walked to the edge of the platform, then lowered herself to sit, legs dangling over the edge. "This is the first show totally under my direction."

Kent eased down beside her. "I didn't know that."

At her admission, relief swept through her, releasing previous inhibitions about her role with the company and her duties.

"I've understudied my oldest brother on a half dozen other exhibits of varying size and complexity. This performance I planned from beginning to end." Unable to contain herself, she waved her hands as she talked. "Every detail—from the mixes of ingredients and which metal salts to add for which colors, to the placement of rockets—was my decision."

"So far, my impression is favorable." He looked over the crowd, his gaze slowing in certain places. "Not like the last show I saw." His voice trailed off at the end, and he shook his head, his gaze focused into the far distance.

"And you didn't like that particular show?" She didn't understand a person who wasn't enthralled by the magic of the miniature explosions.

His body stiffened and his head jerked. "The quality of the show wasn't the issue."

Curious at his abrupt reaction, she studied his face as she questioned him. "Where was that? And when?"

"Ten years ago, at a mine in Montana."

"Ten?" The word whooshed out before she could stop from exclaiming her surprise. "I can't imagine going that long without seeing a display."

"In my mind, I always connect that show with my father's death." He cleared his throat and looked away. "A mining cave-in."

"Oh, sorry." She reached out a hand to touch the back of his, her heart heavy at the idea of losing a loved one. "That explains your attitude the first day."

"That and the fact that I served on the mine's rescue crew." He shuddered and turned, his brows furrowed. "Haven't had a reason to be inside a mine since then. Too confining."

At the sight of his strained expression, she nudged his arm with her shoulder. "I hope this is a more enjoyable experience."

His body relaxed and an arm came around her back. "In so many ways."

And she snuggled closer, her breasts tingling at the memory of their night together. The iron bars, the manacles, the primal sex.

"Uh, Oriana." Kent pointed toward the ground. "Dante is waving a flag like mad down there."

She sat up straight. "Oh, that's my cue." Bracing her boot heels on the wood, she scooted backward on her rear and then stood, brushing dirt off the back of her skirt. "Time for John's speech."

Kent stayed seated but turned to watch her movements, bending a knee and resting a leg on the platform.

Oriana's mental checklist started. Digging into her pants' pockets, she grabbed small squares of flannel and handed two to Kent. "For your ears. The sounds will be a bit loud." She stuffed the fabric in her own ears and turned, her focus already shifted to the next task.

At the end of the rack was a rocket on a stand. She struck a match and lit the fuse, watching the flame catch and burn upward an inch before she backed away. When the flame reached the bottom of the rocket, the end flared with a pop, then shot into the air. The burning rocket burst into a shower of glittering lights.

From below, the crowd gasped and pointed to the sky at the signal for the night's festivities to begin.

"Gather close, folks," John Terrill's voice boomed. "I'd like to say a few words."

The crowd hushed and moved toward the platform, forming a half circle near the base.

"As most of you know, I took over this mine three years ago."

Oriana sat next to Kent. "Not too loud, was it?"

He shook his head and pointed at an ear. "These helped, but I guess you do what you can about the smells."

Anxious for the show to begin, she let her gaze scan the crowd, her emotions tapping into their excitement. "I'm used to them, but at times, the sulfur can be overpowering."

"No, I meant the cinnamon. Nice touch."

She gasped and turned. Was the family's tradition coming true? "You smell that?"

For years, she'd listened to the females in her family tell stories of how they'd know their one true love was for them. Their destiny. *Il destino.*

Could this be her love story coming true?

"Must have used a lot to be able to smell it up here."

"Actually, only a few drops of oil. Then why—"

Heart beating wildly, she jumped to her feet and moved to the closest pail of water, shifting it an inch. Kent's comment echoed in her ears but she couldn't afford the distraction. Distance was what she needed.

As John continued his speech, Oriana walked the length of the platform, making last-minute adjustments to the rockets. She set the box of phosphorus matches near the oil torch and walked to the platform edge, her gaze on Dante.

Nervousness made her movements a bit jerky, and she breathed deep to force a calm. Concentration was the key at this point of her job. She rubbed her hands up and down her arms.

"Cold?"

"No." She glanced over at Kent with a smile. "Just anxious to start."

"Is setting them off your favorite part?"

"Yes, I never get tired of seeing the lights and the colors." Her insides churned with the knowledge he'd smelled the cinnamon smell that illuminated future mates. But she'd have to think about that later. "Don't you love it too?"

"Never saw them as a kid. Just those up north in Montana."

Below them the crowd burst into applause at the end of the speech, and she turned to look at her brother for the next signal. She struck a match and lit the oil torch, holding it near the first rocket.

John Terrill stood with his hands in the air and cheered.

Dante glanced up and tossed the flag into the air.

Oriana held the burning torch near the first cotton fuse and waited, her breath held tight in her chest. Soon her special additions would be displayed for all to see.

She touched the flame to the rocket, counted to four, and then touched another one. She watched the fuse burn and then looked to the sky to see the trailing lights as they sparkled like jewels against the inky darkness of the night sky. A shiver ran through her. The gold dust had worked and the sparks were brilliant, seeming to hang in the sky and dazzle until they slowly faded.

"That was beautiful. I didn't know the lights could be so bright."

A bit of pride swelled inside her chest. "That's a mixture of phosphorus and iron pyrite."

The pop of the rockets at ground level sounded and then a loud scream. They both turned and leaned over the edge.

From down below came a gunshot.

Kent jumped to his feet and pulled Oriana behind him, his gun drawn, sweeping the area.

Two minutes later, Kent strode toward the gathered crowd, aware that Oriana followed closely behind. "Stand back, folks." He glanced at the person on the ground, and surprise grabbed his chest.

John lay on his side, a hand clamped on his upper arm just below a bloody spot.

Had he overlooked a potentially dangerous situation because of the enticements this woman offered?

Or was someone determined to cause John injury? The board on the platform, the shot at the wagon, this mishap.

"Let me help." Oriana pressed close to his side.

He held out a restraining arm and shot her a warning look. "I want Doctor Sutton to look at this."

"I've done this before, Kent—Sheriff Wyman." She nudged him with a hip and dropped onto her knees next to John.

Kent took a good look at his friend. John's mouth was pulled into a tight grimace, but his skin wasn't pale. The sleeve of his shirt near his shoulder was torn and burned, blood seeping into the denim.

Oriana's head rose, and she scanned the crowd pressing close. "Dante, are you nearby?"

The young man edged into the circle. "I'm here, Ori."

"Find something to put the fragments in. A bowl or maybe some paper." She gestured with her hands. "I want to study what went wrong."

Kent brushed a restraining hand against her shoulder. "Oriana, let the doctor work here."

She whipped her head around and glared, dark eyes flashing. "Why make your friend hurt longer than he needs to? I can help." Her gaze studied his expression, then widened. "Kent, I'm not involved with this mishap. I stand behind our company's quality. You saw me work that day. Packed by our methods, none of our rockets could have gone astray. They have been tampered with."

He remembered their conversation of only a few minutes earlier. Excitement and pride in her accomplishments and her role in this evening's events had shone through in her words. But he couldn't allow his growing feelings for her or the fact they'd bedded on two occasions affect his professional judgment.

The personal obligation to his friend and the sworn oath he'd given to the people of Buckskin had to come first. He needed to figure out what was happening in his jurisdiction. Kent forced a chill into his gaze and a distant note into his next words. "Only if you share the evidence."

Her body jerked as if she'd been struck. "Of course." With one last stricken look, she turned her attention to tending John.

Kent registered the pain in her dark gaze and clamped his jaw with regret. Maybe he should have kept his doubts to himself and talked to her in private.

John struggled up onto one elbow. "Just get me to the office. All I need is a bandage."

A murmur passed through the crowd and people shuffled aside.

"Where is he?" a woman's strident voice sounded.

Kent recognized the nasal tones of John's wife and stepped back, dreading what trouble the woman would rustle.

"I'm all right, Velma. Just a scratch."

The tall woman dressed in a stylish red jacket and skirt with a matching parasol stepped close and looked down. "But you're bleeding." Her upper lip curled in disgust. She whirled with a narrowed gaze and stared at Kent. "Sheriff, what are you doing about this? Where is the stupid and unprofessional person responsible for these obviously dangerous fireworks?"

6

Oriana slowly rose to her feet and squared her shoulders. "I'm Oriana Donato Ignacio, and I represent the Donato Pyrotechnic Company."

With a flourish, Velma lifted her parasol and pointed. "You did this to my husband. You and your company's faulty business practices."

Kent closed the distance between he and Oriana but angled his body to face the irritated woman. "Velma, calm down. No sense in accusing anyone until I'm done with my investigation." When he glanced around the area, he noticed the intent looks of those near enough to hear what was being said. Not what John's mine or Oriana's company needed.

Oriana's brow was wrinkled into a frown, and her dark gaze flitted repeatedly from the crowd to Mrs. Terrill.

He could only imagine the concern Oriana must be feeling for her company's reputation. "Folks, let's make some room here. Give John the chance to breathe some fresh air." He used his most commanding voice and walked a slow circle of the group. "John's going to be fine. This was just a minor accident." When the crowd didn't seem inclined to leave, he debated about calling in the security force he'd hired. He had no doubt they'd clear the area in only a couple minutes.

Reverend Whitley stepped forward and nodded. "Now, folks, there's a table yonder just bursting with home-baked cakes and pies. The first dozen or so in line will have a chance at a slice of my Doreen's blackberry pie."

Several people shifted, looking over their shoulders in the direction he indicated. But no one moved.

Not to be daunted by a few skeptics, the gray-haired man circled his hand over his head like he was lassoing cattle. "Come on, I know one of Buckskin's fine bakers has brought a treat guaranteed to tempt your sweet tooth."

For the first time that he could remember, Kent followed the reverend's lead and waved his hands in a herding motion. "Great idea, Reverend. Please, everyone enjoy some dessert while we get this situation sorted out."

Velma huffed and squared off opposite Oriana, towering over her by several inches. "I will be holding your company responsible for the catastrophe that has befallen my husband. An injury like this involves pain and suffering. What if his ability to work is compromised?"

Oriana shot Kent a questioning glance before stepping forward. "I wouldn't call this a catastrophe. John's been hit with something, but the injury is minor." Her tone was calm, her words spoken with even cadence.

"I want the best care for my husband." With a toss of her head, Velma turned and then cast a condescending look over her shoulder. "And you can believe I will be expecting your company to pay the bills."

"No, Velma." John's voice was firm. With one hand braced on the ground, he pushed upward and grimaced.

Kent stepped close and grabbed his friend under one arm, hoping to provide support. "Stay down. Wait until someone looks at that cut."

John shook his head. "Help me to the office," the mine owner's voice rasped with pain. "I'll get tended there."

"Good idea." Kent draped John's arm over his shoulders and wrapped his arm around his waist. "Oriana, follow us."

Velma strode ahead, clearing a path through the few remaining bystanders with wide swings of her parasol.

In the office, Kent stood in his usual spot by the window, watching as Oriana tended to John's wound. Interesting to note that, although she vocalized about the horribleness of his injury, Velma stood near the door, no closer than three feet of her husband. Not one comforting word, not a single gentle gesture of concern. Just venomous spouting about blame and lawsuits. Interesting.

Oriana approached his position at the window, a metal cup clenched in her hand. "I'm doing as you asked. This is what I pulled from his shoulder."

He took the cup and tilted it toward the oil lamp on the desk. A metallic rattle sounded. He peered at a twisted piece of metal. "What am I looking at?"

"I'm not sure." She shrugged but didn't meet his gaze. "I thought you might know. I don't use metal like this in my rockets."

He looked closer and straightened away from the window. This was the remains of a soft bullet. No accident relating to the pyrotechnics had happened. He turned so Oriana was the only one who could see his face or hear what he was about to say. "Don't talk. Go along with what I'm saying. I'll give you details later."

An hour later, Dante hurried Oriana through the camp, wending their way around the few remaining attendees, an oil lantern swinging at his side. "Do you believe the way the sheriff talked to us? That was rude."

She stumbled and felt his grasp on her elbow tighten. "He's doing his job."

"But what about the insinuation we did something to our own equipment?"

For some strange reason, she didn't want to admit to her brother how much Kent's words had hurt. Maybe she didn't want to say the words aloud because then they'd become a truth she couldn't bear—especially after the night they had shared. "Do you want to stay and work out how we will respond to such an insinuation?"

Dante opened the door to the small cabin assigned for her use and entered. Within a few steps, he crossed the floor to light the oil lamps in the wall sconces, then turned to face her. "You're always telling me I'm not the publicity person on this team." He shrugged and a sheepish grin crept across his lips. "Besides, there's a poker game at the miners' bunkhouse."

The little-boy look on his face made her laugh. "Life in the Old West suits you."

He approached her and rested his hands on her shoulders. "Don't let this incident bother you, Ori. You and I know the rockets were done right." With a quick kiss on her cheek and a wave, he was out the door.

She watched until the dark night swallowed his lantern light and then went inside the cabin. For a few minutes, she moved around the small living space, straightening and rearranging her meager belongings. She sat and tried to get interested in the next installment of stories by her favorite author.

Somehow, reading Wild West stories of daring bank robberies, dangerous cattle drives, and exciting stagecoach runs didn't take her mind off her troubles. They only reminded her of the excitement she'd experienced since being in Colorado.

A knock sounded at the door and she jumped up, glad for

any distraction. Maybe Dante couldn't find a game and had returned to visit. She opened the door. When she saw who stood on the small porch, her hand tightened on the knob.

He'd come.

Kent stepped over the door's threshold, a scowl drawing his features tight. "Oriana, you didn't look through the curtain," his voice growled in a low rasp. "How did you know who was calling at this hour?"

These words were not what she wanted to hear from him. She jammed a hand on her hip and narrowed her gaze. "Did you come to reprimand me?"

"I came to talk. To tell you what I'd discovered."

She stepped back and swung open the door. "Come inside, I do want to know about the incident." When he stepped past her, she smelled the outdoors—pine trees and crisp night air. "Would you like a cup of coffee?"

"Always."

In the time needed to stir the embers and add a log to the stove, Oriana's brain raced at what she would ask. Primo would expect her to get all the available facts and prepare a formal report. She fussed with the cups, spoons, and sugar bowl, and then brought the filled cups to the table.

Kent accepted his cup and waved off the offer of sugar.

To be polite, she sat and took a couple sips of the fragrant brew. Then her impatience won out. "Tell me what you learned."

"The metal *was* a bullet fragment." He sat with forearms resting on the table, hands around the cup.

"I thought so." A relieved sigh escaped her lips, and she lowered her cup to the table. "But I wanted confirmation. Kent, you know that metal did not come from one of Donato's rockets."

His head dipped with a sharp nod. "I know that, Oriana. I saw how thorough you were about checking and double-checking the equipment against the items on your list."

She leaned forward on her elbows, wishing she dared reach out a hand to touch him. At the other end of the table, he seemed too remote, unreachable. "Thank you for believing."

"Damn it." His fist slammed on the table, and he shot to his feet, eyes blazing. "Someone took a shot at John. And in my territory." Running a hand through his hair, he paced to the door and back, his steps jerky. "I've got to find out who is responsible. That's my job."

"I want to help. This involves my family's good name."

He crossed his arms over his chest and spread his legs in a wide stance. "I can handle this."

"I don't doubt that." She stood and braced her hands on the table. "But I want to keep Donato Pyrotechnics clear of any hint of a scandal. I have to keep our firm's name in the running for consideration for the Colorado statehood celebration. My family has worked hard to be in this position and is counting on me to do this."

"No, I don't want you near this investigation." He hesitated and shot her a dark look, his brows drawn low. "Besides, I'm still not convinced you weren't the target."

"Me?" She couldn't keep surprise from raising the tone of her voice. "I know professional jealousy exists—"

"Professional! The incidents seemed much too personal." He held out his hand, counting off the items on his fingers. "The firecrackers, the runaway horses, and the shot on the wagon."

At the realization that his brusque behavior revealed his true feelings, she held back a smile. Any worries she'd had about pushing him too far the previous night in the jail cell were gone. She hadn't scared him off. The knowledge gave her confidence. With slow steps, she crossed the room to the door and twisted the key in the lock, then turned and leaned back.

"What?" His gaze narrowed. "Why are you smiling?"

"I like your protectiveness." Her gaze boring into his, she

stepped close and pressed her hands to his chest. "I like how you care for those people around you." As she spoke, her hands circled down over his stomach and held on to the side of his waist.

He widened his stance and rested his hands on her shoulders. "Maybe one person in particular." His hands rose to her jaw and cupped it, thumbs grazing her chin.

At the tender gesture, her eyelids closed for just a moment; then she stretched on tiptoe to brush her lips across his. If this was to be their last night together, she knew exactly how she wanted it to be. Tonight, they would both be naked and they would share a real bed. She pressed her lips harder against his and rubbed the ends of her breasts across his chest.

His arms came around her and hugged her tight.

When his tongue invaded her mouth, she matched it with her bold strokes. His kisses excited her like none had before, making her feel wild and wanton.

She hooked a hand inside his belt and tugged him backward toward the bedroom, a small room that held a narrow bed and a table on which sat a single candle.

He resisted and broke the kiss, moving his head away. "Oriana, I should be—"

She covered his mouth with a finger and shook her head. "No, you shouldn't. For right now, this is where you need to be." After a long, stroking caress of his cheek, her hands went to the row of buttons at the top of her blouse.

His gaze followed the trail of opening fabric, a slow grin tweaking the edge of his mouth. "You are so right." With a glint in his eye, he mirrored her movements.

Within moments, they were inside her bedroom, snuggled under the bedclothes, limbs entwined. Moonlight shining through a gap in the curtains cast a wide shaft across their bodies. For the first time, soft female skin lay alongside lean male skin.

As he ran soft kisses along her cheek and jaw, his hand moved between her breasts, stroking each plump one and rubbing the tips of her nipples between his fingers.

The tempo of this lovemaking was slow, which excited her more. Her blood raced, and she pressed her thighs together against the heaviness swirling low in her belly. Moisture wet her pussy, and she tossed back her head to give him better access to her neck.

Kent lapped at the hollow in her neck and she shivered, tightening the pearled buds even more.

He shifted in the bed, and his warm lips covered a breast, sucking it deep into his mouth.

Tingles ran straight through her body and she arched off the bed. With a sigh, she settled back to the mattress, running her fingers through his thick brown hair.

When his lips ran along the underside of her breast and down over her stomach, she reached for his head and held him still, stopping his progress. "I owe you something we didn't get to last night."

His head shook. "You don't owe me."

"Then chalk it up to another of my fantasies."

She scooted around on the mattress until she knelt at the side of his hip. Her hand stroked along his thigh, over his knee, and down his shin. She enjoyed the contrast of coarse hair and hard muscle—so different than her own body.

His cock was a magnificent thing. Jutting upright from a thatch of brown curls, the rigid shaft with the rounded tip pulsed with each of his breaths.

She ran a fingertip from the base to the tip, circling it once, and then sheathed his cock with her hand. As she lowered her head, her hand stroked the length. Then she encased him with her mouth, sucking him inside and pressing her tongue along the bottom of the head's ridge.

The experience was new and she wanted to taste him everywhere. Her questing mouth ran along his cock from tip to base, swirling her tongue as she moved. When she reached his balls, she gently sucked one into her mouth while she worked the other with a rolling motion.

His legs stiffened beneath her, and his breath rasped.

Emboldened by his reaction, she straddled his leg and bent her head over his cock, taking as much of his length into her mouth as she could. With long strokes of her tongue, she worked her mouth along his cock.

He raised his leg and pressed against her pussy, zapping shots of sensation through her clit.

A moan slipped through her lips. She arched and huffed out an excited breath.

He flexed his hips, driving his cock along her cheek. "Ride me."

"Later." She shook her head and bent her head back toward his groin.

His hands cupped her shoulders, holding her still. "How about indulging in one of my fantasies?"

Through the haze of her building excitement, she recognized the hungry look in his eyes. The acknowledgment he'd thought about them in this position went through her, heating her insides. With hands braced by his shoulders, she tossed her right leg to the other side of his body, centering herself over his protruding cock. Only a small movement of her hips lowered her pussy and teased the tip of his cock, inching down and then backing away. Using a slow rhythm, she moved on him several times, stroking a bit deeper each time.

"I said ride me, lady." He grabbed her hips and held her steady, then thrust upward. "Like this." He raised her up and down on his cock, pulling her forward against his groin, and let out a low groan.

The girth of his cock impaled her, and she gasped at the stretched feeling. With a whoosh, the air left her lungs and she grappled for her balance. The intensity of his thrusts fueled her excitement, and she circled her hips against his, seeking every last bit of satisfaction. In this position, she swore she could feel his cock hitting her womb.

Then his strokes slowed and his large hand cupped her breast, flicking her nipple into a tight nub. He thrust, she pushed—and the excitement built. Her pussy dripped with slippery juices, and her belly clenched with anticipation.

Kent held her gaze, raised a thumb to his mouth and licked it, then pressed it to her clit. His way eased by her dewy essence, he circled the nub and then flicked it with his fingernail.

That single flick took her over the edge. Tingles shot through her and she tossed back her head, reaching to anchor her hands on his thighs and flex her hips in countermovement to his thrusts. Stars and sparkles lit behind her eyes, and her breathing rasped. Waves of completion racked her body, but she fought her body's natural urge to relax. She kept sliding her hips until she heard the catch in his breathing and felt the pulsing of his orgasm deep inside her. Only then did she slump forward onto his damp chest and feel his arms enfold her in a tight embrace.

He blew out a breath and chuckled. "Now that was a ride." Idle fingers brushed the damp hair from her cheek.

Surrounded by his strong arms and the musky scent of their arousal, she could barely think. As her breathing slowed to a normal rate, one thought rose to the surface.

Safe and secure, she wanted this feeling to last forever.

7

A pounding sounded on her front door and Oriana jerked awake. Her hand shot out to the side, but the sheets were cold—and empty. She swept waves of hair off her face and squinted at the sunlight streaming through the curtain.

"Ori? You in there?" Dante's voice grew louder. "Hey, wake up."

Even in her sleepy state, she recognized the note of urgency in her brother's voice. She scrambled to the end of the bed to reach her nightrail, her movements stirring the scent of lovemaking. "What is it, Dante? What's happened?" In a flash, she'd clothed herself and dashed across the room to the bedroom door, opening it a few inches.

Head down, Dante paced the short distance across the room and looked up, his dark brow creased with worry. "There's been an accident."

Her mind stumbled over how this could affect the company. Today the platform was scheduled to be disassembled. "Is it one of our workers? Should I grab bandages?"

He approached and grabbed her hand. "A cave-in."

Her hand rose to her throat. "Oh, how horrible."

"Kent's inside." His grip tightened.

"What?" Her blood chilled. She clamped his hand tight and grabbed with the other for the doorjamb. "Tell me what you know."

"The camp is in an uproar. This is what I've been able to piece together." His stare was intense and serious. "There was a note with a clue about last night's shooting. He and John went to investigate. An explosion went off that blocked the entrance, and they're trapped."

"Stay right there." She pointed a shaky finger in his direction before running back into her room to pull on her work clothes. This couldn't be happening. Last night had revealed what she wanted most. What if—? She shoved aside that thought and grabbed her boots. "Let's go."

They ran and walked through the compound, asking those they met for directions. The answers were vague and confused. By the time they approached the crowd milling outside the southern mine entrance, Oriana was filled with dread that no one seemed to be attempting any rescue.

"Dante, you know more of the mine workers." She waved a hand in the direction of the group of men. "Please ask what is being done."

She clamped her arms over her churning stomach as she watched Dante ease his way through the crowd, stopping for a moment here or there to speak to workers. Unable to keep to the back of the crowd, she moved along the perimeter until she could see into the entrance.

Dante approached, his expression drawn. "Their foreman went inside thirty minutes ago, and they're waiting for his evaluation."

"Thirty minutes! That's too long." She pushed past him toward the entrance.

He grabbed her arm and held tight. "Wait. These guys are superstitious about women in the mines."

Just then a group of men emerged, their faces covered in dust and dirt.

Shaking off his grip, she ran up to the group, ignoring the men's curious stares. "What's the situation?"

A gray-haired man turned, his gaze scanning her from head to toe. "Who are you, miss?"

"Oriana Ignacio. I'm part of the pyrotechnic team responsible for last night's show." Impatience filled her, but she kept her words calm. "What needs to be done?"

"We're working on that here." He turned back to the circle of men. "The rocks are wedged in tight. We need—"

"Excuse me, which of you is the mine's engineer?"

The men exchanged glances.

A thin man stepped forward and answered, "With the mine closed for the celebration, Tolliver went to Denver for supplies. He's expected back tomorrow."

"That's no help." She shook her head and waved her arm in the direction of the cave. "Have you heard from them?"

The man looked over his shoulder, his bushy eyebrow raised. "What?"

"Did you shout to them or hear their shouts?"

"Didn't hear anything."

The terror of thinking Kent lay crumpled under the rocks clawed at her heart. "Dante, go to John's office and search for maps. Anything that might show the layout of the tunnels." Shooting a scathing look at the group of men, she charged inside, grabbing a lantern from a peg at the entrance. From outside came yells for her to come back out, but she ignored them.

She trudged down the tunnel, pushing aside the small rocks that studded the ground until she reached a wall of larger stones. Scrambling along the lower edge, she cried out, "Kent? Can you hear me?" At the top of the pile was a small opening; she climbed awkwardly toward it, slipping on shifting stones while trying to keep the lantern from tipping. "Kent! Are you there?"

A faint yell sounded, but she couldn't tell who spoke. She shoved a couple rocks away to make the opening bigger. They rattled and bumped down the mound. "It's Oriana. We're working on a way to get you out."

When she shoved at a couple more rocks, they didn't budge. Frantic to know he was okay, she lay flat and pressed her face into the opening. "Kent. Answer me!"

"Quit being so bossy. I hear you, Oriana."

At the sound of the familiar voice, she blew out a sigh of relief. He was alive. Now to figure out how to get him out. "How are you? Any injuries?"

"Cuts and bruises from the falling rocks. One arm took the brunt of my fall, but I don't think it's broken."

She closed her eyes and whispered a prayer of thanks to the cosmos. "How about John?"

"His arm's bleeding again, but he's doing okay."

Her hands gripping the rocks shook. "Hold on. I'm going to check about the rescue and be back."

The scrape of boots on rocks sounded through the opening. "Oriana, hurry." His voice was closer.

She heard the tension in his words. Frustration made her tear at the stones on the top and only one moved. "Are you telling me everything?"

"Yeah, just these damn walls are closing in."

The cave-in years earlier. She remembered the stark expression on his face when he recounted his last experience with fireworks. "I'm here, Kent. You're not alone." She extended a hand through the hole, wishing she could touch him, to give him comfort. "Ask John about another way out."

"No good. There were two explosions, front and back. We're boxed in."

Warm fingers grazed the tips of hers; then she heard the tumble of sliding rocks.

"Be careful. I don't want you to get hurt now. I'll be back in a few minutes." She lowered a foot to start the descent.

"Oriana!" A hand grasped the top of the rocks and then part of Kent's face appeared in the opening.

Her heart soared and she stretched to one side to clasp the back of his hand. "I'm still here."

"Don't do anything stupid."

"Stupid, like rescuing you?"

"No, something that puts you in danger. The miners have done this before." He cleared his throat. "Stay outside."

He was protecting her again, trying to keep her from being close at hand should something go wrong with the rescue. Like when he'd found his father. Her throat grew tight, and she blinked against the sting of tears at the back of her eyes. "Don't you dare give up. I *will* get you out."

"That's my little firebrand."

To her ears, his teasing words sounded like endearments. Suddenly, all she wanted was to see him as he spoke. With as much speed as she dared, she climbed down and ran out into the sunlight.

Dante squatted within the circle of men, a map spread out on the ground.

"Dante!" She rushed up to the group.

The men's faces turned her way, and some rose to a stand.

"Both men are all right, only cuts and bruises. So, what's the plan?"

One man stepped forward. "We're studying on whether going through the front or rear entrance is the best."

"Studying?" She looked around the circle but didn't sense that any of the men were motivated to move quickly. "There were two explosions, and rocks are penning them in both directions."

Heads shook and discouraged murmurs sounded among the men; they turned back to her, their brows pulled into scowls.

She stomped up to Dante. "We need to get them out now."

Dante cast a glance at the other men, then pulled her aside. "Ori, I understand you want to help, but these guys have seen this situation before."

"I know they have, but they should be doing something." Stomach clenched with worry, she paced away from her brother and back, her thoughts racing at the tone in Kent's voice and how she wanted to reduce his wait. "I give them five more minutes."

She forced herself to sit on a nearby stool and slowly count. When she reached 120, she couldn't wait any longer. She approached the circle of men, peeking over the shoulder of the man who seemed to be writing. "Well, what have you decided?"

"We're dividing into teams, and we'll gather the tools needed for rock removal."

Oriana dashed back into the mine and clambered up the pile of stones. "Kent, are you there?"

"Right where you left me. I thought I told you to stay outside." His gray eyes appeared in the opening and he winked. "What's going on out there?"

"No one seems to be in charge. The group is dividing into teams for removing the rocks." She waved her hands in the air. "But this is taking too long. I don't want to wait."

"Oriana, we're fine." His voice was firm but quiet.

Her heart went out to his effort to act brave. "Kent, I know you don't like small spaces. Let me help get you out."

"And I want you to stay out of danger."

"Did you happen to notice what I do for a living?" Her comment sparked a thought. What remained in her stash of supplies that she could put to use? Part of her process was to be precise in the amount of explosives she packed. Safety in shipping was one of her father's rules, and only a small amount of gunpowder remained after the celebration. "Hey, what explosives does John use? Blasting oil or nitroglycerin compound?"

"I don't know."

She fought against rolling her eyes at that comment and had to force a nice tone into her voice. "Ask him, please."

After a couple minutes, Kent returned with a question. "Do you know how to handle dynamite?"

"Never seen it, but I've read articles." The excitement of exploration and discovery was irresistible. A new substance just posed a new set of questions to be answered. "Tell me where to find it."

"No, Oriana. Let the crews do their work." His tone was terse, his words clipped.

She flattened herself against the opening and reached her arm through, snapping her fingers until she felt his large one clasping her smaller hand. "Believe in me, Kent. I want to help you."

"I know you can." He squeezed and stroked his thumb across her knuckles. "Damn it. I hate that I can't keep you safe."

She swallowed against a suddenly dry throat and forced a smile. "If you believe in me, you'll tell me where to find the dynamite."

He huffed out a long breath, loosened his grip on her hand, and pressed cool metal into her palm. "The key goes to a metal box in the storage shed. The block of dynamite is wrapped in burlap, and the fuses are in a smaller box on the top shelf."

"Thanks, Kent. While I'm gone, be looking for the best place to get as far back as you can."

"I know." He brushed a kiss across her knuckles.

Ten minutes later, Dante and Oriana huddled at the base of the stone pile, several lanterns lighting their implements as they worked. None of the miners had agreed to enter the cave, so they worked alone.

Dante unrolled a length of cording and held it out. "How long do you want the fuse?"

With a nervous nibble on her lower lip, she eyed the cord and the small blocks of dynamite dough. "I think a piece as long as your forearm is what we want. Cut two." That should give them enough time to get into a side tunnel. At least, she hoped it would.

"Hey, Kent, are you and John well back?"

A faraway call in the affirmative echoed through the small opening.

With her hands cupped around her mouth, she yelled one last instruction. "Good, put your fingers in your ears." She looked at Dante with a raised eyebrow. "Can you think of anything else to make this safer?"

Dante looked at the setup and shook his head. "You've done everything possible."

With shaky hands, she struck a match against the strike plate and held it to the cord. Once it started burning, she moved to the other one partially around the base. Murmuring a prayer that their choices were the right ones, she jerked a thumb over her shoulder. She and Dante scurried back to the nearest side tunnel and waited, mouths buried in their shirts and fingers pressed inside their ears.

As they waited, Oriana ran through the variables in her mind. With too much explosive material, the rocks could fly to where Kent and John huddled deep in the cave. With not enough, they'd have to live through it twice. The second time with dust-filled air.

The explosion blasted and shook the rock along her back. When the roar subsided, she moved her hands to cover her nose and mouth. Small pebbles skipped and hopped along the passage, and dust rolled in thick clouds past the opening.

With one hand, Oriana felt along the tunnel wall. With the other, she waved, impatiently trying to clear the swirling dust so she could find her way to the back of the cave. Her heartbeat quickened, and worry for the safety of the trapped men pressed her forward.

Two dust-covered figures crawled over the piles of rubble, stumbling into view, each supporting the other.

She had no trouble recognizing Kent's broad shoulders and rushed to his side, slipping her arm around his waist. "You're safe." She wished for the freedom to run her hands over his body, checking every inch of his skin. In the dim light, she couldn't see any bad scrapes.

"We're fine." His arm came around her shoulders and clasped tight. "Just get us out of here."

His words must be for show, because his arm around her shoulders was heavy. "Dante, come help John." Oriana waited until Dante took John's weight onto his shoulders and the pair moved slowly ahead.

"We'll be right behind you." Kent waited until the figures disappeared, then turned and walked her backward, pressing her against the wall. "That was a hell of a blast, lady."

His commanding manner made her breath catch. "Are you sure you're okay?" She pressed her hands gently over his arms and chest, worried he'd hidden a horrible injury.

"I'm fine." He held his arms out from his sides until she finished.

The realization settled that he really wasn't hurt, and irritation burned in her blood. "What clue was so important to send you willingly into the mine?"

"The note was found in John's office early this morning. You were blamed—"

"Me?" She slapped a hand against her chest. "I was up on the platform."

"Hey, I know that." His hand soothed up and down her arm. "John knew it too. I had to investigate the information.

The note further stated the claim could be proved by the evidence stashed in the mine. So I went inside to find the 'evidence.' And walked right into that trap."

She gasped, her throat tightening. He'd overcome his fear to prove her innocence?

"Unfortunately, while we waited for rescue, John recognized Velma's handwriting. He revealed their marriage hasn't been happy for a long time, but he never believed her capable of harming him."

"Oh, poor John."

"What about poor Kent?" His head bent low and he captured her lips in a searing kiss, sweeping his tongue inside.

Opening her lips to accept his probing tongue, she melted against his chest, her hands gripping his shirt. All her worry fired into passion. With a moan, she responded to his kiss, leaning her hips against his hard thighs.

Arms wrapped around her back, he nudged her cap from her head and nuzzled his nose deep into her hair. "I will never tire of your cinnamony scent."

Again, he mentioned the scent that tied to her family's matrimonial tradition. Too much had happened for her to put words to her feelings, but the knowledge that he was *the one* settled deep into her chest.

"We're expected outside." His lips pressed against her forehead, and he stared into her eyes. "But I consider this unfinished business."

Arm in arm, they walked toward the smoky sunlight. Just inside the opening, Oriana dropped her arm and moved away from his side.

He turned, his brows raised in question.

"Go do your sheriffing. You know where I'll be."

When Kent emerged, the crowd of waiting miners moved forward, shaking his hand and clapping him on the back.

Oriana watched for several minutes, then skirted the group and walked to her cabin, anticipating the evening to come. Already, her thoughts whirled with indulgences and fantasies.

Hours later, Kent stepped onto the porch of Oriana's cabin and knocked on her door. The curtain pulled back a few inches, emitting a soft light and the outline of Oriana's head. So the lady had listened.

The door opened just an inch or so, and from the back side she leaned her head around. "Good evening."

Curious at her odd behavior, he tried to look into the room, but all he saw was flickering light. "Ready for our unfinished business?"

The door swung wide and he got his first glimpse of the candle-lit room. What stole his attention was the sight of Oriana walking deeper into the shadowed space. Her hair swung along her bare back and filmy skirts swished against her legs. A strip of cloth wrapped her generous breasts. Through the open stove door glowed an orange fire. On the floor in the front room was an array of pillows bunched on top of the mattress.

With a flourish, she spread her arms wide. "Enter Oriana's den of pleasure." Slowly, she sunk to her knees, rested clasped hands on her thighs, and looked up from under lowered lashes. "Tonight, sir, your wish is my command."

He shrugged out of his coat and tossed it on a nearby chair, crossing the floor with slow, measured steps. "That's where you're wrong, lady."

Her dark eyes flashed and she tilted her head. "Oh?"

"Tonight is just the first of many nights of pleasure."

Turn the page for an excerpt
from P.J. Mellor's novella,
"Hard in the Saddle,"
from ONLY WITH A COWBOY!

On sale now!

1

Madison St. Claire feigned sleep, listening as her fiancé, Alan, moved about their darkened hotel room. If he knew she was awake, he might want to have sex again. The thought clenched her stomach.

In hindsight, agreeing to marry Alan Hunsinger was not one of her brighter ideas. Their lackluster love life proved it. She planned to discuss their hasty engagement with him as soon as they returned to Detroit. When he'd encouraged her to leave her engagement ring at home while they traveled to set up a new business in the little podunk town of Slippery Rock, Texas, she had hoped Alan was having the same misgivings.

Unfortunately, they had been stuck in *Hooterville* for almost three weeks now and, quite frankly, she smelled a rat.

And she was increasingly concerned she may be engaged to it.

The door clicked shut and she breathed a sigh of relief, snuggling down farther under the blankets. Thanks to the sleeping aid she'd taken, her mind drifted. Who knew when they would be able to go home? She'd discuss everything with Alan when he returned.

Loud knocking on the door of her room awoke her. Before she'd done much more than open her eyes, blinding light filled the room through the open doorway.

The silhouette of a woman stood framed against the sunlight. "Sorry!" The woman's twangy accent set Madison's teeth on edge. "I said housekeepin' before usin' the pass key. I thought the room was empty."

Madison struggled through the sleep-induced fog, silently cursing Alan for convincing her to take the sleep aid the night before. "Well, obviously that's not the case."

The maid visibly cringed and Madison immediately regretted snapping at her. But before she could apologize, the maid was gone, closing the door on her way out.

Battling the sheet, Madison got to her feet and walked to throw the privacy bolt to ensure her shower would not be interrupted.

As she turned to make her way to the bathroom, something white on the floor caught her eye. She bent and picked up the paper. Walking to the bedside table, she flipped on the lamp and sank to the mattress to read the motel bill.

Evidently she and Alan had checked out: obviously a mistake. From what she'd seen of Slippery Rock business practices, mistakes happened all the time. Why would the motel be any different?

The front desk picked up on the first ring.

"Hello, this is Madison St. Claire in room 302. Yes, I received the summary, but there must be a mistake. He did? Well, why didn't you just put it on the card we used when we checked in? Oh. That's not possible. I—" She listened for a few moments, jaw clenched, then said, "I understand. What do you mean my room has been reserved? Yes, I know hunters make reservations in advance. Yes, I'll be down soon and give you another card. Sorry for the inconvenience."

What was Alan up to?

After her shower, she packed her bags and loaded them into the car, then headed to the office to straighten out her bill. With the opening of hunting season, it might be difficult to find another motel room. Bad enough Alan had dragged her to the tiny town in deep southern Texas, but for him to have taken off and left her there was unconscionable. As soon as she paid their bill, she was going to call him and find out where he was and what he thought he was doing.

The old man at the counter looked up from his paper at the sound of the door chime.

"I'm Madison St. Claire, room 302."

"I know who you are." He took a sip from a mug emblazoned with the slogan HOT GRANDPA. His hazel gaze was hostile, at best. "Ran your card again. Denied. Again. Called the company. Card is canceled."

"That's not possible. There must be some sort of misunderstanding. My company will look into it. I—"

"Called them, too. Said you don't work for them anymore."

"What? That's ridiculous!" As soon as she paid her bill, she would call Hunsinger Properties and get everything straightened out. The old man was obviously mistaken. What a surprise. She rummaged around in her purse. "I must have left my card case in the room. I'll be right back with another card."

"Take your time. I'll be here."

With a withering glance, she stomped out of the tiny office and up the stairs to her room.

Once inside, she literally turned the place inside out, tossing bed linens, towels, and papers, moving furniture, opening drawers—all to no avail.

Her mind flashed to Alan slinking around under cover of

darkness. At the time she'd thought he was being considerate. Now she knew better.

She checked her wallet.

The rat had not only abandoned her, he'd taken all of her cash as well as her credit cards.

Swiping at the wetness on her cheeks, she paced the length of the room several times, attempting to calm down and formulate some kind of a plan. What was wrong with her? She always had a plan. Why, then, couldn't she wrap her mind around a course of action for this horrible scenario? The only thought she could come up with was to go back to Detroit and strangle Alan with her bare hands. And even that would not be enough.

Sinking to the edge of the unmade king-size bed, she reached for a tissue and sniffed. What was she doing? She never cried. Never.

She'd obviously lost her touch. By getting involved with Alan the Rat Hunsinger, she'd dropped her guard, become lax.

Darkness descended while she sat there, wracking her brain for a plan. She was a woman of action. Women of action . . . acted.

She retrieved her briefcase and opened her laptop, only to cuss a few seconds later when she was denied access to the corporate Web site of Hunsinger Properties. What was going on? After trying a few more times, she logged out and back in as Alan. Just as she'd suspected, he'd neglected to change his password. She clicked on the Projects file.

"Son of a bitch!" Flopping back against the pillows, she ground her teeth, blinking back fresh tears. Damn. It was even worse than she'd expected. There was no Slippery Rock project. No construction bonds to sell.

She'd been set up. A few more clicks to various files confirmed it.

A glance at the digital clock surprised her. Boy, it was really dark for four-fifteen P.M. The clock was obviously wrong.

She shoved back the sleeve of her raw silk suit to check the gold watch strapped to her wrist. The clock was correct.

Thunder rumbled, vibrating the bed.

It was past checkout time. What was she going to do? Where was she going to go? She flipped open her cell phone and punched the speed dial button. The phone emitted a chime. She squinted in the darkness to read the letters on the screen.

No Service.

"Stupid building probably has tons of crap insulating it, blocking my signal." Stalking to the door, she stepped onto the balcony and tried again.

Chirp. No Service.

Fat raindrops dotted the pavement of the parking lot, splattered the steps leading to her floor.

She had to get out of there. The manager would soon be looking for her, wanting his money. Money she didn't have.

Damn Alan!

Keeping a wary eye on the office window, she made her way to her Camaro, not taking a deep breath until she'd reached the safety of the leather interior.

She winced when the motor began to purr, casting a nervous glance at the office as she eased the car toward the exit.

Stopping at the end of the drive to decide which way to turn, she remembered her gas card. Rummaging through the console, she closed her fingers around the hard plastic and blinked back tears of relief.

It was the first credit card she'd ever had and had been rarely used in recent years. Alan probably didn't even know it existed. She kept it in the car for emergencies. Her current situation certainly qualified as an emergency.

Now she didn't have to worry about getting a new motel room. Assuming the card was still valid, she could use it for gas and food, sleeping in her car on the way back to Detroit. Although the idea of sleeping in her car was personally repugnant and very likely dangerous, what other choice did she have?

There may be a perfectly logical reason for Alan the Rat deserting her. She'd decide if she wanted to hear it after she strangled him.

The card worked. With her tank full and loaded down with snacks from the gas station's convenience store, she set off down the highway toward the interstate, windshield wipers beating in time to the pouring rain.

She touched the stiff paper in her pocket and silently pledged to send a cashier's check for her motel bill as soon as she got back home.